SURROGATE CHILD

She took a deep breath, took hold of the door and slid it open. Solomon stood there looking out at her.

The rope burn on his neck looked even more hideous this close up, but what was more revolting was the way his eyes bulged and his lips thickened. His skin was scaly and pale, his hair disheveled. He said nothing: he simply stared, that hateful smirk on his face.

"You pushed him, didn't you?" she said. "You pushed him so he'd fall off the ladder."

"He's clumsy, awkward. He fell himself. I didn't have to push him."

"You pushed him and I know you did. He knows it too."

"That's a laugh. He doesn't know anything unless I want him to know it. Actually, now that I see what's going on, I'm rather happy you brought him here. Things were getting rather boring watching you and Joe mope about the place. Now I have someone to play with . . ."

SURROGATE CHILD

Andrew Neiderman

A Legend book
Published by Arrow Books Limited
62-65 Chandos Place, London WC2N 4NW

An imprint of Century Hutchinson Limited

London Melbourne Sydney Auckland
Johannesburg and agencies throughout
the world

First published in 1988 by Berkley Books, New York
Legend edition 1989

Printed and bound in Great Britain by
Courier International Ltd, Tiptree, Essex

ISBN 0 09 962100 2

For Dr. Bernard Bloom,
who was first and foremost
a friend to all his patients.

Prologue

"I like him," Martha said. She and Joe stared through the window into the office and looked at the foster child. "He's Solomon's age and Solomon's height. He'll be able to wear all of Solomon's clothes."

"Maybe he'll want to wear his own clothes," Joe said.

"He won't have much to bring with him. Mrs. Posner told us that."

"Maybe he'll want us to buy him new clothes."

"Why?" She turned around, her eyes wide. "You remember how Solomon was about his clothes, how everything was kept so neat and clean. Most of it still looks brand-new anyway."

"He just might not like wearing someone else's clothes," Joe said in a subdued tone. Martha looked at him a moment and then turned to look back through the window at the boy. She considered him, and she considered what Joe said.

"I don't think that's a fair thing for him to do or a grateful way for him to behave."

"I'm not saying he definitely won't wear Solomon's clothes. I just said he might not want to."

"He'll want to," she said. "When he sees all those

beautiful things, he'll want to," she added, and nodded her head.

"Well, for that matter, he'll just have everything that Solomon had," Joe said.

"Yes," she said. She took a deep breath.

"You want to go in now and meet him."

"Wait . . . just a few more moments. I want to look at him without his knowing." She continued to study the boy. Joe shifted the weight from his right foot to his left and looked down the corridor of the county government building. Soon someone would see how they were just standing there looking through the window of the door to the child-care agency. He was impatient and nervous.

"We can't stand here much longer, Martha. Besides—"

"All right, all right." He started to reach for the knob, and she seized his wrist. "Do you realize the color of his hair?" she said. He paused and looked through the window.

"Yes," he said. "It's the same color as Solomon's was."

"Do you think that's just a coincidence?"

He studied her for a moment.

"Of course, Martha. I mean, except for what we told them about the age of the child we wanted and the physical measurements you gave . . . you didn't call Mrs. Posner and add color of hair, did you?"

"No, of course not. That's why I'm asking you whether or not it's just a coincidence."

"It's not such a rare color, light brown, you know. Of course, it's just a coincidence," he repeated, but she smiled up at him as though she knew something he didn't and then turned the doorknob herself.

He hesitated, for the first time feeling that this was the greatest mistake of their lives.

1.

Martha Stern stood by the front door of her house and stared out through the small panel windows at the quiet, country back road beside which they had built their modest three-bedroom two-story home a little more than sixteen years ago, one year after Solomon had been born. Joe and she had picked the lot out years before they could afford to build their own home.

She recalled how during their first two years of marriage they often drove down Old Creek Road and stopped by this location. They played a game with their imaginations then. In the springtime, they would get out of the car and walk through their imaginary house, calling out the locations, pretending to do things in different rooms. They even had a picnic lunch in what they dreamed would be their kitchen. The back window would look out to the west, and if the window was big enough, they could sit at the kitchen table and watch the sun set behind the soft, rolling blue-ridge mountains that shaped the horizon.

When it came down to the actual construction, though, the window didn't turn out to be as big as they would have liked. Reality had a way of pinching and squeezing dreams. Costs had to be considered, and in order to meet the limits

3

of their mortgage, a great many of their original plans were modified.

Despite that, those early days lingered in Martha's memory like a beautiful old tune in a fragile music box. Sometimes, for no reasons she could see, it would start playing, and the images, the sounds, the laughter, and the blue skies would flow. She could close her eyes and sit back and be twenty again.

The long silences that often fell between her and Joe now didn't exist then. They were always at each other in little ways, touching, kissing, talking excitedly. Even if there was a silence between them, it was a different kind of silence. They looked at each other with longing and exchanged thoughts with their eyes.

Perhaps the worst part of being without Solomon a little over a year, she thought, was the silences. The emptiness and the void had quickly slipped into the spaces once filled with Solomon's laughter and talk, even his tears. This silence spread like a cancer and infected every aspect of their lives. They caught it as they would catch a cold, and the conversations that had once linked Joe and her together dwindled until they practically disappeared. Monosyllabic words replaced whole sentences. Without Solomon to talk about and ask about, they stared at each other like patients in a mental ward, both bankrupt of thoughts, their minds filled with echoes.

It was no wonder, then, that she looked forward with such eagerness to the arrival of Jonathan. It would be so good to hear another voice in the house, to hear someone else's footsteps besides hers and Joe's, to be concerned with someone else's needs and wants, and to drive the silences away. The decision to take in a child about Solomon's age was not an easy one. They both recognized that there would be pain. She saw that Joe was visibly afraid of it, and she realized he was not just afraid because of her. He was afraid because of himself.

"It's going to be hard, starting again," he said. "I

don't know if I can do it. I don't know if I'll be good for such a kid. He's got his own problems to deal with, much less mine, too.''

''We'll help each other,'' she told him. ''It won't be easy. I'm not saying it will be easy, but it will be good for us and for him. You'll see. Trust me.''

And so they began their search for a foster child. It was her idea that the child be similar in age and appearance to Solomon. Joe wasn't for that. He said it would be too painful because it would stimulate memories.

''And comparisons. You won't be able to help making them, and you could be very disappointed. You might even take out your disappointment on the child.''

''I would never do that.''

''Sometimes . . . often, we do things we can't help,'' he said. Even though he said it with a tone of sadness, it also carried a note of warning.

Nevertheless, she persisted until he gave in, and they went to the agency. Mrs. Posner, the woman in charge, was surprisingly sympathetic and apparently saw nothing unusual in their request, not that she had had any like it before. She made a point of saying that. Joe thought she was sympathetic because she was desperate to find homes for foster children under her care, but Martha thought her sympathy was drawn from a well of common feeling, since she was a wife and mother herself.

It took time before they found Jonathan. They were presented with a number of other boys who were about Solomon's age, but there was always something about those others that made Martha hesitate. Joe didn't understand her reasons for rejecting one or the other, but he didn't pursue it. At this point there was a sameness to all teenagers for him.

But as soon as Martha set eyes on Jonathan, she knew she had found the boy she wanted in her house, the boy she wanted to sleep in Solomon's room and wear Solomon's clothes and use Solomon's things. It was instinctive; she couldn't explain it.

Joe didn't see what she saw—at least, not at first—but later he admitted he sensed resemblances. Once again he warned her that this might not be good for any of them, but by this time she was committed to the child.

Now she stood by the doorway and awaited Jonathan's arrival. The agency was delivering him. She was sorry that Joe couldn't be home when Jonathan first arrived, but he couldn't get out of his assignments. He was the chief IBM repairman for an area nearly seventy-five miles across, and today he was needed to service some word processors at an insurance agency forty miles away. There was no way to get out of it.

When she complained, he said, "It isn't the same as being there when you gave birth. I know it would be better if I could be there, but I'll have plenty of time to get to know him, and he'll have plenty of time to get to know me."

She was disappointed that he didn't have the same intensity about the boy as she had, but then, in a strange way she was happy about it. It was almost as if she didn't want to share the pleasure the way she had shared the pleasure of Solomon. Sometimes she resented the fact that Joe loved Solomon as much as she did. Maybe that was just the possessiveness of motherhood, she thought, but in any case, it was there, the feeling existed, and she couldn't help it.

Martha stepped to the side when the agency car drove into their driveway. She was anxious to see Jonathan's expression when he first set eyes on the house, but she didn't want to appear obvious about doing it. She made up her mind she wouldn't be obvious about anything. She remembered Joe's warnings. In no way would she intimidate this child. She could frighten or discourage him if she did, and that would ruin everything.

She pulled a corner of the curtain back and peered out at

the car, confident that neither Mr. Frankel nor Jonathan could see her doing so. Jonathan stopped as soon as he emerged from the vehicle. She saw that he carried a small suitcase. It reminded her of the time Solomon insisted on having his own little suitcase when they took that motor trip to Toronto. How cute he looked carting it about . . . a little man dressed in his sport jacket and slacks. Everyone fell in love with him no matter where they went.

They could fall in love with Jonathan, too, she thought. At fifteen he was already five feet eight inches tall. He had the same thick, light brown hair with a natural wave, and like Solomon, Jonathan had a medium build, but with broad shoulders and a narrow waist. He would grow into a handsome and physically impressive man, just the way Solomon would have if he hadn't—she couldn't say it, much less think it.

She saw the way Jonathan squinted at the house, scrutinizing it carefully, almost scientifically analyzing, weighing, judging. Solomon had been just as exacting. Unlike most young people his age, he was rarely impulsive. Whenever he was asked a question of any importance, she could practically see his mind working. In school he was the play maker for the junior varsity basketball team. The coach told her Solomon was unique.

"He has a maturity about him. He doesn't lose his cool out there; he holds the others together and forces them to get back into position."

She saw what he meant when she went to the games with Joe and sat quietly in the stands. Other parents were boisterous and active, but she and Joe sat quietly observing and admiring Solomon for his grace and his skill, and yes, his poise. Occasionally, he would look up at her in the stands, and she would nod and smile.

Maybe Jonathan will go out for the team, she thought. He should get involved in the extracurricular activities. It's the fastest way to make friends.

She saw Mr. Frankel come around to Jonathan and offer

to take his suitcase or his small carryon bag. He reached out for one of them, but Jonathan simply glared. Oh, how Solomon could do that, she thought. He could drive people away with a cold, piercing look. He didn't need words.

She opened the door as the two of them came up the walkway.

"You found us," she said. The detailed directions she and Joe had given to Mr. Frankel left him concerned. He had a bad habit of getting lost on back country roads, he told them. He said it was easier for him to find his way around Brooklyn.

"The road signs up here are so small, and some roads have homemade signs painted on slabs of wood," he explained.

"Thanks to Jonathan," he replied, stepping forward to shake her hand, "we found it." Jonathan came forward, expressionless. "I nearly made the wrong turn twice, and twice he stopped me. It was almost as if he had been here before," Frankel said.

Martha smiled. Her gaze met Jonathan's and for a long moment, they simply stared at each other. The silence embarrassed Sam Frankel. It made him feel like an intruder at a dramatic homecoming.

Frankel knew that Martha and Joe Stern had had a very good first meeting with Jonathan. Although Jonathan wasn't an overtly difficult child, there was something about his personality and his manner that made all his previous foster parents nervous and uncomfortable. His most recent pair of parents admitted to locking their bedroom door at night. Obviously, that couldn't go on.

Frankel thought he knew what they meant. He and Jonathan had barely exchanged a dozen words during the entire trip up here, yet he felt a tension the whole time. It wasn't something easily explainable. No adult liked to admit to being afraid of a child, but after spending only a short time with Jonathan, he could understand why the boy's most recent foster parents locked their bedroom door at night.

"Well, you certainly have a nice piece of property out here, Mrs. Stern. Great views."

"Thank you."

"I'm surprised other people haven't grabbed up the adjacent property."

"Oh, people have been trying. We bought ten acres on the left a few years ago, and the land to the right is tied up in litigation. Relatives are all arguing with one another as to who owns what portion."

"Very convenient. If you like privacy, that is . . ."

"We do."

"Well, you can't get into much trouble out here, Jonathan," Frankel said jokingly. Jonathan didn't laugh. He shrugged and looked off to the right as though he saw something or someone familiar.

"Let's go inside. Would you like something cool to drink, Mr. Frankel? It has been unusually warm for autumn, don't you think?"

"Yes, it has. Thank you."

She opened the door and stepped back.

"My husband couldn't be here. He's on a major service call that he wasn't able to put off."

"Oh. Very complicated work, nowadays, servicing computers."

"Yes. He's constantly going in for retraining. There's a computer in Sol . . . in your room, Jonathan."

"I know," he said.

"You know?" Mr. Frankel asked.

"Mr. Stern told me."

"Oh, don't call Joe, Mr. Stern, Jonathan," Martha said. "He'll hate it."

"I won't," he said. His face softened.

"Just put your suitcase down a moment, and we'll all go into the kitchen for a cold drink," she said. Jonathan did so immediately.

"A pretty house," Frankel said. "Looks comfortable, livable," he said, even though he noted how neat and untouched everything looked. The living room off to the left of the alcove was bright with a light blue rug and a thick cushioned couch and settee done in a blue and white cotton fabric. There was a built-in glass-door bookcase to the right of the bay window. The walls were done in a pressed board of even brighter light blue. There was a rocking chair in the far right corner. Beside it was a magazine rack with just the right number of magazines in it. They looked as though they had been placed there more for decoration than for use.

Jonathan had a different way of looking things over. It was almost as though he had a photographic memory and simply snapped images as he went along. His short, quick looks left him with an expression of quiet satisfaction. Frankel thought he looked more like a drill sergeant who had found things as they should be.

Frankel couldn't help studying the boy and looking for his reactions to things. He hadn't been working for the child-care agency that long, but he had grown to expect certain responses when a child was brought to a new home. Some looked frightened, some looked angry, and of course, some looked happy. All of the reactions, whatever they would be, were reactions of children who felt insecure. At this moment Jonathan not only did not appear insecure, he appeared arrogant. It was as though he had expected no less.

The kitchen was just as brightly decorated as the living room. It was done in a radiantly yellow flower pattern and had glistening Formica counters and light pine cabinets. It was even more spick-and-span than the living room; in fact, it looked unused. He imagined that Mrs. Stern had spent the better part of her morning cleaning the house for the new boy. Frankel couldn't help thinking Jonathan didn't deserve such a welcome.

"This is very pretty," he said. He could feel how his

wife would envy this kitchen if she were here. She would be justified, he thought sadly, thinking about their far-distant plans to redo their kitchen cabinets. "Good sun exposure."

"We had hoped for a bigger window here, but in the early days, we didn't have the finances. Joe is talking about expanding the window. He wants to tear out the wall, but I just can't stand the thought of all that disruption."

"I know what you mean," Frankel said. It was a good rationalization for his failure to do anything new in his home.

"Sit down," Martha said. She went to the refrigerator and brought out some lemonade. After she poured two glasses, she sat across from them. "I've already contacted the school, so the bus driver has been instructed to stop. Tomorrow we'll get you registered."

"How long is the ride?" Jonathan asked.

"Only twenty minutes. We have a nice school system. Solomon . . . my son . . . was always on the superintendent's honor roll. He liked the teachers. Classes aren't too large," she explained to Frankel, "so the children get a lot of attention."

"That's great. My son and daughter go to a bigger system. I'm still trying to get Junior to open a book on his own, but between the television set and the Walkman and the video games . . ."

"We never had that trouble with Solomon. He was always reading or working on his computer. Do you like to read, Jonathan?"

"Sometimes."

"You'll find a great many books to choose from . . . all sorts of subjects. Solomon had varied interests." He sipped the lemonade and nodded.

Frankel knew that the Sterns' only child had committed suicide. He admired the woman's ability to talk about her son so objectively, and yet he sensed something eerie about it as well. It was more like the boy had gone off to college. He imagined this was the mind's way of protecting itself, and he thought in similar circumstances he might very well act the same way.

"Well, Johnny can be a good student if he wants to be," Frankel said, recalling the boy's past records.

"Do you like to be called Johnny?" Martha asked immediately.

"No," Jonathan said emphatically.

"I didn't think you would. Jonathan has so much more strength to it. Don't you think so, Mr. Frankel?"

"Yeah. I guess it does. Jonathan it'll be. So . . ." he said and gulped down the remainder of the lemonade in his glass, "I'd better be going. You have all the information you need, and you know now to contact us should there be any need."

"There won't be any need," Martha said softly.

Frankel looked at her and then at Jonathan. They were both looking at him now as though he were the one who needed supervision. He got up quickly and pushed his seat in.

"Thanks for the drink," he said. Martha stood up, and Jonathan followed. They walked Frankel back to the front door. When he turned around before stepping out, they were standing side by side, looking at him as though they had been together for years and he had merely paid a visit. "So long, Jonathan," he said. "Good luck."

"Thank you," Jonathan said.

Frankel stepped out, and Martha Stern closed the door behind him. He didn't understand it, but he had broken out in a cold sweat. Feeling ridiculous, he hurried to his car and drove off, looking back through the rearview mirror only once. The house, quiet and sedate, remained in his vision for a few moments after, fading slowly like a frightening memory.

Joe Stern slowed down after he made the turn onto Old Creek Road. There was no way to delay things any longer.

He had decided to clean up some loose ends at work even though he could have easily put them off until tomorrow. And when it was clear that there was nothing left for him to do but go home, he drove at least ten-miles-an-hour slower.

Everything he had agreed to do, he had agreed to do for Martha's sake. When she rejected one after another of the foster children Mrs. Posner had presented to them, he felt confident that she would eventually end her search, and the idea of taking in a child would die.

But then she set eyes on Jonathan, and everything changed. Although he didn't want to admit it to himself, he finally had to agree that the boy resembled Solomon in many ways, and not just physical ways, either. He caught a similar look in his eyes and saw the same calculated hesitation before he spoke.

There were many reasons why he and his son hadn't been as close as a father and son should be, he thought, but after all the rationalizations were lifted and all the explanations sorted, the primary reason had to be confronted: He simply didn't understand his own son, and he could never really penetrate the shell to reach the core. Certainly, he hadn't been able to forestall what had happened.

Scanning the past, Joe realized that from the moment Solomon could formulate his own opinions, his son had been disdainful of him. When Solomon was only eight or nine, he would often glare at Joe hatefully. Why? He never hesitated to offer companionship. He took Solomon with him wherever and whenever he could. He bought him most everything he wanted. And yet a real relationship between them never developed.

He never thought there was anything peculiar about Solomon, not in the way some fathers viewed their sons. Solomon was athletic; he had many friends, and he had girlfriends. He watched the television programs other kids his age watched; he had the same film and sports heroes;

he was so good with home computers, he could take one apart and piece it together again in an afternoon. He wasn't queer or effeminate. Joe had no reason to be ashamed of him.

And Solomon had no reason to be ashamed of him. Joe had provided well for his family; he was a respected member of the community and had even served two terms as a town councilman. And yet, the wall between them thickened. Toward the end it got so they could barely speak to each other.

Joe thought he should have seen the tragedy coming; he should have done more to prevent it, but it was almost (and God forgive him for this), it was almost as though he no longer cared.

He remembered finding it difficult to cry at the funeral. He was grateful for Martha's hysteria and his need to take care of her. It kept his mind off his own failure to mourn properly. When he finally did break down, it was because he recalled Solomon as a baby. It was almost as if his son had died at age three rather than at age fifteen.

For months afterward he had the feeling that Solomon was still alive, but keeping to himself, locked in his room and glued to that computer screen as usual. He didn't miss the small conversation they had between them. He didn't miss the rejections of his offers to do things together. In short, he wasn't saddened by the loneliness because he had been lonely so long.

What he had done was cling to the belief that somehow, someday, he and Soloman would become close. Solomon would mature into a fine young man and realize how valuable his father was to him and they would eventually do many wonderful things together. Whenever he thought about that, he became mournful. The future had died, and with it had died the potentiality of a fruitful father-and-son relationship.

He didn't want to admit it to Martha, but the real reason he didn't want another child in the house was because he was afraid of failing again. He certainly hadn't changed very much, and if this new boy was anything like Solomon, there was no reason to hope for any success. It was just a personality clash, one of those inexplicable, illogical, mystical events.

But then he thought, how could any new boy be just like Solomon? There had to be essential differences. Maybe he could capitalize on those differences and maybe he could build a meaningful relationship with the boy. He had to try, if only for Martha's sake. This was the first thing that had really brought her back to life.

For months after Solomon's death, she was like the walking dead. Nothing made her laugh; nothing made her smile much. She went through the paces, doing the things that had to be done, working and living like some kind of animated mannequin. It got so they had had little to say to each other. He began to feel he was living with a shadow.

Sex, which had once been a pleasurable and loving thing between them, died away altogether. Even a kiss good-bye had become perfunctory. They rarely touched.

And then, she got the idea to pursue a foster child, to seek one who would drum away the silences and light up the shadows. After he finally agreed to the idea, she was resurrected. There was music and sunlight and, most of all, there was affection, the old affection, the warm and loving affection.

They made love as though for the first time. They took walks in the fields and the woods; they held hands like school-age lovers, and they talked for hours at a time. Of course, her conversation was filled mostly with things she wanted to do for the new boy, but it was still excited conversation. There was laughter and humor. He could stand it.

It was just like . . . just like the days before Solomon was born. That frightened him a bit. He wasn't sure why, but it was eerie. It was as though they had turned back time, cheated fate, outsmarted destiny. A couple of times she spoke about the potential new child and unknowingly referred to him as Solomon. He didn't want to correct her; he let it pass, but it bothered him.

And then they found Jonathan, and it was as if what Martha had predicted came true. She had found a boy who was close enough to Solomon. What worried him now was how would the boy react to all this? No one likes to have his identity taken from him, not even a child who has had a bad life. He still has a clear self-image; he still has an ego, Joe thought.

What he was sure would happen was Martha would push too hard with her comparisons and her challenges. The boy would resent having to fill Solomon's shoes, and eventually, he would opt to leave.

How would Martha react to that? Would she see it as a second death? Would she go back to the way she was after Solomon's suicide?

His job, as he saw it, would be to temper her efforts. He would have to act as a mediator of sorts and get her to understand that she could have a child who looked something like Solomon, who even had some of Solomon's mannerisms, but who couldn't be Solomon.

Solomon was dead.

His body had swung back and forth under the thick, strong branch of the old maple tree. What could have driven him to it? What was too ugly to face?

He read somewhere that suicide was the biggest cause of death among teenagers. What a paradox. With so much of life before them, in their prime, with strength and beauty, they opt to travel "that undiscovered country from whose bourn no traveler has returned." Hamlet was young, and Shakespeare knew the torment and the pressures the young endure. Even in his time, it was difficult to be a teenager.

Joe turned into the driveway and pressed the button on his garage-opener transmitter. The door moved up slowly but obediently. Joe drove in slowly, even more slowly than usual because there was something different about the inside of his garage. There was a change in here, but for the moment, that change eluded him. It wasn't until he entered the house that the change occurred to him. Solomon's twelve-speed bike was no longer hanging on the wall.

Martha greeted him as he entered the kitchen from the rear entrance.

"Oh, Joe," she said. "He's a wonderful boy. It took him only minutes to acclimate himself to this house, and guess what he's doing right this moment," she said, speaking quickly and animatedly.

"Does it have something to do with Solomon's bike?"

"Yes," she said. "You're so observant. He's out back working on it, getting it back into shape. He says he'd rather ride it to school than go on the bus. Just like Solomon," she added.

He grunted and walked past her to look out the patio door. The boy had his sleeves rolled up and the tools placed neatly before him. He was adjusting the gear shift.

"Well, go say hello to him, Joe. Welcome him here, for godsakes."

Joe opened the door and stepped out. Jonathan didn't turn around. He was concentrating fully on his labor. For a moment Joe felt he had fallen back through time. How many times had he come upon Solomon doing something, either in his room or around the house, and waited for Solomon to acknowledge his presence. But Solomon was always too involved in his work, too.

"Hi there," he said. Jonathan turned around quickly.

"Oh, hi." He turned back to the bike.

"That hasn't been used in quite some time," Joe said. He walked around so he could face Jonathan. Even though he had met with him and spoken to him, he had forgotten exactly what he looked like. Whenever he did think about him, he pictured Solomon. He blamed that on Martha and her incessant chatter about giving the boy Solomon's this and Solomon's that.

"Yeah, I know. It wasn't shifting right."

"My son put a lot of miles on that."

Jonathan didn't respond. He checked the wrenches until he found the size he needed and then started to tighten the bolt.

"Need any help with it?"

"Naw, I think I got it now." He put the wrench down and turned the bike right-side up.

"Tires look like they might need air."

"I checked them. They both needed thirty-five pounds."

"That much?"

"Like you said. It wasn't used for a long time."

"Pretty handy, are you?" Joe asked. He intended it to be a compliment, but even he had to admit it came out sounding critical.

"I don't know. I guess."

"I was always like that, too. Diddling in that, diddling in this. I suppose working with computers and typewriters and other business machinery was just natural for me," Joe said. He realized he was concocting conversation, but he felt a need to keep talking.

"That's what Martha said," Jonathan replied. "Well, I guess I'll give it a test ride."

"Sure. Go ahead."

Joe watched him mount the bike and then peddle off around the end of the house and onto the highway. When he turned back to the patio door, he saw Martha standing there, smiling.

"He's fixed it up already?"

"Looks it," Joe said stepping back in. "Looks like you're right—he's made himself at home pretty fast."

"That's because he's never really had a home," Martha said. "Poor thing. We've got to make it different for him, Joe."

"Well, we'll do the best we can. What's for dinner?"

"I made the turkey. In celebration. Don't you remember

me telling you I would? My goodness, Joe. This is an occasion.''

"I suppose it is. Well, I'll go wash up.''

He went upstairs quickly, not understanding why he felt so tense. This was his house, yet he felt more like the one who had just arrived. He paused at Solomon's room. The door was opened and he saw some of Jonathan's things spread out over the bed. He walked in and looked about for a moment. Usually, he avoided this room. Martha kept it like a sanctuary. He knew she spent a good deal of her time in it, just sitting on Solomon's bed or going through his things. He suggested they give some of it away. He could have easily sold the computer. But that was like doing something blasphemous. Solomon had spent so much time working on it. Now the dark monitor atop the computer looked more like a sort of modern tombstone.

Oh, well, he thought. Maybe now some of this will get some use again. Maybe Jonathan would want to learn. He'd offer lessons. He started out and stopped when something caught his eye. It was the picture of himself and Solomon when Solomon was five and they had gone down to the Neversink Dam and caught three two-foot trout. Solomon was holding all three of them up but looking very unhappy about it. Bob Avery had taken that picture, he recalled.

But he also recalled Solomon taking it off his wall and putting it in his closet under a pile of parlor games. That was less than a year before his suicide. He asked him about it, and Solomon said he had other things to put up. But he never put anything up; he just left the wall bare.

Why would the new boy want something like that up on his wall? he wondered, and then he realized that picture was one of the very few pictures of him and Solomon together doing anything. Maybe this new boy longs for a good father-son relationship, Joe thought.

That encouraged him.

But it also, for reasons he didn't quite understand at the time, made him somewhat uneasy, too.

He went into the bathroom to wash up. While he was over the sink, he looked out the window that faced the front and saw Jonathan riding past the house, his body crouched over and his head down. His feet pumped the pedals with the same kind of vigor and anger that had made Solomon a champion at it. Joe used to think it was as if Solomon were attacking the highway. To him it didn't look as though his boy were having any fun.

This boy had the same serious expression on his face. Whenever Solomon wore it, which was most of the time, Joe would think his son had somehow skipped over the happy-go-lucky nonchalance of childhood, and he would pity him for that. There was time enough to bear down on life.

But it was no use to tell Solomon that. In fact, he acted as though he resented that sort of advice.

Maybe this boy would be different. Why shouldn't he be? Just because he was riding Solomon's bike, that didn't mean he had to ride it as Solomon rode it, did it?

Of course not, he responded to his own question.

But then, why was he riding it as Solomon rode it?

2.

Joe expected a certain amount of tenseness and nervousness at the first dinner. Despite the background information they were given about Jonathan and what Jonathan had learned about them before arriving, it was still, in reality for Jonathan and in reality for them, a dinner with strangers. But Joe was surprised.

He couldn't say "pleasantly so" because the instant familiarity between Martha and Jonathan was eerie. The boy came into the dining room and took Solomon's seat without even waiting first for instructions. He went right to it as though he always knew where he should sit. When Martha served the salad, she put Solomon's favorite salad dressing, herbs and spices in front of Jonathan, and he took it without even considering the other salad dressings available on the table. In fact, she seemed to know all the foods the boy favored—string beans, sweet potatoes with a mound of butter, the dark meat of the turkey rather than the white meat. He couldn't help noting that she didn't ask first. He assumed she had gone over the menu with him beforehand.

He realized Jonathan was wearing one of Solomon's short-sleeve shirts, the white one with the thin blue stripes. This is a boy who acclimates himself rather quickly, he

thought. Maybe that came from being shipped from home
to home. Joe felt a mixture of contradictory emotions. On
the one hand, he couldn't help resenting the new boy
taking Solomon's things so quickly, but on the other hand,
he pitied him for being a hobo searching for a handout of
family love.

"So how do you like the bike?" Joe asked. He remembered the day he bought that bike for Solomon. He had
gone into the den and found him glued to television cover-
age of the Tour de France bike race, and during one of
their rare father-son discussions, they talked about biking as
an exercise. He reminisced about his own youth and his
J. C. Higgins Special that had a horn and a light. Solomon
explained why that was unnecessary weight, and Joe could
see that the boy had been doing some reading on the
subject. He mentioned a few bikes, describing their assets
and liabilities. The next day, Joe bought him the Nishiki
International. He remembered being disappointed in Solomon's reaction because the boy behaved almost as though
he had expected it.

"Beautiful," Jonathan said. "Light, fast, great gear
shift."

"You've done some biking?"

"Not really. The people I was with last, the Porters,
lived in the city of Middletown, and Mrs. Porter thought
that riding a bike on the street by her house was too
dangerous. She was a nervous wreck about everything,"
he said, and Martha laughed.

Joe looked up and smiled at her. But his smile faded
when she ran her fingers slowly through Jonathan's hair.
The boy didn't wince or seem to mind it in any way. She
was always touching Solomon—pressing down his shirt,
squeezing his hand, rubbing the top of his back, resting
her hand on his shoulder, and kissing him, always kissing
him. It used to amaze him how his son accepted the
intimate contact and was never bothered, never embarrassed by it, even when it was done in front of others.

Sometimes Joe thought Martha treated their son more like a puppy dog than a teenage boy, but Solomon didn't resent it. If anything, he acted like an obedient dog.

How many times did he come into the den and find them on the couch, Solomon reclining with his head on Martha's lap, and Martha running her fingers through his hair just the way she had just run them through Jonathan's.

"He was telling me about Mrs. Porter," she said. "She sounds like a bundle of nerves. Do you know she made her husband lock their bedroom door at night?"

"What?" Joe looked at Jonathan, but he was concentrating on his food and wearing that far-off look that Solomon used to have whenever he ate. He hated his son's silence at meals. Often he looked as though he were in a trance and his body consumed the food automatically—his mouth working with monotonous rhythm, his hands cutting and bringing the food up to it within a pattern so tightly designed that he seemed to begin and finish each meal within seconds of the same amount of time. "She locked the bedroom door?" he repeated. "What was she afraid of?"

Jonathan shrugged.

"It's so hard for them to find adequate homes for the children," Martha said. "Thank God he got out of that place in time."

"You've been in three places, haven't you, Jonathan?" Joe asked. He meant it to be merely a subject for conversation, but Martha spun around on him so fast, he felt as though he had cursed the boy.

"Joe!"

"I just meant—"

"Yes, I have," Jonathan said. He turned to Martha. "It's all right. I don't mind talking about it."

"Well, you shouldn't have to relive the painful past," Martha said. "We're only concerned with having a good present and a good future. Let's forget about what's been," she added, and slapped her hands together as if the action drove every unhappy past moment into oblivion. "In fact, let's make a pact about it," she said.

Joe groaned. He couldn't help it. Making pacts had been one of Martha's favorite games with Solomon. Whenever something bothered either one of them, she would say "Let's make a pact to never do it again," or, "Never say that again." The pact was usually sealed with a kiss.

"Pact?" Jonathan said, and grimaced. Good for him, Joe thought. "What do you mean?"

"An agreement, treaty, a promise," she said, undaunted by his reaction, and took the knife out of his left hand. She placed it on the table and held his hand in hers. "I swear never to make Jonathan talk about anything he feels is an unpleasant memory." She started to lean toward him to kiss him on the cheek.

"What's his part of the pact?" Joe teased. She gave him her look of reprimand—the corner of her mouth drawn up, her eyelids nearly closed from the agitation.

"I won't bring up any of my pleasant memories," Jonathan said, "or make you and Martha feel you are not doing something as well as some of my other foster parents have," he added. Martha squealed with delight.

The shrewd little bastard, Joe thought. Kids were sure a lot smarter nowadays.

"This will really be a new beginning," Martha said. "For everyone." She and Jonathan turned to him expectantly. He was amazed at the similarity of expression on both their faces. The boy looked as if he could really be her child. Martha had unique eyes. Most of the time they were aqua blue, but when she got angry, the blue darkened considerably, and when she was very melancholy, her eyes looked more like a light green. Right now, both Jonathan's and her eyes were aqua blue. He had thought Jonathan's hair was a shade or two darker than Martha's, but at this moment, the hue of their hair appeared identical.

"There's no need for you to restrict yourself so," Joe

said. "We're not going to be jealous. At least, I'm not," he added.

"He's only trying to please us, Joe," Martha said. She kept her half smile. "And if that's the way he wants it . . ."

"I don't care," Joe said. "This turkey is really moist," he said, determined to change the subject. "One of your best."

"Well, it's a special occasion." She squeezed Jonathan's upper arm. He looked at Joe with what Joe thought was a very smug expression, an expression so like Solomon's that it gave him a chill. "And, I have a homemade apple pie coming up."

"Great," Joe said. "If she promises to cook like this every time we bring in a foster child, I'll go get a dozen more." He leaned toward Jonathan after he said it because even though he had intended it to be a joke, he recognized a tone of sarcasm in his own voice. He couldn't prevent it. Martha was ready to jump on him for saying it, but Jonathan surprised them both.

He laughed and laughed hard. Grateful for the rescue, Joe smiled at the boy. He looked like he expected the gratitude.

"You're both being very naughty. I've got two wise guys," Martha said. And then she sat back and with a far-off look on her face added, "Once again, I've got two wise guys."

Joe didn't say anything. After dinner he took Jonathan for a walk around the house. He described the boundaries of their property and told him about the small pond in the woods off to the left.

"Can you swim in it?"

"No, not really. It's small and muddy. There are some fish in it, sunfish, I've seen catfish. You ever go fishing, Jonathan?"

"No, not really."

"I do some trout fishing. Go up to the Willowemac. If you'd like to try to sometime . . ."

"Maybe," he said, but not with any enthusiasm. Solomon really never liked going fishing with him.

"Anyway, as you can see, there's plenty of room around here to stretch your legs. You can follow the path down the back of this hill, and it will take you out to the southwest end of the village eventually."

"What's that in that big old tree?" Jonathan asked, pointing to some slabs of lumber secured between two thick branches.

"Oh, that was a tree house I built for Solomon. I don't think he used it more than twice. It's still pretty sturdy." He looked back at the house. "I've got to paint the trim soon. You want to help do that?" he asked. It was a test question. Solomon had despised working on the grounds and the house, and anything he did do, he did reluctantly.

"Sure," Jonathan said. This time his voice indicated interest.

"Great. I'll be getting the paint this weekend."

Jonathan nodded. He didn't say anything for a few moments, and then he looked up quickly.

"What really happened to Solomon?" he asked. But before Joe could reply, they heard the back door open and close.

"We'll talk about it some other time," Joe said quickly.

They both turned to watch Martha come down the small flight of steps off the back deck. She was wearing a light green cardigan sweater and a pair of jeans with tennis sneakers. She had her hair down and around her shoulders the way he liked it. Joe thought she looked young and energetic. The new boy hadn't been in their house one full day, yet already there was a remarkable change in her demeanor. Her resurrection was continuing. In fact, she was so rejuvenated, she reminded him of how she was during the first year or so of their marriage. The spring that had been in the air was now in her as well.

She came forward, her arms folded under her breasts.

"It's going to continue to be a great fall," she said. "I just know it. Look at the redness in that sky. It will be warm tomorrow, your first day in a new school."

"Jonathan and I are going to paint the trim," Joe said. "Maybe we'll start this weekend."

"Really?" She didn't sound happy about it.

"Yeah. Why, you think we're going to mess it up?"

"No. Jonathan might just be too busy. You know, he's got to get himself into the flow of things . . . new teachers, new friends."

"Well, Jonathan will tell me if he's too busy," Joe said. "I'm sure."

"I'll see," Jonathan said. He stood there with his hands in his pockets. Martha smiled and threaded her arm through his. The boy didn't pull away, but he looked up at Joe to see his reaction.

"Come on," she said. "I'll show you where the blueberry bushes are. Solomon used to pick the berries in July, and I would make pies and muffins and put them into his pancakes." She started away with the new boy, leaving Joe behind. He watched them for a few moments and then went back into the house to watch the evening news.

It was a good half hour before they returned. He wondered what they could be doing out there all that time, and how Martha was able to think of so much conversation. It had been the same way with Solomon. Things to say just came naturally to her. He always felt as though he were contriving to build a discussion. Maybe it was mostly his fault; maybe he had been working with computers too long and didn't have enough contact with people.

"You can turn the television to whatever you like," Joe said when Jonathan came to the den doorway. "The news is over, and I'm going to do some reading. Gotta catch up on some new technology."

"I'm going up to my room," he said. "See you later."

"Oh?"

He left, and Martha came in. She curled up beside him on the couch and leaned against his shoulder.

"Your cheeks are rosy. Got a little chilly out there?"

"A little. Maybe I'm just flushed from excitement."

"He seems to be taking to us rather nicely," Joe said. "But you can never tell about these things."

"What do you mean?" She sat up. "He is taking to us."

"I just meant . . . I don't know. I hate to build up something and then have a disappointment."

"There won't be any disappointment," she said. He could see she was so determined, she wouldn't tolerate any discussion.

"Good."

She didn't lean against him again. She sat up straight and stared absently at the television set. Joe tried to go back to his reading but found he couldn't concentrate. After a while he put the magazine down.

"I don't think I'll enroll in that presummer course in real estate at the community college after all," Martha said.

After they had determined that Jonathan would be the boy to take in, Martha had revived her talk about getting her realtor's license. A friend of hers, Judy Isaacs, had done so and was now working with the Sandburg Realty Corporation. Judy's children were all teenagers, and she had decided to pursue an independent career. For a long time, even before Solomon's death, Joe had tried to get Martha to do the same sort of thing. He believed she needed outside interests and that her lack of them was the primary reason why she doted on her son.

"Why not? You were so interested in it."

"I think, for the time being, Jonathan's going to need my full attention."

"Oh, that's nonsense. He's obviously a very independent kid. He doesn't need you looking over him twenty-four hours a day."

"We'll see," she said.

"You're going to try too hard and ruin things," he said.

"Let's not argue about it, Joe," she said, smiling. He felt he was being handled, and understood she thought it was beyond him. In her mind he just didn't understand the needs of a child.

"We're going to make the same mistakes," he muttered. He regretted it immediately, but it was too late. The smile evaporated from her face, and the pain came into her eyes.

"What mistakes, Joe? What did I do?"

"I didn't mean that. I meant—"

"I know what you meant. You blame me, don't you?"

"Of course not. If there's anyone to blame, it's me."

"You always blamed me."

"Will you stop it," he said, assuming an angry demeanor in hopes that would abort the error. It didn't. The tears escaped from her eyes, and she got up quickly. "Martha!"

"I'm tired. I'm going up to lie down."

"Dammit," he said, and slapped the magazine against his leg. She left the den.

There was nothing he could do. He realized it would haunt them forever; forever the screaming would echo in his memory; forever those legs would swing back and forth, ticking away the end of three lives, not just the end of one. The shadow of Solomon's dangling corpse, magnified ten times, fell indelibly over the house and darkened the windows. There was no escape from the cloud.

Or was there? Could it be that there was promise and hope in the coming of the new boy? Could it be that Martha was right in her search and in her determination? Perhaps if they did devote themselves to Jonathan, they would be able to push back the darkness and bring back the sunlight.

He couldn't really blame her for treating Jonathan the same way she had treated Solomon. What other way did she know? She had been a mother only once. For some reason, after Solomon's birth, all their other attempts at having more children failed. Martha used to say, "Solomon doesn't want a sister or brother." She said it with such conviction that he began to believe she believed it. He even went so far as to ask the doctor if it was possible for a woman to will herself not to become pregnant. The doctor started to laugh, but when he saw Joe was seriously asking, he stopped and went into a detailed explanation of the biology. He did end by shrugging and saying, "But who knows the power of the human mind."

Perhaps it would have all been different if they'd had another child or two and Solomon hadn't gotten all Martha's and his attention. Maybe Solomon needed a brother or sister to confide in. What would it have been like if Jonathan had been living here then? he wondered.

What's the difference? he thought. It's too late now. Still, Martha might be right. The new boy might end up giving them more than they could give to him. He had to wait and see, but more importantly, he had to give it a chance and be cooperative. For the time being, he decided, he would do nothing to interfere with Martha's strategy. He shouldn't have even questioned her decision to postpone her career plans. If she was willing to be unselfish, why, he had to be as well.

Feeling guilty now, he got up and went upstairs to see if he could make her feel better. He paused in front of the door to Solomon's room and thought, I've got to stop thinking of this as Solomon's room. It's got to be Jonathan's room.

That's it, he realized. One of the first things he could do to help things along was change this room to satisfy the new boy. That way he would feel more at home. The idea excited him. He knocked on the door and waited. Nothing happened. Solomon had the same habit, he thought. He would ignore the first knock; and unless Joe had something he considered very important on his mind, he would give up and go to his own room. It used to amaze him. Why wasn't the kid at least curious about what his father wanted? Because he didn't care, that's why, he told himself. He just didn't care.

He knocked again, this time a bit harder. After a moment, Jonathan came to the door. He was wearing Solomon's light brown, cotton pajamas, the ones that had the initial S embroidered on the top pocket. They did fit him perfectly. How could he take to someone else's clothes so quickly? Joe thought. Despite what he had concluded earlier, he couldn't imagine himself being so easily adaptable, no matter how many homes he had been farmed out to so far.

He was afraid that this boy was so different, almost another species of human, that they would never find things in common and never reach real understandings. It might even be worse than it had been with Solomon, for at least Solomon was his own flesh and blood. There were some genetic links. What linked him to this child?

"Hi. Didn't want to disturb you, but I was thinking about this room," he said. Jonathan turned to look at it as though for the first time.

The room was a twelve-by-twelve with a heavy pinewood bunk bed on the left, and a dresser just to the right of that. There was a wall of attached shelves on the far right wall, the first three shelves of which were stocked with paperbacks and hardcover books. On the top two shelves were some of the model planes and cars Solomon had made from kits when he was only ten and eleven. To the right of the shelves was a large walk-in closet. Against the center wall and between the two windows that faced northeast was the matching pinewood desk and chair.

The year before Solomon died, Joe had gotten him an IBM PCXT with a ten megabyte hard-disc drive. Its capacity was far beyond anything Solomon needed at the time, but being an IBM employee, Joe was able to get a bargain, and he had the notion that he might get closer to his son if he could get him interested in the work he did.

He expected his son would have a million questions for him once he got started with the computer. He gave him an initial lesson and then Solomon started to read the basic manual. If he had any problems, Joe never knew about it, for Solomon asked him nothing. From time to time, he stopped by to watch him work on the computer and offered unsolicited suggestions. He brought him new and different software packages, but after a while, he sensed that Solomon wanted privacy whenever he worked on his computer. Ironically, the thing that Joe thought would have brought them closer together had wedged them further apart.

He always shrugged. Ah, well, with his son's high IQ, he was probably creating new programs. Solomon might be reinventing the field of computers.

The room was papered with blue and white glossy sheets that had pictures of a variety of sports cars scattered throughout. A light blue shag rug carpeted the floor, and Joe noticed it was beginning to show wear.

"What about the room?"

"Well," Joe said, stepping forward. "There's nothing chipped in concrete here. We can replace the wallpaper."

"It's all right," Jonathan said.

"You like cars?" Joe asked, and then shook his head. "Stupid question. All kids your age like cars. Well, this rug is looking anemic." He looked to Jonathan, but the boy only shrugged. "I see you are already learning about computers," Joe said, gesturing toward the IBM. Jonathan had it started and had drawn up a file.

"A little," he said, but Joe thought he looked guilty about it. "We had IBMs at my school, though I never learned much about them."

"After you get settled in awhile, I'll show you more. Could really help you in school." Jonathan didn't reply. The momentary silence made Joe uncomfortable. He kept looking around the room. "Main thing is for you to be comfortable," he said.

"I'm comfortable. You don't have to change a thing."

"Uh-huh. Well, we'll see as we go along. There's time," Joe said. His gaze went to a carton pulled out of the walk-in closet. In it were notes and papers and pictures, all Solomon's stuff, things he wished Martha would have at least put in the basement. It was obvious Jonathan had been spending time looking through it.

Oh, well, he thought. He couldn't blame him for being curious about the boy who had lived here before. Still, he felt uneasy about it. He hadn't looked in that carton himself because he was unable to involve himself with Solomon's personal things, just the way he was when Solomon was alive. He wouldn't think of looking in his son's drawers or through his papers.

"Okay," he said. "If there's anything you need—"

"Thanks," Jonathan said quickly. It was obvious he wanted Joe to leave.

" 'Night, then," he said. The moment he stepped out, Jonathan closed the door.

Why was it, he wondered, that the boy already made him feel like an intruder in his own home?

Martha was still awake. She was lying on her back, staring up at the ceiling, a Mona Lisa smile on her face. He hadn't seen that smile for quite a while. The Mona Lisa smile was attractive, but mysterious. Was it really a smile, or was it a grimace? In the early days, she teased him about it.

"I can't tell if you're happy or sad," he would say.

And she would say, "You'll just have to wait to see."

Usually it was a true smile, but because of the time when it was not, the look remained mysterious.

She was locked into some memory right now; it was obvious. He started to undress, deliberately making more noise than was necessary.

They had what would normally be a comfortable-size bedroom, sixteen-by-twenty, but since they had bought the king-size oakwood bed, the space was significantly diminished. Getting the big bed was more his idea. They were going to replace their queen-size bed with two singles because he was a restless sleeper, but to his mind separate beds added to the chasm that had been growing between them at the time. They bought the new bed a year before Solomon's death. He characterized most everything they did in those terms now.

Their life together was divided into two parts: before Solomon's death and after it. He had a strong feeling it was about to be divided into a third phase: after Jonathan's arrival.

"I was just talking to the boy about Solomon's room," he said, putting on his pajama top. He thought that would bring her out of her reverie. It did. She blinked rapidly and pushed herself up a little in the bed.

He saw that she was sleeping nude again. It was something she had stopped doing after Solomon's death. Why one should relate to the other, he did not know; but it was one of the many things in their daily lives that changed and made them strangers to each other. If he brought up one of these changes and asked her why she had done it, she couldn't remember how it was before or she denied that it was that way before. It had been a while since he challenged anything anymore.

"What do you mean? What about the room?"

"I thought the boy would like things more to his own liking. It would give him a better feeling and a stronger sense of belonging."

"But he likes everything in the room just the way it is," she said, obviously troubled by the suggestion.

"So I discovered. Weird," he added, and pulled on the pajama pants.

"I don't think that's so weird, Joe. Solomon had everything well organized in there."

"It's not a question of that, Martha. Everyone wants to put his own stamp on things; otherwise, it's not his own."

"Obviously this boy doesn't have those ego problems."

She pulled the blanket up against her throat as though she were suddenly very modest about herself. He didn't say anything else. He went into the bathroom and prepared for bed. When he came back out, she was on her side, her back to him. The blanket was draped just below her elbow now and the sight of her naked back stimulated him.

Ever since her high school years, Martha always had an attractive figure, giving credence to the belief that some people hold onto their shape for genetic reasons. No matter how little or how much she ate, her metabolism adjusted to maintain the symmetry in her body.

What was particularly beautiful about her was the way the lines of her features melded. Her neck turned gently into her soft shoulders, shoulders that were developed to the perfect point between femininity and masculinity. Some women, especially those who were involved with heavy exercise, had shoulders more like the shoulders of men, and some had shoulders so frail and bony they were downright unattractive. Martha's shoulders felt good in his palms. Whenever they embraced in bed, he lingered over them and then ran his hand down over her arms until he reached the point where he would move laterally and lift her full and perky breasts toward him. Whenever he strummed her nipples with his thumbs, her kiss would become more demanding. The slight touch of the tips of their tongues lit each other.

Joe wasn't a man with a record of sexual conquests. Twice before, during his college days, he thought he was in love. Now, whenever he looked back, those relationships seemed so insignificant, he had difficulty recalling what, if anything, had given them any intensity. When the lovemaking between him and Martha was good, pre-Solomon's death and lately, since Solomon's death, it was so all-consuming he felt as though they created a new form of life during the act. They were totally involved and gave of each other so completely, their identities merged. For those moments they became a part of each other. After it was over, he always felt it took time to return to himself.

Right now, he wanted that feeling very much.

He slipped into bed beside her and pressed his body up against hers, running his right palm down her shoulder and arm, over her hips and onto her thigh. She didn't respond. He pressed himself against her more emphatically. She could not misunderstand.

"Martha," he whispered. "You look so good tonight."

"Don't, Joe."

"Why not?"

"It's his first night here."

"So?" He pulled back. "What could that possibly have to do with it?" He waited, but she didn't respond, nor did she turn toward him. "Martha?"

"He might . . . hear us."

"Are you kidding? What do you think he's doing, holding his ear to the wall? Come on."

"No, I just feel nervous about it tonight."

"What if he did hear us? He's old enough to know what men and women do, for godsakes. Who knows what he's done during his wild life?"

She turned toward him.

"That's precisely why we've got to set a good example for him, Joe."

"So? We will. What's that got to do with making love?"

"Don't you remember that time Solomon heard us and came into the bedroom just as we . . . just as I opened my eyes and saw him standing there. He looked so angry."

"Not half as angry as I was. He was old enough to respect his parents' privacy."

"Don't talk critically about him. Not now, now that he's gone."

"Well . . . dammit. Do you expect this boy to come spying on us?" She didn't reply, and he thought for a moment. "Was that why that woman, Mrs. Porter, wanted her bedroom door locked?"

"What?"

"Was that the reason? Maybe the kid has a history of perversion."

"Joe!"

"We've got to think about it. They don't tell us everything. If they told the foster parents everything, there probably wouldn't be any."

"That's not fair, Joe. It wasn't his fault. That woman was a . . . was a nut."

"Maybe."

He turned on his back.

"I know what you're doing," Martha said. "You're blackmailing me."

"What?" He wasn't, but now that she had brought it up . . . "Well, if having a kid living here is going to interfere with my love life . . ."

"You're a bastard, Joe." He smiled, but she couldn't see. There was a long moment of silence, and then she said, "All right, but let's be quiet about it. At least tonight."

"It'll be a silent movie," he said, and subdued a giggle. He turned back to her and began to kiss her.

Just before his climax, he heard Jonathan come out of his room and go into the bathroom. He closed the door rather hard and rather loudly. It was close to a slam. He didn't come out and go back to his bedroom until after they were finished and Martha had turned over on her side again. They heard him close his bedroom door.

"Just like Solomon," she whispered. "He senses when we do it."

"For Christ sakes, Martha," Joe said.

But he lay awake for the longest time recalling his son's belligerent attitude the mornings after he and Martha had made love. He had to admit to himself, he had had a thought similar to hers. He just never verbalized it as she just had.

Because it was a ridiculous idea, he thought. No mother and son could be that simpatico.

And anyway, how could this new boy be so tuned in to them so quickly? In the back of his mind, he was afraid of the answer, for he suspected that the answer to this question would be the same as the answer to why he had taken so quickly to Solomon's bike and Solomon's clothes and Solomon's foods and Solomon's room.

3.

In the morning Joe couldn't make up his mind whether Jonathan was sleepy, pensive, or sullen. The new boy's conversation at breakfast, even with Martha, was restricted to short sentences and monosyllabic answers. Martha felt something wasn't right also, and he knew what she believed to be the cause. Before Joe left the table to get ready to go to work, she gave him an "I told you so" look.

"How about us going to one of the fast-food places for dinner tonight?" he offered, in hopes of rescuing the first full day with Jonathan. "Which one's your favorite, Jonathan? They just opened a new Roy Rogers in Middletown."

Jonathan didn't respond immediately. Joe recalled that Solomon had the same technique. Joe got to think of it as a technique because it seemed so calculated. After a while Joe had gotten to feel it was another subtle way his son belittled him—he would keep him waiting, especially when he offered to do something for him. He would do Joe a favor by responding. Usually Joe kept his anger contained, but occasionally, he expressed it by saying something like, "I just asked you a question, Solomon. The courteous thing is to acknowledge."

"I'm going to respond. I'm just thinking about it," Solomon would say. Of course, Martha defended him.

"He's not impulsive, Joe. We should be grateful. So many young people rush in where angels fear to tread."

"He's arrogant," Joe told her. But he didn't pursue it; he just stopped offering to do things.

"It's all right with me," Jonathan said finally, without looking at him. But he looked at Martha after he spoke, and she appeared to read something in his face.

"For the first week, I think I should make dinner for all of us," she said. "We want to get Jonathan into the habit of good, home-cooked meals," she added.

"Fine," Joe said.

"Maybe on the weekend we'll let you take us somewhere, Joe," she said. Joe felt as if she had thrown a bone to him. He shrugged.

"I gotta get moving," he said. "Have a good first day at school, Jonathan." He wanted to pat him on the shoulder, but he hesitated. Why was it that Martha had no inhibitions about touching him? What made him so timid?

Now that he thought about it, though, hadn't he been the same way with Solomon? Had it been Solomon's fault or his?

"Thank you," Jonathan said. Joe left the two of them sitting there, looking after him as he left. He had the same cold and empty feeling he had often had during the last year or so of Solomon's life. Was it something he imagined? Or had his wife and son come to resent him to the point where they welcomed his leaving? Once, when he and his close friend and attorney, Kevin Baker, talked about their relationships with their families, he described this feeling to him.

Kevin was a six-foot-two-inch, burly man with licorice-black hair and deceptive dark brown eyes. It was only because of their years of friendship that Joe was able to tell when Kevin was kidding and when he was serious. For the most part, Kevin liked to put people on. He could carry a joke or a fabrication deeply into a conversation before revealing through his impish smile that he wasn't telling the truth or that he really didn't mean what he said. Joe liked him because he was a bright, witty man who seemed unflappable. He used his sense of humor to insulate him from frustration and unhappiness, whether it involved his personal or business life.

"Maybe it's a reverse Oedipus," Kevin said. "You know, usually the son resents the father's closeness to the mother."

"You think I'm jealous of my son's relationship with his mother?"

Kevin smiled and shrugged. In this case Joe sensed that he was only half joking. He couldn't blame him for having such a theory; he had thought of it himself. In a way the possibility haunted him and made him somewhat paranoid about his own words and deeds.

He respected Kevin's opinion, not only because Kevin was a bright man, but also because they knew each other so long. Kevin and he had been high school classmates. They were lifelong residents of the area who had gone off to college and then decided to return to make their lives here. More and more lately that kind of thing was becoming a rarity. Young people were eager to make a completely new start, distancing themselves from their families and their origins. Kevin thought it was because travel was faster and miles of separation no longer had the same meaning.

"AT&T has made it possible to reach out and nag someone who thought he had escaped," Kevin said. "But I don't blame them for wanting to escape. Don't you remember how much we hated it here when we were in our senior year? It was fashionable to knock your hometown then," Kevin said.

Joe remembered, but he also remembered he wasn't as sincere about his criticism as some of the others were. Perhaps that was why he returned so easily and why he jumped at the opportunity when IBM offered it to him. Kevin had even closer ties, since his father had been a successful attorney in the area, and he could capitalize on his name.

Kevin's father had died when he was in his second year at law school, but when he graduated there was still a place for him at the firm. Joe was already working for IBM, servicing business machines. He met and married Martha after only a year and a half on the job. She hadn't gone to college. Right out of high school, she went to work for her father, who employed her as a secretary in his dairy business in New Paltz, which wasn't that far from the IBM plant. He came to service her electric typewriter and was immediately taken with her soft, and what he considered, naturally beautiful look.

Aggressive women turned him off, even frightened him a bit. Martha had a shyness to her that he found charming. Perhaps it came from being the only daughter in a family with six children. Four of her five brothers were older than she was, and from what she told him after they had started dating, they were quite overprotective and dominating. Her father was a stern, Old World type obviously uncomfortable in the presence of strong-willed and authoritative women.

It wasn't hard to see why Martha was somewhat subdued and lacked self-confidence. Right from the start, it took a great deal of convincing on his part to get her to do anything that involved her with the public. She didn't make friends easily, and most of the women who were married to the men he knew resented her for relegating herself to what they considered the old-fashioned role of wife and mother. To their thinking, she sacrificed too much of herself.

Even Kevin's wife, Mindy, never missed an opportunity to bawl Martha out for not being demanding enough. She wasn't underhanded about it; she would list her complaints about Martha right in Joe's presence. Martha made too many meals and didn't insist on Joe taking her out as much as she should. She should have demanded a cleaning lady.

She shouldn't be looking after her son so much. "Don't worry, children get along," Mindy told her, but Martha thought that Kevin and Mindy's two boys were self-centered, indulgent, unambitious children, logical products of parents who made their own pleasure the priority.

"They accumulate children the way most people accumulate most of their material possessions," she told Joe. He thought she had a good point, only he didn't see where they were having far superior results with Solomon.

Martha could cook; Martha took pride in her housework and believed no cleaning lady would have the same concern; Martha was understanding when it came to finances; Martha watched the budget and didn't splurge on clothing. In short, Martha became something of a threat to some of these women, so they rejected her, avoided her, and ridiculed her. Solomon's violent death seemed to confirm something for them, although they weren't in agreement as to what it was.

Joe's mother, Sara, who lived with Joe's youngest sister, Brenda, and her husband, Gary, in Yonkers now, had been a devoted wife and mother. Yet she was not limited in her vision. She had pushed Brenda into a college education. Brenda was an accountant, working for a big firm in New York City. They had two children: a ten-year-old boy, Stuart, and an eight-year-old girl, Harriet. As far as Joe could see, neither of Brenda's children seemed neglected because their mother was a working woman. Of course, he recognized that his mother was still a big help when it came to raising Brenda's children.

His father had died at the age of sixty-four, and although his mother could get along well by herself, being only fifty-nine at the time, Brenda and Gary were so sincere with their invitation, she couldn't resist moving in with them. Often now, Joe wished he had been smart enough to invite her to live with him and Martha. Perhaps, with her in the house, Solomon wouldn't have been driven to suicide.

He hated that expression "driven to suicide." The implication was quite clear—the boy hadn't wanted to kill himself, but something, some actions on his or Martha's part, perhaps, had pressured him into it. After Solomon's death, he read everything he could about teenage suicide, and whenever the subject came up during a television talk show, he was glued to the set. Martha avoided the subject, but he knew he would search forever for the cause. He was only afraid that Kevin's reference to Oedipus would prove true in another sense: like Oedipus he would seek the villain, only to learn that he, himself, was the villain he sought.

Joe discovered that teenagers were killing themselves today for a variety of reasons: some drug oriented, some associated with the pressures of school or the demands made by parents. Some couldn't tolerate failure in romance. But whatever the reasons were, Joe thought, wasn't it also possible that they had some fundamental weakness in them; something might even be genetic, like a faulty circuit or bad transistor in a computer. Eventually something would cause it to short out, but if the circuit or the transistor weren't faulty to begin with . . .

It made sense to him. He favored such a theory because it helped mitigate any responsibility he had for what Solomon eventually had done to himself. After all, they never pressured Solomon about his schoolwork because he did so well without their pressuring him. They encouraged him and congratulated him on his achievements, but there wasn't any overt influence. As far as they knew, Solomon was never involved with drugs and refused to be friends with those his age who were. And although he wasn't what Joe would classify as a lover boy, he had female interests and a strong relationship with one girl, Audra Lowe.

Kevin was sympathetic to Joe's theory about genetic flaws when they eventually discussed it. Of course, it took a while before he could talk about it, even with his best friend.

"You did the best you could," Kevin said. "You certainly didn't want him to kill himself. You weren't out to hurt your own child. It's got to have something to do with his own psychology. I think you're right: it might have been inevitable. I wouldn't swear for anyone, not even my own," Kevin said. Joe knew that Kevin was referring to his older boy's flirtation with cocaine. They already had him in counseling.

It was good having at least one friend like Kevin. Frequently, especially during the last few years, he found himself talking about more intimate subjects with Kevin than he did with Martha. It took him back to his teenage years when he and Kevin would confide in each other about their feelings and their fears concerning girls and school and their family life. They weren't afraid to expose their deepest thoughts. There was trust, the kind of trust that Joe realized should now be between him and Martha.

For a long time they had had it. Then they lost it, and now he had high hopes they were going to win it back. Recently, they were well on the way toward such a rebirth in their relationship. He had to do all that he could to keep it on track, and if that meant tiptoeing around the new kid for a while, why, he would do so.

The important thing was that she was happy again and that they seemed to have finally put Solomon to rest. The only thing that made him anxious now was the strange idea that the new boy could somehow resurrect him.

But why would he want to? From all of his experience, he knew that teenagers especially had such strong egos. These were the critical years for self-image and identity. Something that Mrs. Posner from the child-care agency had said made him wonder, though.

"These poor children, they're searching for an identity, searching for a place to belong. A name without a family attached to it is . . . is like a kite with a broken string floating aimlessly."

"Not anymore," Martha responded, and raised her hand

to demonstrate her determination. She closed it in the air as though she had grasped the string. "I'm going to take hold of that string and bring it back to earth." She looked proud of the way she had seized on Mrs. Posner's image. Mrs. Posner was impressed.

But who was seizing on whom? Joe wondered, now that he thought about the quick and complete way in which the new boy had taken to his new home and surroundings, even to the point of breaking into the computer, though he had little prior knowledge of how to operate one.

He went off to work, hoping that his anxieties were imaginary and short-lived.

Martha wanted to accompany Jonathan to be sure everything went smoothly, even though the child-care agency had sent all the necessary papers and information to the school. In her mind, the situation resembled the first time she had brought Solomon to school to enter him into kindergarten. He would need her beside him to give him confidence and reassurance.

Only, when she was truthful with herself, she had to admit that Solomon hadn't really needed her. While other four- and five-year-old children were crying and resisting being separated from their mothers and fathers, he quietly took his place and waited. She would never forget Mrs. Scoonmaker's admiration for him.

"Your son is such a little gentleman already. So mature. You've done well by him, Mrs. Stern," she said. Ten years later he would kill himself. If she could start over again, she wouldn't want him to be so self-reliant. At least, not from the very start. That was why she was so unhappy when Jonathan rejected her offer.

"I've had a first day before," he said. She detected a note of bitterness in his voice. Whom did she blame, she wondered, for his lot in life? Did he blame his own parents: a mother who had him out of wedlock and a father who deserted them before he was two years old? His mother neglected him so badly, the authorities finally took him away from her and began placing him in foster homes. And then look at all the failures he had experienced with foster parents since. No wonder he was bitter.

She nodded with understanding, but she could see he wasn't looking for sympathy. And there was no point in her insisting she go with him. She wouldn't push him; she'd made up her mind about that. She recalled how Solomon reacted whenever she insisted he do one thing or another. He would become like stone, refusing to argue, refusing to do it, whatever it was. He would stand there, biting down on his lower lip so hard it made his chin whiten. Once he even drew blood, but he didn't cease. He would wait as though she were a bad spasm that simply had to be tolerated. Eventually, she would give up and he would go on to do whatever he wanted.

"I'll take the bus today," Jonathan said. "Get the route down and then tomorrow, I'll take my bike."

"That's good. You'll want to ride the bus whenever we have bad weather," she told him, and then she thought, Did he say "his" bike?

Martha smiled to herself when she turned away from him at the front door. It was nice that he was taking to everything so quickly. Naturally, she wanted that to happen, but even she was quite surprised at how easily he was adapting to a new home and new parents. Was Joe right in sounding a note of caution?

Poor Joe, she thought. She was doing this for his sake as much as she was doing it for her own. In time, he would see that. He had suffered so after Solomon's death. She knew it, even though he was silent and devoted himself to making her happy. His tears were falling inside. How many times did she see him go out to look at the tree? She never joined him or said anything about it, but just like him, she couldn't look back there without seeing Solomon's body dangling. Once she even suggested they cut the tree down, but he didn't think she was serious about it.

She was. As long as it was there, it haunted her. That long, thick branch loomed larger and longer every time she went back there and envisioned him, his body turning ever so slightly north, northeast, south, southwest. It was as though the corpse were on an arena stage accepting applause from the full circle of admirers.

It was the look on Solomon's face that got to her, and she was sure, got to Joe, too. There wasn't an expression of pain; there had been no last-minute change of heart. There was certainly no fear of impending death. Instead, there was that sneer, that one expression of his that she hated so. He usually wore it when he ridiculed something either she or Joe suggested or did. She could remember him putting on the expression even as far back as grade school.

Solomon was never a whiner; he didn't nag for things. If a request for something was turned down, he didn't cry or beg or even sulk. Sometimes, she wished he had. Instead, he would simply nod and look thoughtful. Joe used to say he was filing his anger away, storing it all up for use at a later date. She refused to believe that. How could a child plot so and be so conniving? Why, when she was his age, she wouldn't have even been able to think of such things, much less carry them out.

But maybe there was method to Solomon's madness, now that she recalled it. After a while she got so she hated that deep thoughtful look more than other mothers hated crying children. The result was she gave in to a great deal more than she would have had Solomon not reacted to rejection in his special way.

She never told Joe, and in truth, she never fully admitted it to herself, but at times, she often felt anxious about Solomon. She had a mother's sixth sense about it. She knew there was something explosive in him. Perhaps her vigorous disagreements with Joe over some of the things

Solomon did or said was a result of her own anxiety. Was she wrong to have ignored it? Maybe if she hadn't . . . she didn't want to face any such conclusions.

Anyway, if she would have listened to Joe's evaluation of Solomon, it would have been almost like believing he wasn't their child, for what in Joe's background or in Joe's personality and what in her background and her personality could combine to produce such a . . . a creature. That's what he would have been if she had agreed with Joe half the time.

What else but a creature would want to set its parents against each other?

"That's exactly what he's trying to do," Joe said once, but she wouldn't even tolerate a discussion about it. She sensed a strain in Solomon's relationship with Joe, but she favored the idea that it was part of being a teenager, and had nothing to do with Solomon's personality.

Joe didn't really think it was that, either. He thought worse. It got so they didn't discuss much about Solomon at all. She sadly admitted to herself that toward the end, they had become more like three strangers in the same house. How did it happen? How did it come to that? She couldn't remember when it had begun. All she could remember was how it had ended.

It wasn't going to be that way with Jonathan. She was determined to make this work. She could understand Joe's misgivings; they were natural, considering what had occurred, but she would overcome it all. This boy was exceptional. The resemblances to Solomon weren't just a coincidence. In time, Joe would see and understand. In time, maybe they would both win back some of the life they had lost.

After Jonathan left for school, Martha went upstairs to work on the bedrooms. She went right to Solomon's old room, enthusiastically welcoming the added labor. But when she opened the door, she was surprised to discover that the room was in perfect order. The bed was made with that familiar military efficiency—the bedspread was taut; the pillow was perfectly centered. There were no articles of clothing left lying about, either on the floor or on the chair and desk. The closet door was closed, and all the drawers in the dresser were closed. Everything on the desk was neatly arranged. There was absolutely nothing for her to do. The room was just as it was when Solomon was alive.

For a few moments, she simply stood there staring at everything. Had this new boy really been here? He left the room in such order it looked untouched. As strange as it would sound to anyone, she felt a sense of disappointment. She wanted to look after Jonathan; she wanted some responsibility. She had expected it, especially after the descriptions of where he had been before he had come here. Those people didn't sound like the type of people who would imbue such a sense of decorum in the boy's life. From where had he gotten it?

Suddenly she had the vivid image of Solomon standing by the right window staring out at the lawn and the woods. It was like so many times before—she would come up the stairs quietly or down the corridor softly and stop to look in at him whenever he left his door opened. If he had his back to her, neither of them spoke, but after a few moments, he would say something that indicated he knew she had been there awhile.

The illusionary Solomon turned away from the window slowly, but it wasn't until he was facing her that she saw the noose around his neck. Beneath the rope, she could see the thick, red ropeburn. His facial features were just as distorted as they were that day he hanged himself, and he wore that same sneer.

She brought her hand to her throat. It seemed to have closed as if her body were shutting itself down. She closed the door quickly and almost immediately felt a shortness of breath. When she touched her cheeks, her face felt clammy. She immediately went to the bathroom and dabbed herself with cold water. Her reflection in the mirror was ghostly pale. Indeed, she felt like someone who had just gazed into a coffin.

Her mind was playing a terrible trick on her. She knew why it was happening—she was feeling guilty. Solomon was being replaced. If he could come back from the dead and speak to her, he would show his anger.

But it wasn't fair. How about her anger? How about what he had done to her? He had no right to be upset; there was no reason for her to feel any guilt.

One thing was for sure: She wouldn't tell Joe about this. That's all she had to do, and it would confirm his misgivings and make everything impossible. She had to deal with this herself; she had to find the strength to overcome it. Determined to do so, she knew she had to face down the illusion immediately. She turned from the bathroom mirror and went back to Solomon's bedroom.

This time when she opened the door, she confronted an empty room. There was no image standing by the window, and all was quiet and untouched. She took a deep breath. Confident and satisfied, she closed the door and went on to work on her and Joe's bedroom.

She had barely completed her morning housework when the phone began to ring. Sally Cirillo called first, followed by Sandy Miller and Mindy Baker. Of course, everyone wanted to know about the new boy and what he was like, but she heard the unasked questions, too. Was it painful to have a teenage boy living in Solomon's room and using Solomon's things? How was Joe reacting? Were you continually making comparisons between the new boy and Solomon? Were you sorry now that you had agreed to do this?

She revealed little or nothing about her true feelings. She never mentioned Solomon once, and she talked about Jonathan as though he had been living there for years. She sensed the disappointment in their voices. Mindy was the only one who was somewhat direct.

"Don't become a slave to the kid like you were a slave to Solomon."

"I wasn't a slave. I never did anything I didn't want to do," she responded. Her voice began to sound small and weak to her.

"The quicker you get them on their own, the better it will be for all concerned, believe me," Mindy said.

"Why do we have children if they're such a burden?" Martha replied. It was her strongest statement of the day. Mindy didn't answer. She simply repeated her advice and babbled on about a new restaurant in Goshen.

"The Coopers want to go, too, so maybe the six of us can go down this weekend. Kevin will talk to Joe."

"Okay," Martha said. There was no commitment in her voice. She was relieved when the conversation ended.

Joe called from the road. He was in Port Jervis, but he thought he would be home by five. He didn't ask anything about Jonathan. She went to the supermarket to stock up on the kinds of snacks and cereals she recalled Solomon liking, and by the time she returned and had everything organized in the kitchen, she heard the school bus pull up in the front of the house. For her, the day just seemed to have flown by. She couldn't remember time passing so quickly since Solomon's death. The days between then and now were all long ones. Time seemed to torment her. She remembered the days she would simply sit and look at the clock and think about all the things Solomon would be doing at this moment or that, if he were still alive.

She went quickly to the front and looked out just as the bus was pulling away. Jonathan came down the sidewalk, carrying his newly issued schoolbooks under his right arm. Just like Solomon's hair would be, Jonathan's was as neatly in place as it had been in the morning. He had the same good posture when he walked—his head held high, his shoulders back.

Martha had always enjoyed studying Solomon from a distance, observing him when he was unaware she was doing so. Most of the time, that was impossible because he usually sensed her presence, but sometimes he was in such deep thought about one thing or another that he didn't seem to know she was peering down at him from a window or looking out at him from behind a curtain. Then again, she thought he did know but pretended he didn't, maybe for her sake.

Jonathan looked deeply pensive as he approached the house. His eyes were small and his face was still, the smooth and remarkably blemish-free skin of his cheeks drawn tightly down to his jawbone. He looked ethereal, otherworldly. Solomon had had a slightly softer chin, and his facial bones weren't as emphatic. In some ways, Jonathan was better-looking, she thought. He already had a more mature, masculine appearance. Again, she thought that could be another thing that was somehow a result of the hardships he had already endured.

In contrast, Solomon's life had been soft and smooth. He was always well protected and well cared for; he lacked nothing and suffered few disappointments, as far as she could tell. All that he had, he had gotten with relatively little effort on his part. There were no struggles that compared with Jonathan's struggles.

She greeted him at the door. He looked as if he had expected her to. Would she have as much difficulty surprising this boy as she had surprising Solomon? Was she so predictable? She made a mental note to ask Joe about that sometime when they were alone.

"Hi," he said, and stopped in the hall beside her.

"Good day?"

"Yes," he said. He nodded with a sincere look of satisfaction on his face. "I like the school, and for the most part, I like the kids."

"Oh, that's wonderful," she said. "I was so afraid the other students wouldn't be as friendly. I know how it can be when you're a new kid on the block." She wiped her hands on her apron even though she had nothing on them. The nervous gesture made her conscious of how closely she was standing to him. She saw the way two little hairs on his eyebrows curled upward.

"No problems. I got to meet quite a few of them, too. Quite a few of Solomon's friends," he added.

"Really?" She couldn't help the way her incredulous smile froze on her face. She had always thought Solomon's friends were special. His friends were the brighter and more talented kids, but they were also somewhat snobby. From what she had learned about them when they were at the house and from the things Solomon had told her, they weren't the types who would take in a new person easily.

"Yea. I hope you don't mind," he said, "but I invited someone over tonight. She's going to help me catch up on a few things. It's hard enough to start classes in the beginning, much less toward the middle of the year."

"Oh, no, I don't mind. That's wonderful. Next time you can invite someone to dinner."

"Thank you. Well, I'd better get a little of this done before she comes tonight," he said, indicating his homework.

"Great. We're having veal and peppers, one of your favorite meals," she said, and then laughed quickly. "I meant—"

"I know. It was one of Solomon's. That's all right. It's one of my favorites, too, although I haven't had it much. See you in a while," he said, and lifted his books again to indicate what he was going to do.

"Great."

She went off to work on the meal when he started up the stairs. She had planned to make an apple cake for dessert, another one of Solomon's favorite foods. Joe was fond of it, too. Now, after seeing how well Jonathan had done at school his first day there, she felt enthusiastic about everything.

Jonathan was still upstairs working on the computer when Joe returned from work. He looked tired, and he explained that he had run into three major problems with a company's computer system, all of which would require him to spend at least two more days there.

"They really need one more serviceman on this route," he said, "but no one wants to believe me."

"Don't do any more than you can, Joe. They'll get the idea soon enough."

"Yeah, sure." He looked about and then inquired about Jonathan.

"He's upstairs, working on the computer. He went right to it, just like—he's very excited about the school."

"Oh? He's spending a lot of time on the computer?"

"He said the students took to him. He's already made friends, many of whom were Solomon's friends."

"You're kidding. You mean like Arthur Griff and Larry Elias?"

"I don't know. He didn't mention names. Oh," she said, "I almost forgot. One of the kids is coming over to help him catch up with some of the work. Isn't that wonderful?"

"Yeah. I guess he's got more personality than I first thought."

"I knew he would succeed here. I just knew it."

"It's great," he said. "Who's coming over?"

"I don't know. I forgot to ask."

Joe laughed.

"What were you, in a daze? You don't seem to know any details."

"I didn't want to seem like I was prying," she said, almost in a whisper. He wondered why she had lowered her voice so, and then he heard Jonathan coming down the stairs. They both turned to him as he approached.

"Hi. Martha says you had a nice first day at school."

"Pretty good. Yeah. How was your day?" he asked. Joe smiled. He couldn't remember Solomon even once asking that.

"Not so good. I've got three malfunctioning hard discs in the PCs at this one firm."

"Maybe he doesn't know what you're talking about, Joe," Martha said. "I don't."

"Yes, I do," Jonathan said, but he looked like he regretted it immediately.

"That's an understatement," Joe said. "Wait until you see what it can do."

"Sometimes I thought Solomon had become attached to it," Martha said.

"A lot of the kids have computers. At least, many of the ones I met today."

"Sure," Joe said. There was a long moment of silence. Joe looked to Martha, who was beaming. He was feeling kind of good himself. "I guess I'll go wash up for dinner. Smells like another feast. And apple cake, too."

"Well, I've got two hungry men to feed," Martha said. "And we want to eat on time tonight. Jonathan's got someone coming over after dinner."

"Oh, right," Joe said. "Who's coming?"

"Her name's Audra," Jonathan said. "Audra Lowe."

For a moment Joe could not speak. He looked at Martha, but she didn't seem as stricken. He decided not to attempt any words. Instead, he nodded and went upstairs, pursued by the vivid memory of Audra Lowe and Solomon all dressed up and seated in the back of the car. He was taking them to a school dance.

But that was more than a year ago, maybe a month before Solomon's death. She hadn't been back since, of course. And they hadn't seen or heard anything from her. Why should they? he thought. She was just a kid, a friend of Solomon's who had, as far as they were concerned, died along with him, just as all his other friends had.

But after only one day, the new boy had resurrected her, along with all the memories and all the pain.

4.

Audra Lowe was mature for her age in more ways than one. She always seemed to be a little ahead of herself, a little too perceptive and sophisticated for her age group. The second of four children, she was quite unlike her two younger brothers and her older sister, Debbie. She was rarely involved in sibling rivalries and most helpful to both her parents. As early as the age of seven, she was helping her mother in the kitchen. She was very dependable as a baby-sitter for her two younger brothers, when she was only ten herself.

Her sister, Debbie, behaved more like a typical teenager. Her father often said that Debbie more than made up for Audra's failure to waste time on rock music and boys. Debbie had smaller features and did seem more distracted by her own appearance and beauty, although Audra was far from unattractive.

She had long, light brown hair that she always kept well brushed and soft. For the last three years, she had maintained its length at her shoulders, while her girlfriends experimented with every hairdo worn by every teenage star in sight. Debbie was always after her to do something different, but Audra wasn't moved by fads.

Her stability in dress and coiffure separated her from the

pack. She wore jeans and sweatshirts, but also wore simple cotton blouses and skirts of conservative colors. And
even when she wore an old pair of jeans and a sweatshirt,
she somehow looked neater than most of the other girls.

Audra had a soft-spoken, easy manner that bespoke
self-confidence and maturity. Her teachers loved her. She
was a reliable and responsible student, concerned about
her homework and her grades, but also able to look past
the marks to the real purpose for studying the subject.

Her physical maturity developed right along with her
mental and social maturity. At fifteen, she stood five feet
eight, had a full bosom and a narrow waist and hips that
made older women drool with envy, yet she didn't flaunt
herself about. She seemed to have a quiet understanding
about sex that ironically turned many boys off. They felt
outclassed. To the high school boys, going out with Audra
would be like going out with a girl who had already
graduated from college. Except for Solomon Stern and
some boys she was rumored to see occasionally in New
York City, she was rarely involved with anyone.

But that didn't seem to bother her. She wasn't as intense
and as concerned as most of her girlfriends were about
their romantic relationships. Her patience confused them.
Was there really something she knew that they didn't?
Some sensed that she did because they came to her for
advice. No matter how trivial the matter, Audra gave it
serious consideration and made them feel that they were
talking to someone much older.

It seemed natural to them that Audra would have been
close with a boy like Solomon Stern. He was so deep
and so intelligent, most girls felt uncomfortable with
him, especially when he was witty and sarcastic. Only
Audra seemed to be able to contradict him openly. Only
Audra seemed to understand what moved him. Only Audra
seemed to care.

The truth was Audra was comfortable with Solomon
Stern because, like her, he wasn't frivolous. He, too, seemed

to have skipped over that period of youth characterized by waste and nonchalance. He didn't appear threatened by his failure to be popular with most other teenagers, and when it came to romance and sex, he also had a calmness about him that suggested more maturity. They gravitated toward each other more and more, linked by every critical comment about other students and by their seeming unity of perception when it came to how people should conduct themselves.

What bothered Audra the most about Solomon's suicide was that she had absolutely no inkling that it was about to occur. She had had a telephone conversation with Solomon the night before he killed himself, and no matter how many times she went over that conversation in her mind and reviewed each and every word, she couldn't see where he had been reaching out or in any way indicated what he was about to do.

In fact, when Sally Kantzler called her to tell her, her first reaction was that Solomon was murdered and his death made to look like a suicide. She kept expecting such an announcement to follow, but, of course, it never did. She told no one about her idea because she thought it made her sound as though she were looking for justification for not being perceptive enough to see Solomon's problem and prevent the suicide. But she never once thought that Solomon blamed her for not coming to his aid.

All the while at the funeral, she imagined Solomon beside her making sarcastic comments about the conduct of the ceremony and the manner in which people behaved. The fantasy was so vivid she had to check the people who were really standing beside her to see if any of them were hearing what she was hearing. At one point she nearly broke out laughing because she heard Solomon singing, "I did it my way . . ." She was sure that if he could come back from the dead, he would do that.

She really did like him. She liked his offbeat sense of humor, the way he could suddenly stop talking and stare into her eyes, confident she could finish the thought, and she loved the way he handled people, whether they were teachers or fellow students. He could turn sincerity on and off like a faucet and always be convincing. A good deal of the time, she wasn't sure herself whether or not he meant what he said. She would have to ask him afterward. Sometimes he was cagey and said, "What do you think?" But most of the time, he wanted to share his true feelings with her.

If there was one thing she could point to in their relationship and say, "This is why I liked him so much," it would be the fact that he never betrayed her. No matter what she told him, it remained with him. He knew when she was intense and when she wasn't, and he knew, almost instinctively, what was important to her and what was not. She could trust him with her most intimate thoughts. In a real sense, Solomon Stern was the best friend she had ever had, and she mourned his death as though a part of her had died.

That was why she was most intrigued when she heard about the coming of the new boy, the boy the Sterns had taken in to live with them. She knew he would live in Solomon's room, and although she couldn't imagine anyone taking Solomon's place, she knew that he would fill some of the terrible gaps in the Sterns' lives. Who had Mr. and Mrs. Stern chosen to do such a thing?

The moment Audra set eyes on him, she experienced a chilling familiarity. The physical resemblances notwithstanding, she saw a similarity in expression and demeanor that not only brought Solomon to mind, but gave her the eerie feeling that his soul had somehow slipped into and possessed this new form. She shook the wild idea from her mind quickly. Solomon and she had discussed the occult and the supernatural, and they had both concluded that stories, movies, and television programs that dealt with it were nothing more than fairy tales on an adult level.

"Unfortunately," Solomon had once said, "there is nothing more than what really is. Most of us don't want to face it, so we fantasize. Illusions make truth palatable," he concluded. He had used that theme for an essay in English and gotten an A plus. Mr. Littlefield, the teacher, enjoyed the allusions to soap operas so much he had read the essay aloud in all his classes and insisted that the school newspaper print the essay in its next edition.

In any case Audra discounted her initial reactions to Jonathan, considering it to be a product of her own need to replace Solomon. Since his death, she had become something of a loner. She had not gone on a single date, and she had become a thorough workaholic. If anything, she found herself estranged more than ever from her peers. She kept up casual relationships and remained friendly with what had once been known as "Solomon's crowd," but she didn't socialize with them very much. No matter where they were or what they did, to her it seemed as though the heart had been cut out of them. Like the disciples without Jesus, she thought.

She had intended to introduce herself to the new boy and make him feel comfortable, mostly because she wanted to do something for the Sterns. She liked Martha and Joe Stern even though Solomon often treated his parents as though they were a necessary evil. Actually, he was more like that in relation to his father. His mother he seemed to have treated with more sympathy and understanding. She got the feeling he thought of his mother as the child and himself as the parent sometimes.

And then sometimes she caught him looking and talking to his mother as though she were someone he idolized from a distance. During those times he reminded her more of a teenager doting on a television or movie starlet. Solomon wasn't fond of discussing his mother, though. It was one of the few subjects he treated with an almost religious taboo.

Everyone knew the new boy was a foster child and therefore something of a wandering orphan. Audra, who came from a very close and relatively large family for this day and age, couldn't imagine what it would be like to "borrow a home" and then have to do it more than once. She was intrigued with the new boy because of that as well. She wanted to see what he was like and how being a foster child had affected him.

She had no problem meeting him. In fact, he approached her. It was just after their first class together. She had seen him in homeroom for a few moments because Miss Bogart, the homeroom teacher, immediately sent him to the office for some forms. The forty-five-year-old spinster was always unnerved by anything that caused her to break away from her pattern of procedures. She practically panicked during the fire drills, screaming orders with a voice shrill enough to be used as the alarm. Jonathan's sudden presence sent her stuttering and fumbling for things on her desk. Most of the students smiled and laughed, but Jonathan stood there, calmly waiting, looking cool and collected. Just as Solomon Stern would have, Audra thought. She was fascinated, and when he turned around and looked at her, she was positive that he knew her. But how? How could he know about her relationship with Solomon?

Did the Sterns tell him about her? she wondered. Such an idea seemed improbable for a number of reasons, not the least of which was her perception of how difficult it must be for them to talk about Solomon, even after this length of time since his death. And she was never sure that Martha Stern liked her that much. Sometimes she got the feeling that Solomon's mother thought he was spending too much time with her, even though Solomon assured her that wasn't so.

She went to her first-period class, but Jonathan, because of the business at the office, came late. He was put in a seat two rows away from her and to the rear. Every once in a while during the period, she turned slightly and looked back. Each time she did so, she caught him staring at her. Once, he smiled at her. Right after the bell to end the period rang, she got up and saw that he was waiting for her.

Her heart began beating rapidly. She couldn't recall being as nervous and excited about meeting anyone, not even when her parents took her and her sister and brothers to see the Monkees in a revival show at the Monticello racetrack and her father managed to get them to meet Davy Jones afterward.

Jonathan lingered at the doorway to the classroom. He didn't take his eyes off her as she walked up the aisle. Some of the other students noted that he was waiting for her, and they were obviously curious.

"Hi," he said as she approached the door. "I'm Jonathan," he added, as though that were enough. It brought a smile to her lips. She brushed back her hair with her free left hand. "I'm the new kid," he said with Solomon's tone of dry sarcasm, and she laughed.

From there it just flowed smoothly and naturally. They waited for each other at the end of each period. In science, he managed to get seated beside her. They sat together at lunch, and she introduced him to many of Solomon's friends. She sat back and watched how he handled them, how he knew just what to say to make them feel comfortable. In a matter of minutes, he grasped each separate identity and seemed to know just what each one wanted to hear and know. Before the lunch bell rang, they were talking to him as if he had been there for years, not hours.

He even seemed to know about Donald Pedersen, the one boy Solomon had absolutely hated.

By day's end, Audra had begun to feel that Jonathan's arrival was something just short of miraculous. A brightness had returned to her life. The dark shadow that had descended since Solomon's suicide lifted. She was excited by the sound of her own laughter. The loneliness that had been wound around her like a sari began to unwind and fall away with every passing moment she and Jonathan spent together. She welcomed the sense of freedom that followed.

Despite the terrible feeling of sadness and horror she often experienced when she went by or even near the Stern residence now, she didn't hesitate to accept Jonathan's invitation to come to the house in order to go over some of the work he would have to review. She couldn't believe how quickly she had agreed to the visit herself. And when she went home and told her mother what she was going to do, her mother stopped what she was doing in the kitchen and looked at her as if Audra had announced she were enlisting in the army.

"You want to go to the Sterns' house?" she asked.

"Yes." Audra became introspective a moment. Her mother's surprise made her self-conscious. She had been behaving like someone under hypnosis.

"You seemed surprised yourself," her mother said, and smiled widely. "You want to help this new boy? A stranger?"

"Well, he's not exactly a stranger."

"What do you mean? You knew him before? Where? When?"

"I don't know," Audra said.

"What?"

"I mean, he reminds me of Solomon."

"My God," her mother said. "What a thing to say and with the boy living in the Sterns' home, too." Her mother looked pensive for a moment. She returned to the batter she was preparing for chicken cutlets and then stopped as if just realizing something very important. "Is that why you're going over there?" she asked.

Audra looked up sharply.

"I don't know. Yes," she said quickly. "But I don't want to talk about it," she added, and fled from her mother's look of amazement, not knowing why she felt she had to.

• • •

The Lowes lived in a rich-looking, brick-faced ranch-style home in what was essentially the first housing development constructed in the Upstate New York, Catskill Mountains village of Sandburg. Audra's father had been one of the early investors in the project; consequently, they had the choice corner lot, which was only a half a block from Main Street, Sandburg. Her father was an accountant who had good judgment whenever it came to investments. Presently, he was one of the investors in a rather large town house project being built to attract the so-called second-home market.

Stephani Lowe found that her anxiety about what her daughter had told her did not lessen as the early evening went on. During dinner, she tried to bring up the subject of the new boy and Audra's intentions to go to the Sterns' to help him with schoolwork, but Audra wouldn't talk about it, and Harry Lowe was too excited about the four new sales at the town-house project to pick up on his wife's tensions. The other Lowe children had heard about the new boy, but none of them had Audra's interest in him. As usual, the conversation at dinner was a cacophony of different discussions with rarely a time when everyone listened to only one speaker.

As soon as dinner was completed, Audra went to her room to get her books. When she stopped by the living room entrance to tell her father she was leaving, he looked up in surprise. He had been sitting there reading the proof of a pamphlet created to advertise the new town houses.

"Leaving? Going where?"

"She's going to the Sterns'," Stephani Lowe said. She was waiting in the hallway by the kitchen, expecting Harry to snap out of his fantasies about making fortunes just before Audra left and realize what she had been trying to tell him at dinner. It was typical of him, Stephani thought; he hadn't heard a word she had said at the table.

"The Sterns'? What for?"

"I'm helping the new boy get started with our subjects," Audra said.

"New boy? Oh, that foster child they took in. It's a boy, huh?" he said, as though Martha Stern had given birth again. "How old?"

"How old? Harry, don't you listen to anything I say?" Stephani said, stepping forward. "He's the same age as Solomon would have been. He's in Audra's classes."

"No foolin'. What'dya know about that? And you're going to help him, huh? That's nice."

"Harry."

"What?" He looked up at his wife, puzzled.

"Oh, what's the use," Stephani said. She really didn't know what to say herself. He had never had the same anxieties about Audra's relationship with Solomon Stern. Even after Solomon's suicide, he was unable to understand why Stephani was so uptight about Audra's having spent so much time with Solomon. But Harry was always like that when it came to people, Stephani thought. He was always blind to the nuances in character or the quirks in personality that she thought were obvious. Harry had a tendency to stereotype and classify people. Teenagers were all the same, just as were doctors and lawyers and small businessmen. They were categories on a tax form.

Another thought came to her mind as she searched for a way to make him see some danger. "I don't think you should be riding your bike at night, Audra."

"Why not?"

"It's too far to go on a road without streetlights," she said.

"But you never complained before. Why is it suddenly too far?" Audra didn't whine; she never had to whine. Even as a little girl, she was somehow perceptive enough to cut right to the heart of something. It was difficult to deal with a child who could be so logical and right. Most of the time, Stephani would simply say, "Because it is," and leave it at that. It was easier to deal with Debbie because Stephani was more like Debbie.

Audra took after Harry's side of the family in looks. Debbie had Stephani's small, slightly upturned nose and emerald green eyes. Audra's eyes were deep blue, thoughtful, and penetrating. When she spoke to someone, she held her gaze firmly. She didn't have Stephani's and Debbie's shy and somewhat coquettish manner of looking quickly and then down or away.

Audra was already an inch taller than Stephani and two inches taller than Debbie. Sometimes Stephani thought that the physical differences and the differences in mannerism between her and Audra were what made it so difficult for them to understand each other.

"Well, I should have complained about it before," Stephani said.

"What's the problem?" Harry said. "I'll drive her."

Stephani looked at him with both shock and annoyance. Couldn't he see that he was contradicting her?

"Thanks, Dad," Audra said.

"You'll have to pick her up," Stephani said, hoping that would discourage him. Why she was so intense about this, she couldn't say, but she was, and it was something she couldn't help.

"Maybe. Maybe Joe Stern will drive her home. You're not staying there very late anyway, right, princess?"

"No, Dad."

"Problems solved," Harry Lowe said. "Tonight, I'll do anyone a favor." He got up and joined Audra at the door.

"Audra," Stephani said.

"Mom?"

"Be careful."

"Of what?" Harry said. "The slide rule or prepositional phrases?" He laughed loudly at his own joke, but Stephani Lowe didn't even crack a smile.

She couldn't help it. It had always bothered her that

Audra had been so close to a boy who committed suicide. There had to have been some great danger there. If someone could do harm to himself, why couldn't he just as easily do harm to others? she thought. Who knew how close Audra had come to something terrible and now she was returning to that house and going to help a boy she said resembled Solomon Stern.

Why would a mother want to bring another child into her house who resembled her dead child, especially if her child had committed suicide? she wondered. Stephani had never really liked Solomon Stern. She always thought there was something weird about him. She felt Audra's relationship with him was illogical. Her daughter had such a good mind and a sensible way about her. Why would she choose to keep company with someone so sour all the time?

She recalled how the boy gave her the chills whenever he came into the house. He was polite enough, but there was something about the way he looked at her. It was almost a lewd expression. Whatever it was, she was made uncomfortable by it, and when Solomon committed suicide, she was, God forgive her, almost happy about it. At least he couldn't influence Audra anymore.

But now Audra was returning to that house, and for Stephani Lowe, it was as if all of it were starting over again. What a ridiculous idea, she thought, now that she did give it thought. Just because Audra said the boy reminded her of Solomon and just because the boy was about the age Solomon would have been had he not killed himself doesn't mean the boy would have Solomon's personality.

Still, he was a foster child, Stephani thought, and one didn't know what kind of background he had. This was a whole other problem. Oh, why couldn't Audra be more like Debbie, she concluded, and chase only the handsome, athletic types. At least you were guaranteed they were normal.

She went back into the kitchen to finish up. Usually the girls helped her, but occasionally she wanted to be alone after dinner. She needed the peace and quiet, especially if the conversation around the table was as boisterous as it was this evening.

Debbie and the boys were all in their rooms. She knew Debbie was on her telephone; it was practically attached to her ear. As a joke, Harry once pinned a cartoon on her door. In the cartoon a doctor is delivering a child, and the child is born holding a telephone receiver to its ear. The mother is looking up, anxious to know whether she had given birth to a boy or a girl, but instead of saying "boy" or "girl," the doctor in the cartoon says, "It's a teenager."

Audra rarely spoke for long periods of time on the telephone. She said she wasn't fond of talking to people unless it was face-to-face. Stephani remembered that Audra had quoted Solomon about that. "People can rarely hide their true feelings from being exposed in their eyes."

"Except Solomon," Audra had said. "He's very good at that. If he wanted to, he could even get Donald Pedersen to believe he likes him."

"Why don't they like each other?" Stephani asked her. "The Pedersen boy seems nice enough, and his mother is very nice." She made it sound innocent, but she meant to drive a wedge between Audra and Solomon.

"It's a matter of chemistry," Audra said. And then, realizing the weakness of her answer, she added, "Donald's jealous of him. He's always mocking Solomon, and trying to embarrass him in front of his friends."

After his suicide, Solomon became something of a forbidden topic. Stephani wasn't unhappy about that; she was just unhappy about the reason for it. She could tell that her daughter somehow felt responsible for Solomon's death. Audra once said, "Of all people, I should have sensed it."

"Shouldn't his parents have been the ones to sense it?"

"No. I should have been the one," Audra insisted.

Stephani shook her head and retreated from the subject.

She didn't want to know why Audra felt that way; she didn't want to learn about the intimacy between her and Solomon. She had hoped that Audra would get over it and go on to have more sensible relationships.

But she didn't, and it was hard not to compare her with Debbie. Debbie flitted from boy to boy with the grace and smoothness of a butterfly, but Audra didn't see anyone socially, even though she was far from the ugly duckling. It was as if she had no interest in ever finding anyone else. Stephani first thought Audra might be afraid to have another boyfriend. She wanted Audra to understand that all boys weren't like Solomon Stern, but Stephani was afraid to get into such a conversation with her.

Whenever Debbie, she, and Audra would sit around and talk, Debbie's conversation was filled with descriptions and anecdotes about this boy and that. Audra would listen with interest, but she had nothing similar to say. The way Audra listened and gave advice to Debbie made Stephani feel as though Audra were closer to her age than to Debbie's. In any case, Stephani noted that she hadn't gotten as excited over anyone since Solomon's death as much as she was excited about this new boy.

It disturbed her because it was as if she had been waiting for him to arrive, as if she knew eventually he would come.

Joe Stern stared incredulously at Audra Lowe for an embarrassingly long moment after he had answered the doorbell and opened the door to face her, even though he expected her arrival. During that long moment, it was as if all the terrible events of the past year or so had been part of a bad dream. He had fallen asleep in the living room watching television, and he had dreamed Solomon's suicide and Martha's depression. All the misery was imagined, for here was Audra as usual, coming to spend time with Solomon.

What they used to do in his room all those hours, he

didn't know. He never asked his son about it. He never even made a humorous comment about it, hoping to extract some information. There was nothing Solomon held so dearly as his own privacy. Whenever he did tell Joe anything about himself, whether it was some achievement in school or something that drew his interest in a book or magazine, Solomon always made it sound as though he were granting his father the privilege of knowing some deep secret, no matter how simple or insignificant the information was.

Actually, Joe was surprised at Audra Lowe's continual interest in his son. Solomon was far from being an unattractive boy, but Joe thought his personality would be a turnoff when it came to girls, and Audra Lowe, a rather mature and apparently outgoing young girl, looked as though she could have her choice of male companions.

The truth was Joe found her attractive himself and was somewhat envious. Of course, he told himself it was ridiculous for a man his age to have any interest in a fifteen-year-old girl, but Audra Lowe did not look fifteen or act fifteen, and besides, just seeing her sent him rushing back through his memories, clamoring for that carefree age when his biggest problem was what he and his friends were going to do on the weekend.

He found it hard to believe that Solomon would know what to do with a girl like this—how to keep her interest, how to make her happy. He imagined Solomon bored her with his model airplanes and cars or his talk about his computer. Yet, if he did bore her, why did she keep coming around? Obviously, Solomon had more to offer. The mystery surrounding his son deepened with every passing day for Joe, and the harder he tried to understand him, the more frustrated he became. It was easier to simply retreat.

"Hi, Audra," he finally said. She had said, "Good evening, Mr. Stern," and waited patiently for some response. He heard a horn beep and saw Harry Lowe waving from his car as be backed out of the driveway. He waved back and then stepped away from the door to let Audra enter.

"Jonathan's expecting me," Audra said. He was still standing and holding the doorknob and staring at her. She was dressed in a tightly knit, light blue sweater over an off-white blouse with the frilly collar out. She wore a straight dark blue skirt, ankle length, which had the effect of making her look even taller and older.

Most of the time whenever she came to visit Solomon and Joe was home, Joe would be the one to greet her at the door. That annoyed Joe because he felt if Solomon was anticipating her arrival, why couldn't he come out of his room and greet her at the door? He sat up there and waited like some monarch, Joe thought. But the girl didn't seem bothered by it. He would say, "Solomon's up in his room," and she would smile, nod, and go up to him. He heard her knock on his door and then enter. If he went upstairs and paused by Solomon's door, he heard little more than the classical music Solomon played on his tape deck, music he said was more conducive to studying.

Joe didn't want to admit it, but he was intimidated by his son's taste in music and art and literature. Here at the age of fifteen, he was already far more knowledgeable about these subjects than Joe had ever been. Solomon was also up on popular music; he knew what Joe considered to be the things typical teenagers should know, but he also knew more. Solomon's variety of taste amazed Joe. He couldn't help comparing himself at his son's age to his son. He had never had such range.

Sometimes he heard Audra and Solomon laughing, but most of the time, if the music wasn't playing, their voices were far too low and indistinct for him to make out enough words to understand what they were saying. He didn't want to linger by the door long, either. Martha might come up behind him, or Solomon or Audra might come walking out and find him listening in. But he couldn't help being very curious about them.

From what he could see when they were together in his presence, there wasn't any overt affection demonstrated. They didn't touch or look at each other in a way that suggested sexual involvement, but Joe felt he couldn't be sure about it. They both also had that air of superiority, the look of grown-ups who knew they had to restrain themselves in the presence of children. That was it, he thought, they made him feel like the child. He resented all this, but he had no way to express or explain it to Martha, who, he was sure, even if he could explain it, would think it all ridiculous. All of it just added to his frustration.

"So you met Jonathan," he said. It was a stupid comment. Why would she be here, if she hadn't met him? he thought. Why was it he never knew the right thing to say when it came to young women?

"Yes. We have all the same classes."

"Who is it, Joe?" Martha called from the living room. He closed the door.

"It's Audra."

"Jonathan's up in his room, Audra," Martha called back. She had done it the same way so many times before that hearing her do it and seeing Audra's reaction once again put Joe into that reverie. Audra had a familiar expression on her face. He sensed that she didn't like being spoken to through walls and doors. She turned to him to say thank-you and then started up the stairs. He watched her as he had done before, thinking about the way her legs and hips moved under that long skirt. He heard her knock on the door, and he heard Jonathan welcome her. In a moment, she was gone, and he was left wondering.

"I'm surprised she was able to come over here," Joe said when he reentered the living room. Martha looked up from the novel she was reading. If she felt what he felt, she wasn't willing to show it.

"Why?"

"Why? Because . . . it's obvious why . . . the memories."

"Kids are more resilient, and besides, I told you, Joe, Jonathan's a very special boy, as was Solomon. He's already impressed the other kids at school."

"But Audra Lowe . . ." He shook his head. It was incomprehensible to him.

"She's just another teenager, Joe. I don't know why you make a big deal out of it."

"She was so close to Solomon."

He saw something flash in her eyes. It looked like anger, but he had no reason to believe she could be angry. He hadn't said anything that would make her angry.

"She wasn't so close," she said softly, with an obvious good deal of self-restraint.

"She wasn't? For a time there, they were inseparable. I remember you commenting about that."

"Teenagers. Have you forgotten what that was like? Teenagers don't really understand their emotions, do they, Joe? What are you going to tell me, that they were in love?" She smiled widely.

He didn't like being ridiculed. This was something she rarely did to him, but when she did do it, he could see the resemblances between her and Solomon. Kids can tap on the most dormant and latent characteristics of their parents, he thought. What qualities of himself that he did not like had Solomon inherited from him? he wondered.

"No, not in love exactly, but certainly seriously interested in each other, comfortable with each other."

"They had some common interests, that's all," she said, and looked back at her book to signal she was through with the subject. He stared at her a moment and then looked up at the ceiling as if he could see through the walls into Solomon's room.

He shook his head, sat back in his heavy-cushioned easy chair, and picked up his magazine again. He was halfway down the page when he heard the music, a piano piece he recognized as a Rachmaninoff. Solomon had played it often enough. He looked at Martha, but she acted as if she didn't hear it. He didn't understand how that could be; she couldn't be so involved in that book, he thought. He waited. She looked up a few times, but she said nothing about the music.

"You want something from the kitchen?" she asked him.

"Huh?"

"I'm getting something cold to drink."

"No, no, thanks." He waited for her to respond to the music, but she didn't. If he was able to hear it, she certainly could. Why didn't she think that remarkable? A fantastic thought brought the blood to his cheeks. Maybe the music wasn't playing; maybe he was imagining it because Audra was here. Should he ask Martha if she heard it, too? She would think him mad.

Finally, he could take it no longer. He got up and put on the television set to drown out the sound of the music even though there wasn't anything on that he particularly wanted to see. When Martha returned, she went back to reading her novel. He stared at the television set, mesmerized by the light and the sounds, but hearing or seeing nothing.

Some time later, Audra came down and stopped by the living room to say good-night. Jonathan, as Solomon often had, remained in his room.

"I saw you didn't ride your bike this time," Joe said.

"No, my mother was worried about me riding in the dark."

"Is your father on the way?"

"I've got to call him," she said. "May I use your phone? I didn't realize the phone in Solomon's room wasn't working."

For a moment there was a terrible silence. Joe hadn't had Solomon's phone disconnected for months after his death. The symbolism of the act was too severe for Martha to take at the time, and when he did have the phone company do it, it brought a fresh new round of sorrow and pain.

"Of course," Martha said. "But, Joe, you can run her home, can't you?"

"Sure," he said.

"I don't want to be a bother."

"Nonsense. You gave your time to help Jonathan. It's the least I can do." He got up.

"We'll have to see about reconnecting that phone, Joe," Martha said. "Jonathan's going to need it after he makes more friends," she added, stressing the importance of "more."

"Right. First thing tomorrow, I'll call the phone company."

"Good night again, Mrs. Stern," Audra said. Martha gave her a perfunctory smile, and then Joe led her into the garage and to his car.

"So, Audra," he said after he backed out, "how have you been doing?"

"Good," she said.

"Bet you're still on the honor roll all the time, huh?"

"Yes," she said, but without any enthusiasm.

"Well, I'm sure your parents are proud. And you should be proud."

"I am," she said.

"Do you think Jonathan's going to be a good student? From what I can see, he has the potential."

"Yes, he will," she said, her voice coming alive.

"It's nice of you to do what you've done for him. He's probably not used to other kids being so kind so quickly."

"I don't mind. It helps me, too, to review things."

"None of this is easy," he said. "But we've got to try. For everyone's sake," he added. Audra didn't respond. He felt he was already talking too much and sounding his usual awkward self in her presence, so he sped up and got to her house moments later. " 'Night," he said when she opened the door. "And thanks again."

"Good night," she said. "Oh," she said, nearly closing and then opening the door, "I nearly forgot. I made a mistake and told Solomon we had lab tomorrow, but there's an assembly that period. Tell him he doesn't need to do those pages in the manual until Thursday."

"Right," Joe said. She closed the door. He watched her walk to her house; and then he pulled away.

He was nearly all the way home before he realized she had called Jonathan, Solomon.

5.

The next day, Joe contacted the telephone company and requested Solomon's phone be reactivated. The business representative looked up the records and told him that as unusual as it was, they would be able to give him the same phone number. Did he want that? He hesitated. Normally, he couldn't see what difference a telephone number would make, although he imagined that the same people who worried so much about their car license plate numbers would probably worry about their phone numbers.

Even though there was something unnerving about getting Jonathan the same number Solomon had had, he simply couldn't tell the operator no. He said it would be okay. When he told Martha what the number was going to be, she didn't seem surprised. She was as nonchalant as she had been when Jonathan had announced Audra Lowe was coming over. What made her so strong suddenly? he wondered.

And then he thought it was all part of her revival. Why question it? Things had gotten off to a relatively good start, and as long as she was happy about it all, he was. That was the main purpose for his agreeing to taking in the foster child, wasn't it? How could he complain about her being too casual and content?

As Jonathan's first week with them continued, Joe noticed Martha and the boy growing closer quickly. Despite the half-serious arguments he and Charley Lewis, another IBM serviceman, had about woman's liberation and the roles of the sexes, Joe had to admit that there was something unique about a woman's relationship to her child. Perhaps it was a result of the child being part of her body for nine months, but whatever the reason, he used to marvel at how accurately Martha could anticipate Solomon's needs and wants. Joe thought she was far more in tune with Solomon's moods and attitudes than he was.

When the boy got up in the morning, she knew whether he'd want a big breakfast or not. She could look at his face, a face Joe found inscrutable most of the time, and ask him why he was upset. She sensed when something good happened at school and when he had to go somewhere, a party or class event; she knew what clothes he would want to wear and had them ready for him.

In short, Joe thought a man could cook and clean and cart his children around, but could he be as receptive and simpatico as a woman could? He thought this simply because he was so unsuccessful when it came to that sort of thing with Solomon. According to Martha at least, Joe never seemed to ask his son to do things with him when he was willing or eager to do them. He always asked him at the wrong time. Of course, he was defensive about it.

"The kid shouldn't be so moody, and we shouldn't have to tiptoe around him. He's a kid."

"He's a human being. Just because he's young, it doesn't mean he lacks feelings, Joe."

She had such patience. He thought that was particular to a woman, too.

"Women spoil their children faster than men do," he told her, but she didn't see the point.

Why should she? How was Solomon spoiled? Did he waste things they gave him? Was he in continual trouble at school? Was he into drugs? Didn't he do well in school, and wasn't he well behaved in front of other people?

"Tell me, Joe. How have I spoiled him?" she asked.

He thought for a moment. What would he say? That Solomon didn't respect him as much as he wanted him to. The truth was he was rarely, if ever, insubordinate. He didn't have to chastise him for leaving his room a mess or being nasty to his mother. What could he say?

"It's . . . it's nothing specific," he told her, and she grimaced. He knew this was not a battle he would win, and after a while, he lost his taste for the war. He sat back and let events take their course, hoping that something would change as Solomon grew older. But Solomon never grew older. Solomon broke his neck at the end of a rope.

And now here was Martha hitting everything just right with the new boy.

"You didn't sleep too well last night, did you, Jonathan? Here's a good breakfast. It will help you get through the day.

"It's so bright today, Jonathan. Wear the blue shirt with those pants. Today's a day for rich colors.

"Something funny happened in school today, didn't it, Jonathan? I can see it in your face. Tell us."

Joe simply sat back at the breakfast or dinner table and watched like some invited guest, an observer brought in to see how successful the Sterns were with the foster child. But what was his contribution to this success so far?

He could say he was a good listener. He was attentive and interested when Martha told him things about the boy. She was always waiting after he came home from work. Jonathan would usually be up in Solomon's room doing his homework, and they would have an hour or so to unwind from the day. Sometimes, they had a cocktail, although Martha was a little leery of doing that after Jonathan had arrived. She didn't want him to get any wrong impressions about them.

"I don't want to stir up any bad memories for him," she said.

"That's ridiculous," he told her. "We're no alcoholics. He's got to see the difference between us and his real parents."

"And some of those foster parents, too, Joe. You don't know half of it. He's been telling me more and more. Little by little I'm getting him to trust me, and what he's been describing makes it seem like it's a miracle he's as good as he is."

"Maybe most of it is in his imagination," he said. It was as if he had called the boy a deceitful and disgusting criminal. Her face collapsed in shock. For a moment she was unable to respond.

"What are you saying? He's making it up? Why would he do such a thing?"

"To win your sympathy. Why else?"

"That's cruel, Joe. You don't know how cruel that is. If you only spoke to him more."

"I talk to him."

"Not as much as you should."

"Martha, we talk at dinner. Right after dinner he's on the computer or listening to Solomon's music, or he's on that damn phone with Audra Lowe."

"How do you know who he speaks to? Are you listening at his door?"

"Of course not."

"I don't want him to feel he's being watched. That happened to him at the second home," she said, and went on to describe a paranoid foster father who insisted Jonathan leave his bedroom door wide open and who was not unaccustomed to walking in on him at odd hours. "Why, he'd bust in on him in the bathroom, suspecting he was doing drugs. Can you imagine what the boy went through there?"

"No," he said. He was in retreat. Her face was bright red from anger and excitement. The furthest thing from his intentions was to get her upset. Why did he make such comments anyway? he wondered. Maybe he was jealous of her quick-building and obviously successful relationship with Jonathan. But then he thought, he had really no one to blame but himself for not getting just as close to him. He simply hadn't had the time to invest yet. It was a particularly busy week, and he had been doing some unusual traveling. It all made him very tired. He was looking forward to his week's vacation next month.

Soon he would spend more time with the boy and get a more balanced view of things, he thought. It was just that he couldn't help having the feeling that everything was moving too quickly. As strange as it seemed, Jonathan was slipping into the relationship Martha had had with Solomon as smoothly and as comfortably as he was slipping into Solomon's clothes.

And he was doing that more and more. There seemed to be nothing in Solomon's wardrobe that Jonathan didn't like. There were a few things Martha had to adjust: pants she let down, a sports jacket she had tailored.

One night when Joe came home from work later than usual because he had had to travel to just about the boundary of his territory, he found Martha and Jonathan in the kitchen. Jonathan was wearing Solomon's dark brown sports jacket, and Martha was marking and pinning it for the tailor. They hadn't heard him come in; they were too involved in the clothing, and he did sort of sneak up on them. He was curious.

"You're growing so fast," she said. "These sleeves have got to come out an inch. And those shoulders—they were never as broad."

For a moment Joe couldn't speak. She was talking to Jonathan as if he had lived with them for a long time or as if she had known him before. What was going on? Why didn't the boy react to that?

"Hello," he finally said, and they both turned around

abruptly, both wearing the same look of annoyance at being so surprised.

"Joe! For Christ sakes, why'd you sneak up like that? You nearly scared me to death."

"I didn't sneak up," he said, but their expressions of condemnation made him feel so guilty and so small, he could only laugh awkwardly. "What's happening here, anyway?"

"There's a dance at the high school next weekend. I thought it would be nice if Jonathan wore this sports jacket, but it needs some work."

"Formal dance?" he asked. Solomon's taste in clothing always amazed him. He could dress in the casual, nearly sloppy garb of a typical teenager, but he was also cognizant of style and liked to look sophisticated. Joe recalled a boy from his high school days, Bernard Hartman, who was usually dressed in a tie and slacks during the regular school day. Instead of coming off sophisticated, however, he was considered weird, what the kids today called a "nerd."

Yet from what he saw when Solomon was around other kids his age, no one considered him in that light. It was as if his friends had expected him to be more elegant and mature in his clothing. Yet Joe was sure (in fact, he knew from driving Solomon to school for the dances) that most of the other kids dressed casually for these affairs. He would have thought Jonathan would want to be casual, too.

"It's a dance," Jonathan said. "No one said anything about how we should dress."

"It doesn't hurt to look nice," Martha said.

"No, of course not."

"I'll have your supper out in a minute, Joe."

"That's all right. I want to take a shower first today. I feel like I've been driving for days," he added, expecting her to ask about the jobs and the places he had been. She usually did, but right now, she not only seemed not to have heard him, she seemed totally uninterested in anything but Solomon's sports jacket and the way it fit Jonathan. They both turned away from him. "I'll go shower," he repeated, and left.

By the time he came down for dinner, Jonathan was already sequestered in his room. When he walked past the closed door, he heard the beginning of *Madame Butterfly* and shook his head in amazement. Downstairs, Martha had his supper ready. The sports jacket lay folded over what used to be Solomon's seat at the table.

Now that he saw her alone, Joe realized how radiant she was. Her complexion, which had become what he thought would be irrevocably pale after Solomon's death, was returning to its previously rich and smooth state. He had always been fascinated with Martha's skin. It was a thrill to simply run the tips of his fingers gently over her cheeks and press his lips to her forehead. She was one of those women who would never look their age. Wrinkles would come almost as an afterthought, probably when she was well into her seventies. And her eyes would deceive and confuse the most astute physician, who would be unable to accurately guess her age because of the youthful and vibrant look within them.

Wasn't that something that happened often already? People who didn't know her couldn't believe she was thirty-eight. Dress her in jeans, sneakers, and a sweatshirt and she could easily pass for a college coed.

But age seized her with the appetite of a leech after Solomon's death. The brightness left her eyes, her hair dulled, she stooped when she walked, and her gait was slow and heavy, more like the walk of a woman carrying the burden of years of manual labor.

Now she had drunk from the fountain of youth. There was a lightness in her laugh, a brightness in her eyes that illuminated her whole face with a smile, and a youthful vigor in her mannerisms and gestures. It was truly as if they had turned back time. This was the girl with whom he had fallen in love. His heart beat with such happiness, he could think of nothing but good days and wonderfully passionate nights. And just as it used to be when he came home from a hard day's work and saw her, he, too, felt revived. The mere sight of her washed away the fatigue.

"Feeling better?" she asked.

"Yes. A shower is a wonderful thing. I had a rough day," he said, expecting she wanted him to describe it as usual. But she didn't pick up on it. She nodded quickly, the smile frozen on her face. She was looking through him.

"Isn't it wonderful how he fits into Solomon's old clothes. He fills out the shirts and can wear most all of his pants. Why, there are even some shoes he can wear."

"What do you mean? They don't have the same size foot."

"Solomon had a nine, and he wears an eight, but some of Solomon's shoes were a little too snug, especially the older ones. Solomon kept all his clothes so well, Jonathan thinks everything is brand-new. Do you know what he asked me?" she offered, following her question with a short laugh.

"What?"

"He wanted to know if we had continued to buy Solomon clothes even after . . . can you imagine?"

"How could he ask such a thing?" Joe sat back, unable to prevent an expression of disgust.

"It was just a matter of speaking. Like a joke," she said.

He stared at her.

"Like a joke?"

"He just couldn't believe the clothes were that old, Joe. Don't forget what he's been through."

"How could I?" he said, and immediately regretted how sarcastic it sounded.

"I thought you would enjoy his reactions to things," she said. "It's part of the pleasure of having a child."

He nodded and continued to eat.

"I suppose I'm just very tired," he said finally. She accepted the statement as an apology and patted his hand.

"Just relax after dinner. I see the Knicks are on television tonight."

"You noticed the Knicks were on television, and you want me to watch?" He sat back with a smile so wide it could fit well on a clown.

"Well, to be honest . . ."

"Yes? Come on," he said, expecting she would be asking for some favor.

"I wasn't the one who noticed. Jonathan pointed it out."

"What?" He sat forward.

"He overheard you talking about the Knicks, and he spotted the game in the television guide and told me to remind you about it."

"He never mentioned that he likes watching basketball."

"I don't know that he does, Joe. He was thinking of you."

"Really?" He thought for a moment. Solomon never did that, he thought, and then he chastised himself. Why was he always comparing the boy to Solomon? This was something he was afraid Martha would be doing and here, he was the one who was doing it. "Well, that's nice of him."

"I know. He's a nice boy, Joe. Give him a chance. Try."

"I am. I will," he said defensively.

"That's all I ask," she said. "That's all he'll ask either," she added with the authority of someone who knew she could speak for someone else. He nodded without speaking and went back to his meal.

After dinner, he did go in to watch the Knicks game. Martha decided to do her supermarket shopping because she said it was less crowded and easier in the evening. She was going to meet Judy Issacs for coffee right before going to the market, and then they would both go. He was glad about that. He liked Judy because she was a strong and independent woman, almost always optimistic and up about herself. He thought that Judy, of all Martha's friends, was the best influence on her. He hoped Judy would get her to reconsider taking the realtor's course at the community college.

Just before the halftime break, Jonathan came down. He stood watching the game for a while. Joe invited him to sit, but he said he had to study for a test.

"You keep up with professional basketball?" Joe asked him.

Jonathan hesitated as if telling the truth might be painful. He shook his head.

"Not really," he said, but Joe sensed otherwise. He wondered why he wanted to hide his interest in such things.

"Well, if you want, I can get us tickets to a game at the Garden next month. One of my clients has good connections for that sort of thing. We could get a box seat. How's that sound?" Jonathan's eyes widened and then, as if someone turned down the lights, his face darkened, and the heat that had been in his eyes cooled.

"I don't know," he said. "Maybe," he added, but without any enthusiasm. Joe turned back to the game, and Jonathan went to the kitchen to get himself a glass of milk. He stopped on the way back.

"The Knicks are ahead by six," Joe said, thinking that might be what he wanted to know.

He barely acknowledged the information.

"Oh," he said. "I was wondering about something maybe you could fix."

"What's that?"

"This watch," he said, and held his wrist out. Joe stared, the smile fading quickly from his face. It was

Solomon's gold quartz, the watch he had bought him for his thirteenth birthday. After his death, the watch along with his gold chain and the clothes he wore that day were put in a plastic bag, and the bag was buried deep in the corner of his and Martha's walk-in bedroom closet. Joe knew for a fact that she hadn't touched it since the day he put it in the closet.

"Where did you get that?"

"Martha gave it to me to use. She saw I didn't have a watch, but it's not working right. I think the battery's dead. I think you need a special tool to replace it, right?" He dangled his wrist in front of Joe, but Joe didn't respond. Finally, he nodded.

"I'll get a battery tomorrow," he said.

"Thanks. I'll just keep wearing it anyway. It looks good on me," he added, and smiled.

Joe said nothing. He turned to the television set, and Jonathan walked out of the room and back upstairs. The way Joe looked at the remainder of the game, it would have made no difference if the television picture tube had blown out. In fact, when Martha returned and asked him who won, he couldn't tell her.

He was going to ask her about the watch before they went to sleep, but every time he phrased the question in his mind, it sounded so critical, he was afraid he would start an unnecessary argument, the result of which would be to turn back all the progress she had apparently made. In the end, he would feel small and stupid for making something out of giving Jonathan Solomon's watch. After all, they were giving Jonathan Solomon's room. He was wearing Solomon's clothes, riding Solomon's bike, and especially using Solomon's computer. What was so special about the watch?

What was special about it, he thought, was the same thing that was special about the gold chain and the clothes he wore that day: They were on his body when he died and that fact made them sacred. It was why he understood putting all of it in the bag and keeping it in their room. It was why they had never touched any of it up until now.

This was what surprised him about Martha's actions—her sudden ability to do and say things that had been forbidden for the last year and a half. It just seemed that she not only accepted Solomon's death now, she diminished it. If he was dead, why let anything of his go unused? The stoicism inherent in such actions was uncharacteristic of her. He wasn't sure he liked it, even though he was happy with her escape from depression and sorrow.

His similarly contradictory feelings about the new boy continued that first week. He wanted to like him; he wanted to give him a chance, just as Martha had requested, but he couldn't help resenting the way he ingratiated himself with Martha and assumed Solomon's things as if they belonged to him all the while. It was hard, if not impossible, for Joe to point to anything specific and complain about it. What he felt was subtle, and just as he couldn't ask about the watch, he couldn't ask about other things without seeming stingy or cruel.

And then again, the boy had many qualities that recommended him. Joe liked the way he continually asked him about his work and the way he offered to help with things around the house. He wasn't smarter than Solomon, and he probably wasn't any more dexterous, but he was willing to do things Solomon never thought about doing.

On Thursday night, for example, when Joe returned home from work, he found that Jonathan had repaired the garage door. Occasionally, it would come out of its track and the door would get stuck half up or half down. The garage wasn't heated and the changes in the weather played havoc with the runners, but like a shoemaker without any shoes, Joe didn't repair it as well as he should have or as well as he repaired other people's machinery. On the way out that morning, it had gotten stuck. He told Martha he would fix it when he got home that night.

But when he pulled into the driveway, he saw the door was down properly. Puzzled, he pressed the button on the transmitter that raised and lowered the door and found it going up smoothly. He drove in, suspecting that Martha had gotten tired of the constant breakdown and hired a repairman.

"Who fixed the garage door?" he asked as soon as he entered the house. He was annoyed with himself for not repairing it right once and for all because he imagined what it must have cost to do it. He stood in the living room doorway. Martha was watching a late-afternoon soap opera and was so entrenched in the story, she didn't even hear him enter, much less ask a question. He laughed to himself and went upstairs to change his clothes.

When he came down, she was in the kitchen getting the supper out. She had the radio on at low volume and was moving to the music. For a moment he stood there quietly and watched her as though he had walked in on a magic moment and was afraid that the sound of his voice would break the spell. Finally, she caught sight of him.

"Oh, hi. You know, I didn't even hear you come in."

"I know. Thanks to 'Passions Forever' or whatever program you watch." She laughed, and he went to the table. "I even spoke to you, but you didn't hear me."

"Really? What did you say?"

"I asked who fixed the garage door?" he said. "Don't tell me you called Billups Construction." He put his hands over his ears as though to block out the ugly truth. Billups had built the house, and Joe was finding more and more fault with their workmanship as the years went on and things happened to the structure and foundation. She laughed at him. The magic moments continued.

"No, I didn't call Billups. I didn't have to call anyone. Jonathan fixed it," she said, her eyes sparkling with amusement and pleasure.

"Huh? The kid fixed the door?"

"He went to it when he came home from school. I

didn't ask him to do it, either. He went upstairs, changed into his own clothes, and went out to the garage. Next thing I knew, the door was working fine.''

"Well, I'll be . . . where is he?"

"Some of the kids in school wanted to go to Pizza Hut tonight, and I thought he earned it. Gary Isaacs got his driver's license. Judy's already pulling her hair out with worry.''

"Can't stop them from growing up," he said. Actually, he was happy that he and Martha would dine alone. He thought it would give him a chance to talk about other things, things they hadn't talked about since Jonathan's arrival.

He wanted to see if she had reconsidered her decision not to take the realtor's course; he wanted to talk about his work. He was considering a winter vacation on one of the Caribbean islands. He had gossip about some of the people in his office. He felt stuffed and choked with information and ideas he had been unable to express all week.

And indeed, when he began to talk while they ate, he spoke like someone who had just been released from a month's solitary confinement. He babbled and barely acknowledged her response to things he said. About halfway through their dinner, he realized he had been conducting a monologue. She had served the dinner and been eating throughout it, but she hadn't said much or even looked at him much. He stopped because he wondered if she had heard anything. The answer came when he saw that she wasn't aware he was no longer talking.

"Martha? Haven't you heard anything I've been saying?"

"Why, of course."

"You seem distracted."

"I can't help that, Joe. We don't just have each other to worry about anymore. Things come to mind, things that have to be done.''

"What things? What are you talking about? You weren't like this when Solomon was alive."

"Of course I was, Joe. You just never took note," she said, smiling.

Was she? he wondered. Maybe she was right; maybe he wasn't as observant. Maybe that was a major part of the problem—he was in his own world, not she.

"Well, what's so important that you can't stop long enough for us to have dinner and talk?"

"We can talk. I'm listening. You said Ralph Levine is getting divorced, and Kevin is going to handle it for him."

"I said a lot of other things," he muttered.

"So? I'm listening. Talk."

He looked at her. She wore such an understanding expression. He felt foolish, and anyway, the excitement had been dissipated. Maybe the boy wasn't here at the table, but he was here. He chalked it up to the novelty. It was only natural. As soon as the boy had been here awhile, Martha's intensity about him would diminish. He had to be fair about it.

"The rest is nonsense. What's worrying you about Jonathan now?"

"Nothing's worrying me, Joe. I spoke to Mrs. Posner today, and we agreed that Jonathan should get a dental checkup this month. I made an appointment at Dr. Baxter's. Remember how much Solomon liked him. He never complained about going to the dentist.

"Oh, and Jonathan wanted to get his hair styled and asked if I would take him to Barbara Jean."

"Barbara Jean? How did he know about her? You told him?" Barbara Jean was a hairstylist who worked for one of the biggest style shops located in the Concorde Hotel, a major Catskill resort, but for years she had been taking in work on the side at her own home in Sandburg. Solomon had liked the personal attention.

"He just knew about her. I suppose the other kids told him."

"Um."

"And he needs new sneakers. He went out for the basketball team and made the first cut."

"Did he?"

"I've got to get him more sweat socks and a new gym uniform. They're not using the old one anymore. Oh, and I was wondering whether we should sign him up for ski lessons this winter. All of Solomon's friends are into skiing. He'll be left out."

She went on and on and assumed the style of monologue he had abandoned. He turned his attention to his meal, nodding when she asked a question occasionally, but her chatter drove him into a quick retreat to the living room. She brought him his coffee and some new cupcakes she had purchased because Jonathan told her he liked them.

"Aren't they good?" she asked. They were, but he didn't say so. He watched the news and felt like someone drifting through his life.

A little more than an hour later, Jonathan came home. Joe noticed that he was quite a bit more animated than usual. He had obviously enjoyed his dinner out with his friends. Joe was pleasantly amused by his enthusiasm. He was more sociable than Solomon had been, and Joe thought that was healthy.

He saw the way Martha listened to him when he spoke. She bathed in the light of his excitement, glancing at Joe once in a while to demonstrate her happiness and pride. There was something contagious about the boy's energy. Joe concluded he was bringing a new warmth into the house, maybe even more so than they'd had with their own flesh and blood son.

"Oh," Joe said, "by the way, thanks for fixing the garage door. You did a great job."

"That was nothing," he said.

"Where did you learn how to do that?"

"There was a garage door like this one at my last foster home. I watched my foster father fixing it."

"He's got an aptitude for fixing things, Joe."

"Maybe he does. I'll have to have him look at hard disc one of these days," he kidded. Jonathan nodded thoughtfully.

"I wouldn't mind seeing some of that stuff," he said. "Martha says you have to make a call this Saturday."

"Yeah. I thought I'd get started on that paint job, doing the trim, but it'll have to wait until Sunday. If it doesn't rain. They're calling for showers."

"I'd like to go along with you, if you don't mind," Jonathan said.

"Huh?"

"He means along with you on your service call on Saturday, Joe," Martha said slowly, as if she had to translate from another language.

"You would?"

"If you don't mind."

"Hell no. Great. We'll leave right after breakfast."

"Fine," he said. He looked at Martha. "Thanks for the money for dinner."

"Oh, that's nothing," she said.

"It's still nice of you," he said.

There was a moment's pause and silence during which Joe felt as if ice that had lingered in the air and over the walls of their home since Solomon's tragic death was instantly melted away.

Jonathan took a few steps toward Martha, who was sitting at the corner of the couch. If she had anticipated his intent, she didn't know it. Jonathan bent down, leaned toward her, and kissed her on the cheek.

It was a kiss that took her across worlds, through the darkness of sorrow, back through time. It was the fantasy kiss that could bring a dead princess back to life, and indeed, Jonathan's eyes, when he turned them to Joe, lit up with a sense of power.

No one said a word. Jonathan turned and walked out to go up to his room. It was so still, they could hear his footsteps on the carpeted stairway. Martha sat back and looked down at her hand in her lap.

After a moment they heard the beginning notes of Tchaikovsky's "Sleeping Beauty" waltz. The music escaped under the door of Solomon's old room and nudged the ghosts of old memories asleep in every dark corner of the house. Joe could almost feel them float by, drawn by the melodious tones up the stairs and into the room from which they had fled that fateful day.

Who was this boy whom they had taken into their home? Joe wondered. Had they found him, or had he found them?

6.

Jonathan's desire to accompany him on his Saturday service call filled Joe with a renewed enthusiasm and excitement for his work. Ever since he was a young boy, Joe had a fascination for mechanical things. All children enjoy taking things apart, but even as a child Joe enjoyed putting them back together as well. Mechanical things, no matter what they were, had an aura of mystery about them. He saw a kind of magic in the way things fit or the way something could cause another thing to behave in a particular pattern.

Joe could never understand why most people had a fear of handling mechanical things. He had always been more comfortable with things electrical and mechanical because they followed permanent and orderly laws, laws that were not affected by emotions and feelings. Unlike human responses and decisions, there were no whims, no moments of depression with which to contend. If something went wrong with a machine, it went wrong for explainable reasons. Usually, there was no debate and no conflict of theory, and even if there were conflicts like that, there was the assurance that eventually the truth would be discovered: only one theory could be right.

The same could never be said about people and why

they behaved as they did. Just the small amount of reading on the subject of teenage suicide that he had done showed him how inexact and theoretical social science was. It seemed that for every statement made by one so-called expert, a contradictory one was made by another.

No, as far as he was concerned, machines were much easier to deal with than people. He still delighted in successfully repairing something and especially took pleasure in the repair of computers and their associated hardware. Because most of the people who used computers, even those who were expert in their use, had no interest in or knowledge of how the computers actually worked, he was seen to be some kind of specialist. He liked to compare himself to a medical specialist, a neurosurgeon called in when all else failed.

In any case, he was more than a mere repairman, and he was confident no one would simply call him a mechanic. He was a technician, highly respected and in great demand. Joe knew he was unnecessarily defensive about this, especially in the company of Kevin Baker and some of his lawyer friends. True, he didn't make as much money as they did, but the value of what he did was not diminished by that in his eyes.

At times, Joe thought that Solomon had belittled what he did for a living. He had little interest in getting to know exactly what his father's work was like. Joe thought he deliberately minimized the significance of computers and the value of his own computer, even though he was always using it, just to illustrate his disrespect for Joe's vocation. Even professional men whose fathers had been menial laborers had respect for the work their fathers had done, for it was this work that kept the families intact and provided the opportunity for them to go to college and become professional men. Joe sensed that Solomon didn't respect his work, but they never argued about it; they never discussed it. It remained one of the many unspoken thoughts that kept them separated and made them strangers.

Despite the pride Joe took in his work, the manner in which his son viewed what he did had a depressing effect on Joe's enthusiasm. Except for Martha's polite attention whenever he came home with what he thought to be a particularly interesting or exciting problem he had solved, there was no one with whom he could share his accomplishments. Of course, he could discuss things at the office, just as everyone could or did, but it wasn't the same as finding appreciation in the lay world, especially in the family.

When he expressed this unhappiness to Martha and mentioned Solomon, she reacted in character.

"You're work is so technical, Joe. How do you expect a teenage boy to understand or care about it?"

"It's his father's work," he said, but he knew his point was lost.

He couldn't help being jealous of Kevin Baker when they went out together and Martha took great interest in a particular case he had. He realized there was often human drama involved, but what of it—the human drama was all built around some interpretation of law, some view of words, things technical, too, weren't they?

After Solomon's suicide, he tried on a few occasions to interest Martha in something he was doing. He wanted to cheer her up, but he also wanted her to be a part of what and who he was. After all, he thought, they really had no one but themselves now. It was important that they draw even closer to each other. As always, she showed interest, but her interest was polite and aloof. There was even less sharing than there had been before Solomon's death. He could just as well have been a counter clerk at the supermarket for all it mattered during the long period of bereavement.

Jonathan's sudden interest, however, changed things. The boy was more than just a good listener; he asked excellent questions, questions that enabled Joe to go on and on about systems, software, and a comparative analysis of different computers. During their ride to Pine Bush, Joe realized he was conducting an introductory seminar on computers and their uses. However, whenever he thought he was talking too much and paused, Jonathan asked him another question that forced him to explain things further. The boy showed no boredom and seemed to grasp concepts well.

Joe had to go to a travel agency that was having systems failures with their computer, and since so much of what they did was now tied to computer communications with the airlines and resorts, the agency was at a standstill. The owner, Faye Brenner, a rather elegant-looking woman in her mid-fifties, greeted him with such overt and dramatic appreciation, he was a little embarrassed.

There wasn't anything she wouldn't do to make him comfortable. She wanted to send out for coffee and for things to eat. When he asked for nothing, she offered to get things for Jonathan, even though he was obviously just along for the ride.

As it turned out, the problem was much simpler than he had imagined. He replaced a chip in the computer's mother board and did it so quickly, Faye couldn't believe things would be all right. He had to run an entire systems check in front of her to prove that the computer was repaired. When she saw it was true, her flattery rained down in a string of superlatives that left Joe laughing and shaking his head. He smiled at Jonathan. The boy seemed impressed.

Filled with pride and elation, Joe started for home. He began the return journey by explaining what he had done to locate the problem and why the faulty chip caused the failure. Feeling more confident about Jonathan's interest, he went on to talk about other repair jobs, ones that had been a great deal more difficult. In fact, he was about to go on about that IBM AT up at the community college that had stumped not only him, but his supervisor, when Jonathan interrupted with a question that seemingly came out of nowhere.

"Did Solomon take a lot of interest in his computer because of you?"

"In the beginning. Then he was mostly on his own. It became his most personal possession," Joe said, not quite hiding his bitterness. "Once he learned just the very basic things about it, he stopped asking questions. I tried getting him to do more."

"He learned how to use the word processor software," Jonathan said, but he said it as if there were something inherently evil about that fact.

"But he could have done so much more with that computer. He was satisfied merely using it as an advanced typewriter. I was still trying to work with him just before he died."

"Martha says that, too," Jonathan said. There was a half smile on his face, the smile of an adult amused at the actions of a child.

"Says that? Says what?"

"Just before he died. Makes it sound like he had a disease or a heart attack."

"Well, you can understand how painful it is to describe exactly what happened. She's made remarkable progress recently."

"But you do the same thing. You avoid it, too."

"That's natural," Joe said. "I was his father. It was painful for me. It still is painful."

"Not as painful as it was for him," Jonathan said. Joe looked at him. The boy didn't look like he was being amusing. He looked angry. Joe had to look away. There was a long moment of silence between them. Then Jonathan added, "It's too bad people can't be fixed as easily as computers."

"I agree," Joe said. "Unfortunately, in Solomon's case, I never had the opportunity to try. What happened was a total surprise."

"Was it?" Jonathan countered. The skepticism was so thick, Joe had to look at him to be sure he was talking to someone who had been in their house barely a week.

"Yes, it was. There were no warnings, no notes, no threats, no statements indicating this was going to happen, or even that it could happen."

"You weren't very close, then?"

"I don't know," Joe said. He realized he was ashamed of the truth. "No, I guess we weren't what you would call close. He didn't come to me with his problems, if that's what you mean."

"It was a Thursday, huh? After school?"

Joe said nothing. Jonathan's questions had already triggered a vivid recollection, so vivid it brought tears to his eyes. It was a Thursday, and it was after school. Martha had discovered Solomon's hanging body hours before Joe arrived home from work, but she had done nothing until then.

Apparently, from what Joe gathered then and later, Solomon had come back from school and gone right up to his room as usual. She never heard him walk back down the stairs and out of the house. He went out the front door and walked around to the back. The rope must have been in his room awhile, maybe for days. The suicide was in no way spontaneous. Solomon had planned it with the same attention to detail that characterized most everything he did.

A while later Martha gazed out of the window over the kitchen sink. How many times during those months right afterward did she tell and retell about it?

"At first, I thought it was some kind of joke. You know how Solomon can do something funny . . . or at least, something he thinks is funny. He didn't seem like he was . . .

"I stepped back from the window and shook my head, just like someone might do in a movie, hoping the sight would disappear. I shook it hard, like you would shake a bottle of soda that had been in the refrigerator awhile to see if it still had any carbonation. The shaking brings the fizz back," she explained and laughed at the silly analogy. "Only, the fizz didn't come back, did it? I looked out again and he was dangling there, his arms straight down, his body turning ever so slowly.

"My heart stopped. I know I got terribly white. You even said I was ghastly white when you first arrived. 'Why are you so pale?' you asked. Remember? And I laughed. 'You won't believe what Solomon has done,' I said. And you smirked and said, 'What's he done now?' 'He's killed himself,' I said. Didn't I?"

Martha's hysterical words lingered in his mind, indelibly printed on the very essence of his being, to be erased only by death itself.

Thursday afternoon?

"Yes, a Thursday afternoon."

"I'm not surprised that he didn't say anything ahead of time," Jonathan said. "People who really mean to kill themselves don't let anyone know ahead of time. I knew this kid at the temporary house who was always threatening to jump out windows or cut his wrists. He never went through with any of his threats. He just wanted attention."

"Is that right?"

"Solomon wanted more than attention," Jonathan said. Joe was impressed with his tone of certainty.

"How can you be sure of that? How can anyone be sure?"

"Did you like him?" Jonathan asked.

"What?" Joe's half smile was like a confession. "He was my son."

" 'Doesn't mean anything," Jonathan said. "I'm my father's son; I'm my mother's son."

"Well, it meant something in my house," Joe replied, hearing the anger and the defensiveness in his voice. "This isn't a very pleasant subject," he added. Jonathan ignored him.

"People usually kill themselves because they don't like themselves," he said.

"How do you know so much about suicide? It's not a subject for someone of your age."

"But it's happening to people my age. Why do you suppose Solomon didn't like himself?" he asked.

"I don't know as that's the reason for his actions. Look, Jonathan, I can understand your curiosity, but you have to realize this is still a very sensitive topic in my house. I would appreciate your not discussing it, especially with Martha."

Jonathan didn't respond. They drove in silence for a while.

"Parents can drive you crazy," he finally said. "Look what my parents did to me."

"It's bad; I know. But you're a strong, intelligent boy, Jonathan. I think you're going to be all right."

"Unlike Solomon, huh?" he said. It sounded almost like a joke. Joe looked at him and raised his eyebrows. Jonathan turned away and stared out the window. *He acts as if he knew Solomon all his life,* Joe thought, *and blames me for his death.*

Joe went back to the office and showed Jonathan around the service area. Once again, the boy was interested in the things Joe had to say and asked good questions about computers and the work being done. The upbeat mood returned. Afterward Joe took him to the new Roy Rogers in their area for lunch. They had a good talk about some of the things Jonathan hoped to do in his life. He said he had an aptitude for writing and wanted to do something with journalism.

"Maybe a sports writer," he said. "I like describing sporting events."

"So then maybe we will go down to the Garden to watch a Knicks game," Joe replied. Jonathan nodded, looking more enthusiastic about such a prospect.

Joe sensed that the boy was caught between contradictory feelings. He wanted to relax and be trusting, and yet he was frightened and hesitant. It was understandable, Joe thought. Martha was right about giving him time. They had to move slowly, carefully, and be sensitive to his scarred feelings. He had been abused emotionally as well as physically.

Sitting in the fast-food restaurant and talking to him casually like this was just as encouraging for Joe as he thought it must be for Jonathan. He couldn't remember a time when he and Solomon had gone somewhere alone to eat. The father-son act just wasn't in their repertoire.

He concluded that despite all the similarities Martha had found and was finding between Solomon and Jonathan, this boy really was quite different. He could be . . . yes, Joe had to say it this way . . . he could be normal. Solomon wasn't normal. His reactions to his own son were understandable.

On the way home, Jonathan reminded him about his intention to paint the trim on the house. He said he would have time to help him on Sunday, after all. Joe was cheered by the fact that he was returning home with the same upbeat feelings as when he had left it this morning. In fact, he was so happy about the way he and Jonathan were hitting it off, he almost completely forgot about their intense few minutes discussing Solomon's suicide.

But it would come back to him. Every single word would come back to him, especially Jonathan's statement that Solomon didn't like himself.

The reason why was like a festering sore. Joe would rather keep it hidden, but he was beginning to sense that Jonathan wouldn't let it remain so.

"My God," Martha said at the end of dinner that night, "what did you do to that boy? All he's been talking about since you came back from your service call is you and your work."

"Really?" Joe smiled. Jonathan had gone up to his

room right after finishing his meal to get ready to go with Audra Lowe and some of the other kids to the movies.

"Yes, really. Don't pretend you didn't notice his conversation at dinner. I couldn't get him to talk about anything else but computers. He's impressed."

"Well, he seemed to show some interest, so I filled him in on a few things."

"I'll bet you never shut up the whole time he was with you. I know how you are when you get started on the subject. Especially when you have a captured audience."

"That isn't so," he replied, feigning an angry defense. "If he asked questions, I provided answers. Nothing more."

"Uh huh."

He thought he detected a note of jealousy, but shook the idea off. Why would she be jealous of his success with Jonathan? It was something she wanted all along.

"So," he said, deciding to change the subject, "since the kid's going to be with his friends, maybe you and I should go to a movie, too. We haven't done that in a while."

"I don't know," Martha said. She looked threatened by the idea.

"Come on. We deserve a night out."

"Deserve?" She grimaced as if the word were a profanity.

"Well, we've been working hard at making things comfortable for the boy, besides our regular work, that is."

"You make it sound like a job, Joe. He's not an assignment; he's not some kind of penance," she added, her eyes widening with emphasis.

"Of course, I don't mean it to sound like that," he said. Why does she jump on everything I say about Jonathan? he wondered. "But don't you want to go out on a date and not think about anything else but ourselves? Just for a little while? That's not selfish or sinful. In fact, it's healthy. And," he said, feeling more like a salesman pushing a new item than a husband asking his wife to go out to the movies, "if we feel better about ourselves, we'll treat the boy better. It's only logical."

She was quiet for a moment.

"Maybe you're right," she said. "What movie do you want to see?"

"Not the one the kids are going to. Let's take in that new foreign film over at the Strang. Curt Philips over at the office saw it and said it was good."

"You mean the one about the two sisters who fall in love with each other?"

"Well, it's different."

"Why is it the movies today are either ridiculous or kinky?" she asked. He shrugged and watched her clean up. "All right," she said finally. "I suppose we should do something different."

"Good." Joe slapped his hands together and got up from the table to help clear off the dishes. He began bringing them to her at the sink. "I'm surprised Kevin or Mindy didn't call. I saw Kevin this week and he mentioned something about a new restaurant in Goshen."

"She did call," Martha said without turning around. She continued to place the dishes in the dishwasher.

"She did? So what did you tell her?"

"I didn't think we should go to dinner just yet."

"What? Why not? Because of the boy," he said, answering his own question. "What difference would it have made? You could have made something for him and then we would have gone out with them." She didn't say anything. "Martha." She turned around.

"I thought we'd wait until he was here a few weeks before doing that. He's been through so much loneliness."

"Oh, Christ."

"Well, he has."

"You're babying him. You did the same—" He stopped himself, but her shoulders went up as if he had dropped an ice cube down her back.

Suddenly her expression changed, and she looked very

calm. She took on her Mona Lisa smile and made him feel as though he were a patient in a mental ward who was on the verge of hysteria. Once again, he felt like someone being handled.

"It's not babying him to help him make a smooth transition into a new home, Joe. Apparently, you weren't listening too carefully when Mrs. Posner outlined some of the potential difficulties associated with children in the program.

"Really," she continued, turning back to her work, "sometimes you're the one who acts like a spoiled child, a jealous child."

He said nothing for a moment. Her cool and intelligent tone made him wonder. Was she right? Was he as possessive as a child? He thought about his own childhood and the natural sibling rivalry between him and his sister, Brenda. The competition between them had been for their mother's attention. His father couldn't have been more aloof from their upbringing. Like Martha's father, his father was Old Country, with a clearly indicated set of male responsibilities, none of which included dressing, feeding, and caring for his children. He was there to discipline and to make serious decisions for them, but there rarely seemed to be occasions for any insignificant conversation.

His father was a plumber who appeared forever tired and dirty, weighed down by the struggle to make a living. For men like his father, the scope of what was considered to be trivial was much wider than it was for men today. Joe couldn't ever imagine his father being upset because his wife turned down a dinner party.

He didn't go on with the discussion. Instead, he got up and went into the living room to catch some television news. A little while later, Jonathan poked his head in to say good night.

"And thanks for taking me along today," he added.

"Nothing to thank me for," Joe said. "Glad to have the company."

"See you later," Jonathan said, and left.

Joe went to the window and watched him get into a car to sit beside Audra Lowe. After that, he went back to watching television. It was nearly a half an hour later before he realized Martha hadn't come into the living room. If they were still going to a movie, they had to get started very soon.

She wasn't in the kitchen, even though the lights were still on. Puzzled, he listened for her movements in the house. If she had gone by the living room and up the stairs, she had either done it very quietly or he had been so involved in some news story, he hadn't heard her. Convinced the latter was the case, he went to the stairs and ascended.

Just before he reached the top, he thought he heard voices and stopped to listen. He shuddered when he realized the sounds were coming from Solomon's, now Jonathan's, room. He took another step and then another until he was at the landing. Martha was speaking just above a whisper behind the closed door. He went to it and strained to understand her words. He clearly made out the sentence "I want you to leave him alone."

Unable to contain his curiosity any longer, he opened the door. Before she spun around, Martha was sitting on the bed looking at the pillow as though someone were reclining there. Joe stopped and simply gaped at her.

"My God," she said, "why did you open that door like that? You scared the hell out of me."

"What are you doing in here?"

"Straightening up."

Joe looked around. The room couldn't be any more orderly, nor the furniture more spick-and-span.

"I thought I heard voices. For a moment there, I thought Jonathan had returned and something was wrong."

"Nothing's wrong." She got up. A confident and self-satisfied smile took form on her face. "Everything will be fine now."

"Who were you talking to?"

"I was talking to myself. Don't you do that?"

"Sure," he said. He still felt he had heard another voice.

"So why are you standing there and making a big deal out of it, Joe? What is it with you tonight?"

"Me?" He stared at her a moment and then relaxed. "It's getting too late to go to the movies," he said.

"I'd just as soon stay home and finish my book," she said, and started out of the room.

"Okay," he said. He, too, had lost the desire to go out. He looked around the room again. He noticed the covers were off both the computer keyboard and the monitor.

He turned it on, curious as to what Jonathan might have been doing with it. After it warmed up, he called up the files, noting the dates beside each. One file, nearly one megabyte, the equivalent of a novel, had been written while Solomon was still alive. He called for its retrieval, only to discover it had a password. Without that password, there was no access to the file. It was something Solomon wanted kept as secret as a diary.

He couldn't help wondering why. Perhaps he should work on breaking into that memory, he thought. Could Jonathan have broken into it? Was that why he was working on it so much? He would have had to find the password. Joe searched the desk for notes, but found nothing. He looked about the room, wondering where the password might be hidden. It could be anywhere—in a book, in that carton, even in an article of clothing. Wherever it was, he sensed that it was important for him to find it.

He knew Martha would wonder why he was still in the room, so he shut the computer off quickly and left. He followed her down the steps to the living room, still thinking about the computer.

But he said nothing more about it. Martha began reading her book. Every once in a while, she would pause, press the book against her breasts, and look up at the ceiling. Whenever she did so, there was more of a look of anger on her face than a look of fatigue.

"Everything all right?" he asked her after she had done it a number of times. "You look like that story is getting you upset."

"What? Oh. No. It's very good. One of her best." She went back to her reading. Sometime before the late news, she said she was tired and went upstairs to bed. He lingered to watch some of the news and then went up to join her. He thought she was already asleep, so he didn't put on any lights and moved as softly as he could through the room, but she was awake.

"You left the outside light on for Jonathan, didn't you, Joe?" she asked.

"Sure. What time did you tell him he had to be in?"

"I told him not late."

"That's a little vague, considering it's really his first night out here."

"It's what we used to tell Solomon, isn't it?"

"He's not Solomon. In some ways, Jonathan's more of a responsibility. It's like taking care of someone else's child while they're away," he added.

"What a terrible attitude. As long as you feel that way, he'll be a stranger in this house," she said, and turned her back to him. She was still sleeping in the nude. She had done so all week. He shook his head, feeling very confused, and decided the best thing would be to get some sleep.

The shadowy figure that had been hovering around Donald Pedersen's car stepped away quickly and seemed to simply be absorbed into the night only moments before Donald and his friend Stanley Weiner came out of the Crossways. The Italian restaurant was something of a hangout for the high school students. It was well after one o'clock in the morning.

Donald, a tall, lean seventeen-year-old, lived alone with his mother since his father's desertion, and was somewhat more independent than most boys his age. For the last four years, he had been more or less on his own. During the last two and a half years, he worked in the Shop Rite Supermarket after school and on weekends, as well as the summers, and earned his own spending money.

Although he wasn't an arrogant boy, life had toughened him and made him somewhat intolerant of those who had things much easier. He had never been friendly with any of Solomon Stern's crowd, but he never had wanted to be. To him, they were all spoiled and soft. They were the arrogant ones, and because Solomon was their leader, he was the epitome of what Donald hated. When Solomon committed suicide, Donald felt his feelings were validated. Even though Solomon and his friends were supposedly the more intelligent and the more sophisticated and talented students, they were corrupt and degenerate. And this new foster child living with the Sterns didn't seem any different, even though his background should have allied him more with Donald than with Solomon's friends.

Donald never got into any fights with Solomon; they never exchanged bad words between them. They didn't need to confirm their dislike for each other. They simply avoided each other as much as possible, like two dogs who had a natural disdain for each other but who respected each other's turf. Just in the short time Jonathan was at the school, the same unspoken understanding took effect.

Donald didn't mind. He had his own friends, his own activities, and his own likes. Sometimes paths crossed, but most of the time, he and Solomon's crowd were miles apart in distance and in interests.

Earlier tonight, however, he and Stanley had run into Jonathan and some of his friends at the same movie. He saw from the smirks on their faces that they were mocking him. He and Stanley went to a hamburger spot in Monticello after the film, but they grew bored with the crowd and headed for the Crossways. Fortunately, by the time they arrived, Jonathan and his friends were leaving. They had remained to talk, dance, and even have some pizza. Neither he nor Stanley had any kind of curfew. Finally growing tired, they left the restaurant.

"Hey," Stanley said as he opened the door on the passenger's side, "smell that?"

"Yeah," Donald said. "Gas. Like it flooded."

"Didn't give us any trouble on the way here."

"I put new points and plugs in and changed the filter in the gas line two weeks ago," Donald said.

"Lotta good that did," Stanley said, and laughed.

Donald's car was one of the few things his father had left behind. Now nearly nine years old with a little over a hundred-thousand miles on it, it was battling to remain on the road. The bottom side panels had rusted out, and the shocks were nearly gone. But it still served its purpose, and investing in a new vehicle was beyond his and his mother's financial capacity at this time. The insurance alone ate up a large portion of what he made at the supermarket.

"Jeez," Stanley said, getting in. "Why didn't we smell this on the way here?"

"I don't know." Donald hesitated. "Now the son of a bitch probably won't start." He thought about opening the hood and checking the engine, but he remembered he didn't have a flashlight in the car. "Maybe we'll be lucky," he said, and got in quickly. "Phew." He rolled down his window quickly.

"This floor rug feels soaked," Stanley said.

"Yeah, my side, too. How the hell . . . ?"

"Did you leave a can of gas in the rear?"

"No."

Stanley leaned over the back of his seat.

"Looks like one back there." Stanley reached over and straightened up the can. "Fell over and must've spilled some under the seat."

"That's funny. I don't remember doing that."

"Maybe your mother did it."

"Naw, she hates this car."

"So?"

"I don't know," Donald said. He put the key in the ignition, but he didn't turn it. "I don't know," he repeated. "I can't remember doing that."

"Well, it's too late now. Let's get the fuck out of here. I'm tired."

"Yeah," Donald said. He turned the key. He didn't see the electrical wires dangling from the bottom of the dash. The spark was instantaneous.

The fire seemed to rise up out of the floor as though it had been burning all the while and been hidden and silent beneath the floor rug. To Donald and Stanley, in the moment they had to think and react, it appeared they were sinking into the heart of the flames. Terror rushed into their hearts as fast as did the tremendous and overwhelming pain.

Both boys screamed and lunged at the doors, their clothes aflame. The fire was cutting up their legs, across their backs, and across their stomachs. The moment they opened their doors, they fell to the pavement and began rolling around frantically. Remaining patrons at the Crossways rushed out the door. Someone had sense enough to grab a few tablecloths and began an attempt at smothering the burning clothing on Stanley. Another man did the same for Donald.

They dragged their bodies away from the burning car as quickly as they could. By now the entire vehicle was on fire. No one even tried to quench it, but people who had parked nearby rushed to their vehicles to get them farther away.

By the time the ambulance arrived, Donald had regained consciousness once, but the intensity of pain had driven him into a coma. Stanley never regained consciousness. He died in the ambulance on the way to the hospital. Donald, ninety percent of his body suffering third-degree burns, was rushed by helicopter to the Albany, New York, burn center less than an hour after he arrived at the local hospital. He remained in critical condition all night and died just before dawn the next morning.

A little after two o'clock in the morning, Joe woke abruptly, sensing that Martha was not beside him. He sat up when he saw the light was still on in the upstairs hallway. He heard nothing, so he got out of bed and went to the bedroom door. There was no one in the hallway, but he thought he smelled gasoline. The bathroom door was closed. Why would Martha go to the hallway bathroom? he wondered. He sniffed again. The odor seemed to pass. Confused, but tired, he returned to bed. Before he closed his eyes, he saw the hallway light snap off. He saw the bedroom door open and Martha enter. She moved softly back to the bed and slipped under the cover.

"Where were you?" he whispered.

"Just checking to see that he was back all right," she said.

"He came home kind of late, didn't he?"

"He said none of the other kids had to be in any earlier."

"He had a good time?" he asked, unable to prevent the note of sarcasm from sounding.

"It was all right," she said. "Nothing special," she added, and then she was quiet.

"Nothing special until two in the morning?" She didn't reply.

He lay there on his back, his hands behind his head for a while, listening to the movements in the house and the way the strong evening breeze threaded itself in and out of crevices and over the roof tiles and windows.

Something stirred in his chest. It wasn't a pain; it wasn't an ache. It was more like someone invisible poked him on the breastbone, and he was still feeling the pressure. He looked at Martha. She seemed to have fallen into a deep sleep again.

And then the strange, imaginary nudging he had felt took shape in thought as he realized that Martha had gotten out of bed naked to check on Jonathan. He really never gave it much thought when she appeared naked before Solomon, even after he was into adolescence. They were, after all, mother and son.

But this boy was only in the house a week, and he wasn't their real son. Surely, she must have embarrassed him. Could she have forgotten she was naked? He felt like waking her up to ask, but then he remembered her accusation of jealousy earlier and that made him hesitate.

He could hear her say "My God, Joe, you are jealous of him. Aren't you ridiculous? He's just a child, a lost, lonely child, and you want to deny him any sign of warmth and friendship."

Of course, he didn't want to do that, but she shouldn't be parading nude in front of a boy almost sixteen years old. That wasn't right, was it? It bothered him so much, he couldn't fall asleep until hours later, and after he did, he slept so soundly, he didn't wake up as early as he had intended. In fact, he didn't wake up until Jonathan knocked on the door.

He opened his eyes and realized Martha had gotten up hours ago.

"What?"

Jonathan poked his head in.

"Sorry, but Martha told me to wake you. She said you can't sleep this late if you're going to get in any work on the house today."

"Huh?" He looked at the clock. "Oh, shit."

Jonathan laughed.

"I'll be outside, mixing the paint," he said. "I can start on the lower-level window frames, if that's okay."

Joe scrubbed his head vigorously and sat up.

"Yeah, sure. Damn, I haven't slept this late since . . ."

"Since Solomon died," Jonathan finished for him, and smiled. "I know. Martha told me," he added, and closed the door softly.

For a long moment, Joe simply stared at the closed door. Then he got himself up and into the shower to try to wash away the strange mixture of erotic dreams and nightmares that clung stubbornly to the insides of his eyelids.

7.

Martha had been hearing and seeing Solomon more and more all week. There was little terror and amazement in her reaction; she half expected it, although at first she was surprised these visions and sounds had not appeared and occurred during the period of time between Solomon's death and Jonathan's arrival. It seemed to her that that's when it should have happened. Her longing for her dead child was so intense during those months, it wouldn't have shocked her to see him standing in his room or hear his voice in what had become the terribly empty house.

But none of it happened until after Jonathan came, and this made her more angry than terrified. In fact, she thought it was characteristic of Solomon and his selfishness for him to have kept himself hidden and silent behind the dark walls of death even though he had the capability to appear and to speak to her when she most needed him. She believed that what finally brought him out was not his love for her so much as his jealousy, the same jealousy that she now had to admit kept him from liking and appreciating his father. Joe always knew; Joe always understood. She had been wrong to pretend she disagreed, but she did it to protect Solomon.

His appearances became more frequent as the week

wore on and she did more and more for Jonathan. After
she had found Solomon standing by the window in his
room that first day, he surprised her with his appearance in
the laundry room while she was folding Jonathan's under-
wear and socks. She realized he must have been there for
quite a while watching her. Ordinarily she would have
sensed his presence, just the way he was always able to
sense hers, but she was concentrating on thoughts about
Jonathan.

"Why don't you let him do it himself?" she heard, and
turned around to see Solomon standing there with that
horrible ropeburn still vivid on his neck. It seemed even
wider and brighter, the raw flesh glimmering. He could
make it look that way, she thought. He wanted to torture
her with the sight. "I did all that for myself, didn't I?" he
said, and smirked.

At first she was going to ignore the visions; she was
going to chase them back into the recesses of her mind and
bury them under new memories and new feelings, all
having to do with Jonathan. But she couldn't pass up the
opportunity to express her own anger, and she had to
defend Jonathan.

"You didn't do it for yourself until you were almost
thirteen," he said.

"He's almost sixteen."

"You have no right to be critical of him. He's alive. He
didn't punish his parents with his own death," she said. It
was a cruel, hard thing to say. She knew that, but it
worked. Seconds later, Solomon's image was gone, and
she didn't hear his voice until late the next afternoon,
about an hour after Jonathan had returned from school.
She was working in the kitchen, and when she turned
around, there was Solomon seated at the table. He had his
elbows on the table and his hands clutching his neck,
covering most of the vivid scar. She imagined he was
ashamed of it now. She noted that although he was dressed

in the clothing he had worn the day he died, he did not have his watch, the watch she had given to Jonathan.

"Working like a little beaver to make him his favorite meal," Solomon said. "You used to worry more about what pleased Joe."

"That's not true. I was always making you your favorite things. There were even some things that Joe didn't like, but he ate them just to please you. That's all we ever tried to do—please you. And what did we get for it? Your corpse hanging from a tree."

"That wasn't my fault," he said. "You know it wasn't my fault."

"Why don't you leave us alone? You chose to leave us before. Why are you coming back again and again?"

"I don't like him using my things. Get him his own things. You gave him my watch!"

"You should have thought of that before you rushed out to hang yourself," she said, surprised herself at how hard and tough she could be now. But now she had Jonathan to worry about, and Jonathan was alive. She could touch Jonathan; she could hold him to her.

She turned her back on the image, and when she looked again, he was gone. But he returned every day, sometimes twice, once three times, each time complaining about something she was doing for Jonathan. And each time she drove him away by reminding him that it was he who had ruined things, not her. He didn't want to accept that, but it was characteristic of Solomon to shift blame onto other people. She saw that now; in fact, she saw more of his weaknesses and liabilities now that he was dead and she could compare him to Jonathan. And that became another way to rid herself of the image and the illusion: Force Solomon to see what his inadequacies were by comparing him to Jonathan.

"He thanks us for what we do for him," she told Solomon's spirit when it appeared behind her in her bathroom. She was brushing her hair, and suddenly there he was,

standing behind her as he often did, watching her dress
and prepare herself for the day. "He's very grateful he has
two warm and caring adults looking after him now."

"He's playing you both for suckers," Solomon said.

"Jealous words. Deliberate lies born out of envy. Don't
waste your breath," she said, and then she laughed. She
saw how that got him, so she laughed again. "How can
you waste any more of your breath? You wasted it all at
the end of a rope," she added, and the spirit evaporated.

She thought she had firm control of it and it would do
them no harm, but then Jonathan came to her on Thursday
afternoon to tell her about this feeling he had. He spoke
like someone under hypnosis, and it did frighten her.

"I get the feeling that I'm not alone when I'm in his
room. I can't explain it, but sometimes . . . I'll look up
from what I am reading or writing because it was like
someone just walked by behind me. Of course, there's no
one there, but still . . . it's eerie. Once I looked in the
mirror, and I thought I caught sight of someone reflected
in the window."

For a long moment, she said nothing. Then she smiled
to reassure him.

"It's understandable. You're in a new place, and the
history of the boy in whose room you now live is a tragic
and horrible history. Maybe that's playing on your mind.
Try to forget about it."

"I'll try," he said.

Poor thing, she thought. Damn you, Solomon, she
thought, and she looked forward to the next opportunity
she would have to chastise and threaten him. She wouldn't
tolerate him trying to ruin things for Jonathan. That was
when Joe walked in on her.

For a moment she wondered whether or not Joe would
see Solomon's image, too. He seemed to have heard his
voice. But he didn't see him, or he would have reacted for
sure. It didn't surprise her that Solomon made himself
totally invisible to Joe. He was practically invisible to him

when he was alive, and he wasn't jealous of Joe's relationship with Jonathan, anyway. He was jealous only of hers.

She thought about telling him, but then she thought he might not understand or believe her, and instead he might somehow blame it on their taking in Jonathan. The next thing she'd know he'd want to get rid of the boy, claiming it was too much of a strain on her, so she kept all the sightings and conversations to herself. She was confident she could handle it, anyway. Just as with all the other occasions during the week, she had Solomon on the run. She told him he was forbidden from appearing in what was his room anymore.

"It's no longer yours, and these are no longer your things," she told him. "You gave them up that Thursday afternoon after school when you calmly went out there and ruined all our lives. As usual, you thought about no one but yourself. Well, it's too late now. I want you to leave him alone," she said, and Joe came in.

As long as she had Jonathan to look forward to, she didn't feel any pain or regret in driving Solomon's image away. She shuddered to think of what it would have been like had Solomon appeared before Jonathan's arrival. She wouldn't have eventually searched for a foster child. Solomon would have stolen her out of reality and taken her completely away from Joe. She realized all that now, and she was even more grateful for Jonathan's appearance. He was truly a godsend, and that was why she didn't think it was any sort of coincidence that she had finally confronted him; a boy who resembled Solomon in so many ways, a boy whom she could take into her home and feel comfortable caring for and loving. Joe didn't see the wonder in all of this, but Joe didn't know all of it, did he?

He didn't know all that had happened before, although sometimes she wondered if he did. He didn't know the secrets buried in her heart. Sometimes she wanted to share these things with him, especially months after Solomon's death when they used to sit so quietly in the living room or

at the dinner table. She felt a great urge to confess and
reveal, but something held her back.

Maybe it was Solomon, she thought. Maybe he was
here all that time, but he just didn't let himself be seen the
way he did now.

Yes, that made sense, she thought. That was why there
was so much darkness in the house, why the shadows
looked deeper and longer, why the sunlight stopped at the
windows. He brought the gloom and the heaviness. He
wanted them to suffer.

And that was why he was so angry about Jonathan's
arrival, she concluded; because Jonathan was driving him
away, driving him back to the grave. Solomon's revenge
was ending. His clothes no longer hung like skeletons in
his closet, his bike no longer tormented them unused on its
rack, and his room, which had become a tomb, was now a
boy's room again.

It's over, Solomon, she thought. Give up; don't bother.
To prove it to herself and to him, she went out back and
stared up at the tree. Sure enough, it looked like nothing
more than a tree. Why, the sight of it didn't even conjure
up the terrible memory any longer. There was no cold
feeling, no terror, no revulsion. It was a warm, sunny fall
day, and the tree was filled with beautifully colored leaves.
She took a deep breath, inhaling the rich scents of nature,
and returned triumphantly to the house to prepare for
Jonathan's homecoming.

How wonderful every day could now be. She had things
to do again, things that would fill her life with hope and
with meaning. Perhaps she was a little overenthusiastic
when it came to the boy. Perhaps she doted on him the way
she had doted on Solomon. Maybe Joe's feelings were
understandable, but he would have to understand something more . . . Jonathan was their salvation. She was
confident that in time, he would come to that conclusion,
and once again, perhaps for the first time really, they

would be something of a family. She was prepared to make any sacrifice necessary to cause that to happen.

Joe didn't know whether he saw it because he wanted to see it or because it was actually there, but there was something disturbingly different about Martha's demeanor this particular Sunday morning. She spoke to him pleasantly enough; she looked happy and energetic, but she seemed so aloof. He felt like a boarder in his own home— tolerated, decently treated, but distinctly apart from the family who ran the place. He felt like someone who had died long ago and was forgotten. Martha was moving around and above him, looking through him.

From time to time, she stopped what she was doing and looked intensely at an empty chair at the table, the chair that used to be taken by Solomon and was now taken by Jonathan. Her behavior made him nervous. He ate his breakfast as quickly as he could, listening to the news on the radio and watching her move oddly about the kitchen. When he got up from the table, Martha said she would be out to watch him and Jonathan paint the house trim.

"I can't believe the boy got up so early and got things started already," he said.

"Why not? He's a wonderful boy, Joe. I see so many good things in him, things I didn't see in Solomon," she said. He was surprised. It was the first time he had ever heard her say anything in any way critical of Solomon. He was convinced she could never be objective about him; she was a typical mother, and when a mother like Martha lost her child, her only child, there was a tendency to deify him, to raise his image up on a cross and pay homage to it with compliments that sounded more like homilies.

But Joe could now see that the new boy was helping to crack the hard shell of biased thoughts. That's good, he thought. That's very good. Bringing him into the house may have a great deal more value than he originally anticipated. He looked forward to joining him and working side by side on the house.

By the time he got out there, Jonathan had mixed all the paint and painted two window frames. He was up on the ladder doing the boards that ran just under the lip of the roof.

"You're fast," Joe said. He stood with his hands on his hips and studied the completed work. "And good."

"Thanks. The rollers make this part easy."

"It's never easy when you're working on your own house," Joe muttered. "Especially when your wife is your chief critic." He started on the remaining window frames on this side of the building.

They worked quietly at first, building a rhythm between them that was almost poetic in its coordination. By the time Joe finished a frame, Jonathan had painted the wood above him to that point and moved the ladder accordingly. He talked a little bit about the work he had done on the Porter house when he lived with that family, but Joe could hear a note of disdain in his descriptions. Whatever hard feelings had developed between him and his former foster parents had been mutual.

"Mr. Porter gave me housework assignments as though I were earning my keep. He didn't think I knew that the agency paid him my living expenses."

"This kind of work can be done well only if the person doing it does it with a full heart," Joe said. "That's why I hold off until I really want to do it," he added. He laughed at his own comment, but Jonathan only nodded in understanding.

"Is that why Solomon never did any of this sort of thing?" he asked. "Or why you never made him do any of it?"

"Probably."

"Why did he feel that way?"

"I don't know. He was my kid, but a lot about him was a mystery to me," Joe added with a frankness that surprised even him. He looked up at Jonathan. "He did things for Martha."

"Maybe you didn't spend enough time with him."

"Maybe. Who knows what's enough time?" he added.

Before Jonathan could say anything else, they heard Martha bang on the inside of the next window. She opened it quickly and poked her head out.

"I just heard some terrible news," she said. "From Judy."

"What?"

"You know the Pedersen boy and Gerson Weiner's boy?"

"I don't know them," Joe said. "I know the families. So?"

"There was a terrible accident, a fire in the Pedersen boy's car last night. He had left a can of gas in the backseat. It spilled, and some electrical wires touched the soaked floor when they started the car."

"My God."

"They're both dead. Donald died only a few hours ago."

"That's terrible. Did you know them, Jonathan?" he asked.

"Only vaguely," he said.

"Damn. Spilled gas," Joe muttered. Martha shook her head and retreated, closing the window. "Funny," Joe said thinking aloud, "but I thought I smelled . . ." He shook his head. "Funny."

Joe went back to his window frame, and Jonathan worked above him carefully. Hardly a drop had fallen. Joe was impressed with the boy's dexterity and concentration.

"That's really good work, Jonathan," he said.

"Thanks," Jonathan said without pausing. Not skipping a beat, he added, "Maybe Solomon never felt confident enough to do these kinds of things because you didn't give him encouragement or praise. People, especially people my age, need a lot of that,'' he concluded, sounding more like a child psychologist than a teenager.

"I don't know," Joe said. "Maybe we oughta change jobs when we make the turn around the building," Joe said. He wanted to change the subject quickly. He felt the heat rise to his face. "You look like you're straining now. I really don't have a high-enough ladder for you."

"Why?" Jonathan paused to examine the work he had completed. "Is it looking bad?"

"No, but there's no point in your straining." Jonathan was standing at the top of the ladder at this point, although he did look as steady and as secure as a professional housepainter. In a way, Joe resented that, too. He never felt comfortable on ladders, especially when he was Jonathan's age.

"I don't mind." He held the roller away from himself.

"Nevertheless, we'll change jobs around the corner."

"Whatever you want," Jonathan said. There was no sound of resentment. Joe felt it was more like the boy was talking down to an idiot he had to humor.

They both heard the front door open and close and knew that Martha was coming out to watch. Even though Joe was sorry Jonathan seemed to only want to talk about Solomon, he was unhappy about Martha's impending arrival on the scene. Since yesterday and their service trip, he had permitted himself to believe it was possible to develop a good relationship with the boy, one that was more akin to the father-son relationships he envied in other families. Yesterday he had enjoyed the privacy of their discussions, and he hoped to get back to that feeling today, but he knew it would be different once Martha was here.

"Can't believe that about those two boys. Horrible," he said. Jonathan didn't respond.

Joe turned his back on Jonathan and rushed to complete the final window frame, just as Martha made the turn around the house to join them. But before he had his brush to the wood, he heard her scream and spun around to see

Jonathan fall from the ladder as it toppled. He landed on the lawn, striking the ground first with his right foot and then hitting with his right shoulder and hip. He rolled over on his back and groaned.

"JONATHAN!" Martha was at his side first. "JOE!"

"What the hell . . ." He knelt beside the boy. Jonathan moaned; he closed his eyes, and then he reached for his shoulder.

"Why did you put him on the ladder?"

"He was on it when I came out," Joe explained. "All right, just let him be a moment. Jonathan, how you doing?"

Martha held his head between her thighs, couched against her pelvis as she squatted beside him and brushed back his hair. Jonathan opened his eyes and continued to rub his right shoulder.

"Just a bad bruise, I think," he said, and looked up at Martha pathetically. Joe could see the pain in her face. It was as though she and Jonathan were of one body and what happened to one, happened to the other.

"Maybe he broke his arm," she said. Joe felt along the bone.

"Naw. Like he says, just a bruise."

"That's going to hurt a lot more tomorrow," Martha said. "Those kinds of things always do."

"Can you stand?" Joe asked him.

"Yeah, I think so."

"Why did you leave him on the ladder?" Martha demanded as she helped Jonathan to his feet.

"He was already up there and doing a great job. We were going to change just as soon as we made the turn around the building."

"It's all right," Jonathan said. "It's my fault."

"No, it's not. Joe should have known better. He's the adult here."

"Jesus," Joe said. Martha glared at him.

"How is it?" she asked as Jonathan swung his arm up and down to test it.

"Nothing's broken."

"We should take him to the doctor, Joe."

"Sure. We'll go up to the emergency ward at the hospital."

"Naw, I don't hafta do that," Jonathan said. "I've had bruises like this before," he added, and looked at Martha knowingly. She understood that he was making reference to maltreatment at previous foster homes, and this increased her feeling of sympathy.

"You poor kid," she said. She kissed him on the forehead.

"I just gotta soak it for a while."

"That's right, but if it's still bothering you later today, you're going to the hospital like Joe says."

"What about the foot?" Joe asked. "I would have thought that would be worse. You landed on it first, didn't you?"

"Broke my fall," Jonathan said, "but I lost my balance."

"How did you fall from the ladder? You looked so secure up there."

"How do you think he fell?" Martha said with a tone of chastisement. "He didn't belong up there in the first place. He got distracted."

"I don't know. One moment I was all right, and the next I was falling."

"It's all right; it's not your fault," Martha said.

"I didn't say it was," Joe said. He shook his head.

"Come on. Let's get some hot water on that shoulder," Martha said, and began to lead Jonathan away.

"But Joe needs help," he said.

"He'll finish this himself," she said, turning to Joe, her eyes flashing.

"Yeah, go ahead. I'll just do a little more. One side of the house a week's enough anyway," he said, half kidding. He watched Martha continue to assist Jonathan as they made their way around the house and to the front door. Jonathan was leaning heavily on her, but she didn't seem to mind the weight. Joe had the sense that the kid was enjoying the tender loving care and perhaps playing it up.

He shook his head after they disappeared, amazed at how quickly events had turned on him.

Joe made the turn and decided to complete all the window frames in the rear of the house, but as he began to work on the first, he felt guilty about continuing the effort without first finding out if the boy was truly all right. He put his brush aside for the moment and closed the lid on the paint can. Then he wiped his hands quickly and went into the house through the back door.

He didn't expect them to be downstairs, so he went right to the stairway. Halfway up, he called, but neither Martha nor Jonathan heard him because of the sound of water running hard and fast into the bathtub. They were both in the bathroom. He stopped by the door.

"Martha?"

"We're in here," she said.

He opened the door.

"How's he doing?" he began, and then stopped abruptly. Jonathan was already in the tub, and Martha was kneeling behind him on the tile floor massaging his back and shoulder.

"His neck hurts," she said, without turning to him. "He must have twisted it when he fell and not realized it."

"Sure," Joe said. The warm water continued to rush into the tub, steam rising. Jonathan lay his head back against Martha's breasts. She brought her hands over his shoulders and down over his biceps. "Do you want me to do that?" he asked, conscious of the shakiness in his voice.

"No, I can do it," she said. "We're going to rub in some Ben-Gay as soon as we're finished here."

"Uh huh." He continued to stare for a few moments.

"I'll just finish up out there," he said. "Call me if you need me."

Neither she nor Jonathan replied. He watched her press down on his shoulders and run her hands back over his neck. Jonathan kept his head back, his eyes closed. He looked like he was enjoying it greatly. Joe backed out of the bathroom and closed the door.

He wiped his face with the palms of his hands and stared at the closed bathroom door a moment. Then he turned abruptly and went back to the stairway. He descended slowly, confused by his feelings. He knew that Martha would say she was being a good mother, treating the boy's injury, caring for his pain and discomfort; but he was almost sixteen years old, and he was not her real son. There should be some modesty. Wouldn't most sixteen-year-old boys be too embarrassed to strip down and get into a tub in front of a woman they barely knew? He knew he would.

How had they developed such intimacy so quickly? He wasn't just jealous; he was concerned for good reasons. What was the right thing to do here? Should he be critical? He didn't want Martha to think he blamed her for anything, and yet he was well aware of the definite dangers. He needed some objective advice, but to whom could he go? How could he talk about it without bringing back the painful past? He knew he had to find someone or some way to get Martha to understand, but in the meantime . . . in the meantime, it was best not to say anything, he thought.

And then when he got back outside and thought more about it, he concluded the intimacy probably stemmed from the boy's own longing for motherly concern. He might act and look like an older teenager, but he was really only a disadvantaged child who had been deprived of warmth and love. Such a child would be willing to sacrifice modesty for affection. That was understandable.

However, seeing them like that in the bathroom reminded him of Martha's intimacy with Solomon. Neither hesitated to parade nude in front of the other, even when Solomon was an adolescent. He was gently critical, but she laughed it off.

"Solomon's my child," she said. "He emerged from my womb. He sucked on these breasts. What could possibly be wrong about him seeing me naked or my seeing him?"

"It's just that he's getting older," Joe said. "It might be embarrassing for him."

"If it is, he hasn't indicated so," she replied. "Don't worry about it. I think I would realize if something I did embarrassed Solomon," she added. He had to admit that was true. Two people couldn't be more simpatico. He wasn't protecting Solomon. When it came to something like this, Solomon could very well protect himself.

But he did think it was wrong for Solomon to have such easy access to their bedroom, and he did insist that the boy learn to knock first. Solomon seemed to resent the rule, but he followed it, always managing to make it into something annoying by knocking too hard or at the wrong times.

Even when he was fourteen, Martha didn't think anything of Solomon's crawling into bed beside her. In fact, to Joe's annoyance, they used to carry on long conversations like that. He would usually have to ask the boy to go to his room so that he could get into bed himself.

He was also bothered by the topics of their conversation. Some of it should have been reserved for talks between him and Solomon, especially the conversations about sex. But Martha encouraged it all. Nothing embarrassed her; nothing unnerved her and Solomon obviously felt he could tell his mother whatever he wanted to tell her.

Joe didn't know whether he was angry because he was somewhat left out, or he was angry because, as Kevin Baker said, he was jealous of the relationship his son had with his wife, what Kevin called the reverse Oedipus. In any case, it always annoyed him to find them whispering together in his bedroom.

After a while, he came to accept and ignore their intimacy, an intimacy he traced to the power of blood and genetics. One couldn't underestimate the significance of that umbilical cord, he thought. Yet how ironic it was that Solomon almost strangled on it at birth. It was wrapped around his neck so tightly, his face was blue. The doctor had to work quickly to free him from it.

Perhaps the umbilical cord had strangled him in the end after all, he concluded. But then he quickly repressed all such possible scenarios that could have driven Solomon into taking his own life. It was something neither he nor Martha were able to face.

8.

Martha was ready to accept it as an accident, albeit an easily preventable one. Young boys Jonathan's age were prone to showing off. It was understandable that he would volunteer to go up on the ladder and do the more dangerous work, but Joe should not have permitted it. She thought he should have known better, even though he was never really good with children and teenagers. His role in the raising of Solomon proved that.

As she continued to massage Jonathan's shoulders and arms, she recalled more about Joe's relationship with their son. He was always misreading Solomon, she thought, expecting him to do things at the wrong times, expecting him to have the same interests as a grown man had. Sometimes she wondered whether or not Joe had had a childhood himself. He seemed incapable of understanding the problems of adolescence. It was all so foreign to him.

Whenever she questioned him about it, he invariably referred to those ridiculous comparisons. When he was a boy, he didn't have this or he didn't have that. Nothing came as easy as it came to Solomon, and he had had real chores to do. He was expected to work with his father; he was expected to help around the house.

"In my house no one tolerated moodiness, and that was certainly no excuse for not helping out."

According to Joe, his parents were frugal by necessity, and toys were rare, although he admitted his father bought him a bike. Never would he think of being insubordinate to his parents, subtly or otherwise. His father was intolerant and had a quick and violent temper.

"God forbid I told my father I had better things to do than mow a lawn."

However, from her discussions with Joe's sister, Brenda, Martha concluded that Joe exaggerated his past. She thought he might even be fantasizing about it as a way of avoiding his present failure with his own family relationships. Whatever the reason, Martha believed that Joe either could not understand or refused to understand his own son.

"He can't be a carbon copy of either of us," she once told him when he was particularly frustrated by Solomon's behavior. "He's different because he's an individual, and just as you've got to learn to live with different people at work and in the world around you, you've got to learn to live with him."

Joe didn't argue, but she knew he didn't agree. He walked away from the conflicts whenever she made it clear that she was going to take a firm stand on something concerning Solomon. However, sometimes now, when she thought back, she wished he would have argued. He left too much on her shoulders. Eventually, she became more of a mother and father than just a mother.

She had hoped for both their sakes that things would be different with Jonathan. Perhaps Joe wouldn't feel as pressured since Jonathan wasn't his own flesh and blood. That ridiculous sense of competition that exists between father and son, something she saw occur within her own family between her brothers and her father, wouldn't be. Maybe he had learned significant things from his life with Solomon.

However, now she could see that she would have to control and direct events almost as much as she had when

Solomon was alive. Joe was just inept when it came to young people. This was her conclusion as she looked down at Jonathan in the tub, but then he added new information that challenged her thinking.

"I didn't tell the truth out there," he said, his head yet back, his eyes yet closed. The water was still so warm that the steam rolled off his skin. She turned on the exhaust fan to draw out the moisture. Her own face and neck were wet, and she had to unbutton her blouse.

"The truth? What do you mean, Jonathan? Truth about what?" She traced a ribbon of water down his right cheek with her right forefinger, recalling the many times she had come into the bathroom to wash Solomon's back. He so enjoyed the attention, right up to . . . right up to a few days before he died. He probably knew then what he was going to do, she thought. He wanted his death to be a shock and a surprise. He did it that way in order to punish us more.

"About why I fell," Jonathan finally said. He opened his eyes and sat up abruptly, but he didn't turn to her. He looked down into the water. She realized it was difficult for him to say what he was going to say, and that made her tense. She reached for the towel and wiped her hands quickly.

"What do you mean? Why wouldn't you tell the truth about why you fell?"

"I didn't think Joe would understand what made me fall," he replied, and turned to her. "He might laugh at me, and I didn't want that."

She hesitated to ask him, but he had the patience to wait for her to do so. His silence was demanding. She felt the inevitability of hearing the truth.

"What made you fall, Jonathan?" She was speaking in a whisper now.

"Well, it was like this . . ." he said, twisting his body in the water. "I was just finishing up what was left to do under the roof, and I turned when I heard you coming out of the house," he added, and illustrated the movement. Then he paused again. He wanted her to draw it all out of him. She understood that he wanted her to feel responsible for making him say it.

"Yes?"

"And something . . . someone . . . pushed me."

"Pushed you? You don't mean Joe?" she asked, realizing she asked it hopefully.

"No. It was definitely not Joe."

"I don't understand," she said, even though she did. "What are you saying?"

"I can't explain it, but I felt pressure against my shoulder, and that pressure made me lose my balance."

"It wasn't the wind," she whispered.

"No. It wasn't the wind."

There was a long moment of silence between them. She sat back and stared at the bathroom doorway. He waited, frozen in position in the tub. Finally she nodded as though she could see something through the door.

"You think I imagined it, don't you?" he asked, sounding a note of frustration.

"No."

"Because I didn't. I was pretty secure up on that ladder. Ask Joe."

"I believe you," she said. She stood up. "You keep soaking yourself," she said. "I'll be right back," she added.

"Okay." He closed his eyes and leaned back in the tub to lower more of his torso into the warm water. She studied him for a few seconds and then walked out of the bathroom and stopped in the hall.

Joe had gone back outside. It was quiet in the house. She looked in Jonathan's room, but there was no one there. Then she thought she heard something behind her and saw that her bedroom door was open. She always kept the master bedroom door closed, and whenever Joe went in and out, he did the same. She smiled to herself knowingly and walked slowly to the bedroom.

After she entered, she looked around, but she saw no one. Nothing looked disturbed, either. Then she noticed that the sliding closet door was just slightly opened. She nodded to herself and walked to it, standing in front of it for a moment. She took a deep breath, took hold of the door, and slid it completely open abruptly. Solomon stood there looking out at her. She expected he would be in there.

The ropeburn on his neck looked even more hideous this close up, but what was more revolting was the way his eyes bulged and his lips thickened. His face showed more resemblance to the face of a corpse than it had during any of her previous confrontations with him. His skin was more scaly and pale, and his usually neatly fashioned hair was disheveled, the strands lying over his forehead and down over his ears.

Her eyes went from him to the plastic bag in the corner of the floor. It looked as though it had been disturbed. He said nothing to her; he simply stared, that hateful smirk on his face.

"You pushed him, didn't you?" she said. He didn't reply. "I'm talking to you, Solomon. Answer me. You pushed him so he'd fall off the ladder."

"He's clumsy, awkward. He fell himself. I didn't have to push him. I don't have to do anything to him. He'll make a fool of himself by himself. I don't see how you can continue to compare him to me."

"Jonathan is far from clumsy and awkward. He's as bright as you were; maybe he's even brighter, and he's got a much more outgoing personality. Why, Joe even likes him more than he liked you. Everyone does."

"That's a lie. Anyway, Joe doesn't like him. You'll see. Joe will want to get rid of him. Joe will hate him."

"Never. They're getting along fine, and do you know why? Because Jonathan isn't as selfish as you were. Jonathan cares about other people. He's sensitive to their needs. He doesn't reject them out of hand and leave them frustrated and alone like you did.''

Solomon smiled, but his look was so cold it made her shudder. She embraced herself quickly and bit down softly on her lower lip. He pulled his head back in that familiar arrogant way she used to admire. Now she detested it.

''I'm surprised at you, Mother. I would have thought you would be more discerning. I guess I did overestimate your capabilities and your intelligence.''

''I don't want to change the topic. You pushed him, and I know you did. He knows it, too.''

''He knows it? That's a laugh. He doesn't know anything unless I want him to know it. Actually, now that I see what's going on, I'm rather happy you brought him here. Things were getting rather boring watching you and Joe mope about the place. Now I have someone to play with, someone on whom to tinker.''

''Don't you dare. Don't you dare disturb him, and don't you ever, ever try to hurt him again. Do you understand me? It's too late for you,'' she said, and then, as a way of demonstrating her feelings, she reached in past him and dug down into the plastic bag to fetch Solomon's gold chain.

''What are you going to do with that?'' he asked her, but she ignored him. ''Mother?''

She closed the closet door just as abruptly as she had opened it, shutting him away from her. Then she marched out of the bedroom and went back to the bathroom. Jonathan was just getting out of the tub. He reached for the towel on the rack as she approached.

''Feeling better?'' she asked.

''A little.''

''That's good. I knew the warm bath and the massage would help. We'll rub in some Ben-Gay. You go to your room and lie down and wait for me,'' she said as he wiped his body dry.

"Okay."

"But before you do, I want to give you something. You earned it."

"Earned it?"

"You suffered for it," she said. "Come here." She took him by the arm and set him before the mirror. "Look into the mirror," she commanded, and then she brought the gold chain around and draped it at the base of his throat, clipping it behind his neck. She ran her fingers down over the metal, and they both stared at the image in the mirror—Martha, her face as flushed as his, standing right behind him, his eyes bright and fixed on hers.

They spoke to each other through the image in the mirror. For Martha it was like looking through the window into a warmer and more secure world, a world that was more than ever within her reach once more.

"It's beautiful," he said, pressing his fingers over her fingers that were still on the chain. "I never had one."

"Now you do, and it looks good on you. It looks as if it always belonged to you."

"It was Solomon's, wasn't it?" he asked.

"Yes, but he didn't appreciate it."

"I appreciate it," he said. "I always will appreciate anything you give me."

"I know you will." She put her hand between his shoulder and his neck. "Dear Jonathan."

"Thank you," he said. "I'll always cherish it." He turned around and kissed her on the cheek. Then he walked out of the bathroom and left her standing by the sink, her hand on her cheek, her face on fire from the heat of passion that burned beneath her skin and behind her eyes.

When she got the Ben-Gay out of the medicine cabinet and stepped out of the bathroom, she saw Solomon standing in her bedroom doorway, a look of shock and disappointment on his face. He had his hands over his neck to cover the rope scar. She hesitated in the hallway and smiled at him. Then, like a defiant child herself, she turned away and walked to Jonathan's bedroom.

He waited, sprawled on his stomach on the bed, the towel draped over his buttocks. She paused in the doorway and looked in at him. His skin was still red from the hot water, but it looked soft and smooth.

She looked back. Solomon had stepped into the hallway. He was pleading with his eyes, begging her not to go to Jonathan. But she had nothing more to say to him, and Jonathan needed her. She entered the bedroom, closing the door softly behind her, and Jonathan turned and smiled as she went to him.

Joe continued painting and finished all the window frames before he went in for lunch. Martha told him that Jonathan was asleep upstairs. He followed her into the kitchen, where she made him a sandwich from leftover turkey. He noticed that she looked rather flushed. She had her hair pinned up, and she had changed into her heavy cotton, white bathrobe and wore those green and blue slipper socks she had bought for Solomon last Christmas. She worked quietly, with an afterglow on her face that reminded him of the moments after their lovemaking.

"He felt all right after the bath?" he asked her. He suspected she still blamed him for the accident.

"I rubbed him out. We'll wait and see how bad the pain is after he sleeps."

"I don't know how he fell off that thing," Joe muttered. He was braced for her lecture on how to handle kids. He once angrily asked her what made her such an expert on children, and she calmly replied that she came from a large family and that was enough to make anyone an expert. He wondered. Maybe she was right.

But she surprised him now—she didn't go into any tirade; she didn't bawl him out for the way he supervised the boy. Instead, she turned toward him and took on a look of fear, her eyes wide, her mouth pulled back at the corners. It gave him the chills. He actually turned around to see if there was anyone standing behind him.

"Things can happen to him, Joe," she said softly. "We've got to do more to protect him."

"What do you mean, things can happen to him? Things can happen to anybody. I could have fallen off that ladder, too. Just because someone is older, it doesn't necessarily mean he's invulnerable."

He started to eat his sandwich but stopped to look up at her because she continued to stand so still. She had her hands clutched and pressed against the base of her throat. He noticed that she had turned pale, as if something had frightened her so badly the blood had drained from her face. Yet there were only the two of them in the kitchen, and the house was relatively quiet.

"No, Joe," she finally said. "Things are different for him. He's more vulnerable. We must get stronger and keep him insulated. He's fragile and unprotected."

"Jonathan? Come on. You see the way he handles himself around kids his age and what he can do with tools when he wants to. That boy can be on his own, easily."

"Oh, God, Joe, can't you ever see anything? Kids, tools. He's in terrible danger. Terrible," she added and walked to the edge of the kitchen doorway where she looked up toward Jonathan's room. Joe stared at her and then shook his head and continued to eat his sandwich.

"What terrible danger? What the hell are you talking about?" he asked after taking another bite.

"He must never be alone in this house," she said. "Never. Promise me, Joe. Promise you'll never let that happen." She looked terrified.

"What? Alone in this house? What's wrong with that?"

"Just promise me." She turned on him, a desperate look on her face. "Will you?"

"Jesus, Martha. You're beginning to frighten me. What the hell are you talking about?" She didn't reply, but he thought he saw her fingers trembling. He thought he should end it as fast as he could, whatever it was. "All right, all right. I promise. He'll never be left alone in the house," he said, feeling silly for saying it.

"Good," she said. "Good." And then her face changed abruptly, a wide, happy smile appearing. "If Jonathan's up to it later, why don't we all go out for Chinese food? It's Sunday night, and we all used to do that when Solomon was alive, remember?"

"Sure." Her dramatic reversal worried him. She had roller-coaster moods when Solomon was alive. He never knew what things would be like when he came home from work, and even if the day or the evening started out hopefully, something could happen to radically change it, something intangible and unseen. It was like living on the edge of hysteria. He blamed it solely on the kid and the terrible pressures he placed over her, but he couldn't get her to see that.

Once, and now that he recalled it, not that long before the suicide, he had a talk with Solomon about Martha's fragility. The night before, she had done a lot of sulking and eventually gone to sleep early. He knew it had something to do with an argument she had had with Solomon, but she would not tell him what it was about, and Solomon offered no insights. When he had come home from work the day after, Martha was still out shopping. He knocked on Solomon's bedroom door, waited, and knocked again more emphatically. Solomon opened the door and stepped away, turning his back on him and going right to his computer as if opening the door was some unimportant and annoying chore.

"I want to talk to you about your mother, Solomon," he said. He could see that Solomon was obviously surprised by the announcement. He looked more interested than he had looked about any other suggested topic of conversation between them. Only, Joe felt that the boy had a kind of condescending expression, as if to say "*You* want to talk about her?"

"What about my mother?"

"She seems to be under a great strain lately. I think you're putting too much on her shoulders."

"Too much of what?" He turned from the computer and looked up amusingly. Joe felt his temper inflating like a small balloon within the rear of his skull. It sent a ring of pain around to his forehead. He pinched and squeezed his temples with his thumb and forefinger.

"Too much of yourself, maybe. I don't know. You're laying problems on her, and she's not as strong as you imagine."

"Really?" He turned away and began writing quickly in a notebook. "Did she ask you to tell me this?"

"No, and I don't want you to tell her we had this discussion. That would only upset her more. You know she wants to do all she can for you."

"Yes, I know," he said, but he didn't sound happy about it, and Joe remembered being confused about that.

"You can see what I'm talking about, can't you, Solomon? You see how she's been these past few weeks?"

"Yes, I see," he said in a tone of resignation. "You're right." Joe softened.

"If there are things troubling you, I'd be glad to help. I mean . . ."

"I understand," he said. "Don't worry." He turned around, but his eyes were teary and red. "I won't do anything to aggravate her or frustrate her."

Joe felt the need to say something else about it, to ask other questions, but his struggle for the right words ended in defeat. He couldn't help it; there was something about the way he and Solomon confronted each other, something between them that kept them from being close. He longed to understand what it was and rip it down. He wanted so much to reach his son and have his son reach him, but it seemed as though they were miles apart.

All he could do was nod.

"What are you working on?" he asked, choosing another avenue of conversation.

"An English report."

"Anything I can help with? I was pretty good in grammar."

"This is an advanced placement essay," Solomon said dryly, and turned his back on him again. "They advanced me in English, remember?"

"Oh, yeah, right. Hey, I got a new game for the IBM . . ."

"I'm not interested in turning the computer into an electronic toy," Solomon said quickly.

Joe nodded without speaking even though Solomon kept his back to him. After a moment, he left him. He felt so drained from the experience, he had to go downstairs and sit in his easy chair.

As far as he knew, Solomon said nothing to Martha about their conversation. Martha never mentioned it, and he knew she would if Solomon told her what had transpired. Still, he felt as though his son held it over him. When they went out for a Sunday dinner like the dinner Martha was now suggesting for him and Jonathan and her, Solomon cryptically quipped about the need to handle his own problems. Martha didn't pick up on it, but Joe saw the impish twinkle in his son's eyes and hated him for it.

"It'll be a way of celebrating one whole week with Jonathan, won't it?" Martha said, pulling him out of his reverie.

"Huh?"

"Going out to dinner. What do you think?"

"I suppose. I'll finish up the trim work in plenty of time," he said. He watched her move about with a great deal more energy and shook his head in amazement as he finished his sandwich.

Later in the afternoon she came out to tell him that Jonathan was feeling all right and they would go out to eat. He sat at the top of the ladder, and she stood beneath him, her arms folded beneath her breasts.

"So he's up to it. Good. Then out for Chinese food it is," he said, smiling.

"Just like a family," she said. "Just like we used to be."

"Fine," he replied. "I'm almost done here. I'll finish and then go in to take a shower."

"It's all right. Take your time. He's on his homework, so he won't have to worry about it later."

"Just like Solomon. Always getting it out of the way," Joe muttered. His son's organizational skills always impressed him, but he got to the point where they annoyed him, too. He kept such a rigid schedule sometimes, it was impossible to do anything together spontaneously. Yet he knew there were many parents who would have liked to have to complain to their child that he worked too hard and too well.

Nevertheless, after a particularly frustrating moment, he told him, "Once in a while you can screw up, Solomon. Hand something in late. Show them you're human." Solomon didn't get insulted. One thing he hated to do was show emotion. He'd rather be sarcastic or witty. That was his way.

"Is that what you did, Dad? You showed them you were human?"

"I didn't do so badly," he said, but Solomon had already put him on the defensive. The point he was trying to make was lost, even to him. He retreated from the discussion.

Joe simply expected Martha would agree with him when he said Jonathan was just like Solomon about his schoolwork. After all, she had been pointing out analogies all week long, hadn't she? But she surprised him this time. She looked up at him on the ladder and disagreed.

"No, he's not, Joe. He's doing his work because he

wants to do it, not because it's something Solomon would have done. They're two different people, Joe.''

"Huh?"

She didn't remain to explain it. He watched her hurry off back into the house and shrugged to himself.

Women, he thought. They're so damn inconsistent. Not like computers. He spent the rest of the time working and daydreaming about the future when men would be able to program their wives. And especially their children!

That evening Joe sensed some subtle advances in the relationship that had been developing between Jonathan and Martha. It was as though Jonathan's accident on the ladder had shattered what remained of any formalities and hesitation between them, not that much had. But Martha's assimilation of Jonathan into their family and his involvement with them couldn't be more complete. They joked, touched, and spoke to each other as though they had known each other all Jonathan's life.

Joe wasn't sure how to react, for he saw now that it wasn't simply a reincarnation of the relationship Martha had had with Solomon. There appeared to be a difference, and that difference pleased him. This evening Jonathan was careful to include him in every discussion and wait for his opinion, too, when he asked a question. There were times when Solomon was alive when Joe felt completely left out, even when only the three of them went to dinner. Martha and Solomon would carry on conversations about things Joe didn't know and about things they had said to each other when he wasn't around. He was often ignored.

For this occasion, Martha put on her light blue tweed skirt and jacket outfit with the button-down dark blue cotton blouse, the one that had the white tie hand-painted on it. She washed and brushed out her hair so it looked more fluffed and full and then put on those gold-leaf earrings with the blue emeralds in the center. He thought she looked stunning.

Jonathan dressed in the sports jacket she had had tailored to fit him and wore a pair of Solomon's black leather loafers that were, as Martha had said, practically unused because they turned out to be too tight on his feet.

"It was almost as if he were buying things in anticipation of Jonathan's arrival," she quipped, and Joe looked up in amazement as he polished his own black loafers. He could understand her pleasure over having the boy, but was that pleasure so strong that it wiped away the memories of all the pain? Usually, any references to Solomon left her face dark and her eyes tired. He didn't understand it, but he wasn't sure it was something he should pursue. He was still afraid of spoiling things.

He rushed to finish with his shoes because he was the last to get dressed. They were both ahead of him, and he could hear them talking downstairs. Martha shouted up to tell him to hurry because they were hungry.

As he came downstairs, he heard Martha and Jonathan kidding each other about their clothing and their appearance. The nature of their jokes surprised him. They sounded more like two teenagers. Their laughter was free and natural, and he envied them the warmth between them, but as soon as he stepped into the room, Jonathan brought him into the foolery.

"And here he is—Mr. Munster," he said, and she laughed.

"Huh?"

"He says we look like the Munster family from the old television show."

"I look like Herman Munster?"

"Especially in the sports coat," Jonathan said.

"What?"

"He's right, honey. It's time you bought some up-to-date clothing."

"Is that so? I want you to know I accepted an award in this jacket last year, and no one commented about my being out of fashion."

"Where was the award given, Transylvania?" Jonathan asked. Martha laughed hysterically.

"All right, all right. So it's a little long, and the collar is a little wide. I bet we're still going to be the best-dressed people eating at Hong Fu's," he said.

The rest of the evening went the same way. On the way to the restaurant, Martha acted like a tour guide pointing out the homes of people they knew and the restaurants and stores they frequented. After everything or anything any one of them said, someone made a witty remark or a joke. The mood was light and relaxed.

At the restaurant, they fooled around with the chopsticks and imitated television and movie personalities; they told stories from their past experiences. They weren't loud or ostentatious, but Joe could see that they were the center of attention. Other patrons of the restaurant watched them with looks of amusement on their faces. He imagined that in their eyes they appeared to be the perfect little family.

The only time during the dinner when Joe sensed a break in the mood was when Jonathan ordered egg foo yung. That was Solomon's favorite Chinese dish, and he would order it nine out of ten times whenever they went to a Chinese restaurant. It used to annoy Joe that his son would spend ten minutes studying the various dishes on the menu and then conclude by ordering one of the more simple ones practically all the time. Whenever he commented about it, Martha would say, "Let him eat what he wants. He doesn't like to experiment with food."

"That's boring," Joe said, and left it at that.

However, now, as soon as Jonathan said "Egg foo yung" to the waiter, Martha interrupted.

"Why don't you order something more exotic?" she said. "They have so many wild and interesting things here."

"I like egg foo yung."

"But it's so simple. I could make it for you at home."

"That's all right," he said. "I feel like it tonight."

"There's just so much to choose from," she insisted.

"If that's what he wants . . ." Joe said, and realized that somehow things had been reversed. It puzzled him. Martha was the one who looked annoyed now. She snapped her menu up in front of her and deliberately took longer to order her food. For a while afterward, they were left with a heavy silence among them that reminded Joe more of the old days. But, when the food began to arrive, things loosened up again, and the laughter and relaxation that had earlier characterized the evening continued.

It didn't end when they returned home, either. After everyone changed into more comfortable clothing, Jonathan joined them to watch television. It was something Solomon did less and less as he grew older, but Joe didn't mind because whenever Solomon did watch television with them, he spent most of the time ridiculing whatever they watched, unless he watched something he liked.

Watching television together started out well, but then Jonathan began making comments that Joe characterized as Solomon-like comments. If he closed his eyes and listened, he thought Jonathan even sounded like Solomon.

Martha began changing channels to please him, only nothing seemed to be good. After a while the loose and jolly mood darkened. The three of them ended by staring blankly at the set, no one voicing any preference for anything.

Joe was the first to go up. He was really tired from the house painting, and he knew he had a big day tomorrow. He was nearly asleep by the time Martha came into the bedroom. He vaguely heard her wash up and get into bed.

A little after twelve o'clock, he opened his eyes because he sensed Martha was up and standing by the window that faced the rear of the house. He saw her silhouetted in the moonlight that came through the opened curtains. Before he had a chance to ask her what it was, she turned, somehow sensing that he had awakened.

"What is it?" he whispered. "Why are you up?"

"I heard him."

"Heard him? Heard who?"

"Solomon," she said.

Jesus, he thought, she's having a bad dream, and she's walking in her sleep.

"Come back to bed, Martha. You didn't hear anything."

"He did it because he was angry that we had such a good time with Jonathan tonight," she said. She took a step toward him. "But don't let him frighten you; don't let him stop you from developing a good relationship with the boy."

"Christ, Martha. Go to sleep. Solomon's dead. You can't hear him."

"He was out there," she said. "In the backyard. I went to look, but I knew what he would do."

"What did he do?" Joe asked. He braced himself up on his right elbow. Was it possible to carry on a conversation with someone who was walking in her sleep? She's probably just confused now, he thought.

"He hanged himself from the tree."

"Martha. Martha," he repeated, speaking softly, "that was something he did well over a year ago. You're dreaming."

"No, you don't understand. He wanted to punish me with the sight again, but I didn't scream."

"Martha, come back into bed. Come on," he said, reaching up for her. He took her hand, and she let him lead her around to her side. She slipped under the covers.

"He's just terribly jealous," she said. "It's understandable, but he has no one to blame but himself."

"Martha, go to sleep. Come on. You're having a bad dream."

She looked at him, and then she turned over and did fall back to sleep so quickly, he was convinced she was walking and talking in her sleep. It was nearly an hour before he could go back to sleep. He had to wait to hear her quiet, regular breathing. After that, he couldn't help what he did, even though he felt foolish afterward.

He got out of the bed softly and went to the window himself. When he first looked out, he thought he saw a thicker, darker shadow under the tree. It played tricks on his eyes, and he imagined that's what had happened to Martha when she looked out. Understandable, he thought. In a way, we are being haunted, he concluded, and went back to bed, grateful himself now that in the morning Jonathan would be there to distract them and take their minds away from the memory of that fateful day.

Perhaps we need this boy more than I ever believed we would, he thought.

9.

Audra brought her knees up and embraced her legs. She smoothed down her blue and white-patterned, heavy cotton night gown and rested her chin on her knees to look down at Sally Kantzler, who lay on her side, her head against her hand, propped up on her elbow. For a long moment, the girls stared at each other. Sally was afraid to utter a word and chance breaking the spell. Audra had been speaking about the most intimate things, and Sally, although seventeen, had yet to experience any sort of significant relationship with a boy.

Sally wasn't ugly, but she was terribly shy and afraid when it came to romance. For now, her excitement came only through the vicarious experiences she enjoyed whenever a girl like Audra was willing to share. Few of her friends ever did, and it was especially rare for Audra to talk about these things, but something had happened to make her do so and Sally wasn't about to chance any abortion of the discussion.

As long as Audra could remember, other girls usually confided in her. She was the listener; she was the adviser. She had a strong sense of privacy, especially when it came to her relationships with boys, not that she had that many.

Through her uncle Herman and her cousin Margret, she

had met Steve Salvio, a neighbor of theirs in New York, who was now a freshman at City College, and they had carried on an off-and-on relationship for two years. Steve had known about her friendship with Solomon Stern, but neither she nor Steve had ever suggested they go steady and avoid any other romantic involvements, and since Solomon's death, she hadn't seen Steve or talked much with him on the phone.

It was by no means a coincidence that Audra had chosen to be so open and revealing with Sally Kantzler. They had been friends since the first grade, both good students, both very conscious about their schoolwork. But Audra also saw Sally as somewhat innocuous in the sense that she wasn't the kind who would run off with the tales to gossip in the girls' room at school. Sally wasn't very popular with the other girls, and she was disdainful of what she condescendingly referred to as "teenage business." It was the way she generally characterized almost everything the others did. "They're off doing their teenage business," she would say.

Yet despite Sally's aloofness when it came to things teenage girls were doing, Audra respected her sense of proportion and her understanding of human behavior. In many ways, Sally was mature when it came to dealing with other people. She was the only one of her teenage friends who understood Audra's feelings after Solomon's suicide. She didn't treat it like a front-page story in the *Enquirer*. Audra sensed that Sally empathized and felt the mental anguish Audra suffered. In fact, Sally was more sympathetic than Audra's own mother.

From time to time, Sally would sleep over at Audra's house or Audra would go to Sally's. Audra had asked Sally over this particular evening because she had come to where she felt she had to talk to someone about herself and Jonathan. She had arrived at the point where she was both frightened by him and attracted to him, and she wasn't sure how to go about reconciling the seemingly contradictory feelings.

In the back of her mind was also the idea that she had been permitting her imagination to run wild, and it was because of that that she was in this particular state of mind. She had little faith in this theory, a theory that now seemed more like a hope, and she thought if she could talk about some of it with a girl like Sally, she might better crystallize her feelings and arrive at a closer understanding of what was really happening between her and Jonathan.

Sally had known Solomon and had gotten along with him. Audra even felt certain that Sally had a crush on Solomon. Once she and Solomon had discussed it, and he had made her angry because he seemed so arrogant about it, threatening to play with Sally emotionally.

She bawled him out for having such a devious intention, and he did nothing like that to Sally, even though he teased Audra with the possibility occasionally.

In any case, Audra believed that Sally was the only one of her friends who had an intimate enough understanding of the background and the people involved to appreciate what she was now going through. The two of them had begun the evening by doing their homework and then had changed into their nightgowns and sat around talking and listening to music.

Audra eased herself into a discussion of Jonathan, almost the way someone began a series of sensitive negotiations. She began with references to relatively insignificant details about him, his appearance, and his behavior, testing Sally's perception and seeing whether or not her intelligent friend had picked up as many oddities as she had and agreed on what she now considered the smaller aspects.

"You know, of course, that the Sterns have given him Solomon's entire wardrobe, and most everything fits him well."

"I saw he had on that blue shirt with the gold trim on the sleeves the other day, the one Solomon occasionally wore to school, and it suddenly occurred to me why I kept seeing something familiar about him all the time. I just never thought they'd give him all of Solomon's clothes,'' Sally said, and grimaced. "It's ghoulish."

Sally had a pleasant, if not attractive, face. Her nose was a little long and the bone a little emphatic, but she had warm, light blue eyes and a dark complexion that had always been remarkably free of acne, something that symbolically separated her from the other girls and made it seem as if she had indeed skipped over what she would definitely consider a silly and uncomfortable aspect of adolescence.

She wore her dark brown hair cut a trifle too short for Audra's liking because she thought it brought attention to her round face and baby-faced cheeks, but Sally wasn't the type who enjoyed spending time on her coiffure. She hated makeup of all kinds and favored fashions that made her look older, even when some of the skirts and dresses made her hips look wider than they really were. She rarely wore jeans and a sweatshirt.

"Didn't it amaze you how quickly Jonathan made friends with all of Solomon's friends?" Audra asked. Sally heard the tone in Audra's voice and sensed that she was on an expedition. It excited her to be part of something like this, so she nodded quickly.

"Yes, but then I thought he's . . . more outgoing in some ways."

"It's more than that," Audra said. "He seems to know just what to say, just what they want to hear. It's almost as if . . . as if he knew them as long as Solomon did."

"Really?" Sally sat up, her face became electric, the eyes brightening, her lips growing moist as her tongue moved out and over them nervously. "But how could that be?"

"I don't know. He's bright; he's doing well in school already. I helped him start to catch up, but . . ."

"I'd never be able to tell he wasn't there from the start," Sally said quickly. "He's answering questions, and he didn't avoid taking Palmer's exam even though Mr.

Palmer said he could be excused because it involved a great deal of work that had been covered before he arrived.''

"I know. And he got an A on that.''

Sally thought for a moment and then shrugged.

"So he's bright,'' she said, and started to lie back again.

"No, it's more than that.''

"What?''

"I can't say.''

"What do you mean?''

"I just don't know how to explain it. He's like Solomon in so many ways, and yet . . .''

"And yet what?''

"He's different,'' Audra said, looking up. Sally sensed something very exciting was coming. Her heart actually began beating quickly. She held her breath, but Audra paused so long, Sally thought she wasn't going to continue.

"Don't you like him?'' she asked, chancing the question.

"Yes. And no.''

"What?''

Audra just stared for a long moment again. This time Sally was patient.

"I never told anyone, but there was nothing really going on between Solomon and me,'' Audra said softly.

"I don't understand,'' Sally said. Her voice was almost a whisper, as though Audra's tone was infectious. "What do you mean by 'nothing'?''

"Nothing . . . sexual. Oh, we kissed, but it was always like friends kiss, do you know what I mean?''

"Uh huh.'' Sally did know because that was basically the only kind of kissing she had done.

"He seemed to be restrained all the time, distracted.''

"Always?''

"There were times when I was at his house that I thought something might happen. I suppose I was a little aggressive about it, too; but nothing ever did.''

"You didn't even kiss him on the lips?''

"Yes, but he always seemed so far off. It didn't lead to anything more, and I wanted it to. I wanted him to touch me. I wanted . . . you understand?" Sally didn't speak. She simply nodded slightly. She wanted to swallow, but she didn't even do that. "I kept thinking that eventually he would . . . we would get closer, but we never did. Not that way, at least."

"Well, how come you stayed with him so long?"

"I don't know. Yes, I do," she added quickly. "Solomon was so superior, so perceptive. There was something magical about him. I couldn't just walk away from him because he didn't pursue me the way I wanted him to. And besides," she said sadly, "I kept expecting that eventually he would."

"But nothing happened?"

Audra just stared again. Sally sensed that what she had heard so far, as exciting as it was, was just the surface. She bit down on her lower lip in anticipation.

"I got impatient," Audra began. It was clear that what she was remembering was something so vivid it nearly took her out of the present completely. Her voice was low again, soft and low. "It was at his house when there was no one home. His mother had gone somewhere with one of her friends, and his father was out on a job as usual.

"It was a warm spring day," she went on, "an unusually warm spring day. Maybe a month before he killed himself," she added. "We had decided to go on a hike down the path behind his house. We were both acting kind of stupid, running through the bushes, charging up the hills, acting like a couple of young children. But it was fun, you know what I mean? It was so carefree. I guess the pressure of upcoming exams . . . I don't know. Anyway, it felt good to be like that."

Sally nodded quickly, afraid now to utter a sound.

"We got back to his house, and I decided to take a shower."

"In his house?" Sally couldn't resist the question and immediately chastised herself for asking it.

"Yes," Audra said. Sally saw that nothing was going to stop her now. "As I said, his parents weren't home and weren't going to be for quite a while. So I took a shower, and after I was finished, I came out with just a towel wrapped around me and went to his room."

Sally's face was flushed. She held her breath again and waited.

"He had gone into his parents' bathroom and taken a shower, too, and when I entered his room . . . he was naked."

Sally released some air through her teeth, but she didn't take another breath.

"For a moment, we looked at each other, and I thought this is it, this is finally it. He didn't come toward me, but I thought that he wanted to, so I went to him and we kissed. It was the best kiss we ever had. My towel dropped. We kissed again, only this time . . ."

"What?"

"He wasn't kissing back as hard. Here I was naked, and he was naked . . ." She stopped and put her hands over her face a moment. Sally thought she wouldn't go on, but she lowered her hands and, looking directly at her, said, "He wasn't even excited."

"Pardon?"

"He wasn't excited. He didn't even have an erection. You know what that is, don't you?" Audra asked impatiently. Sally nodded quickly. "I could have just as well been dressed," she said, but she sounded more sad than angry about it.

"What happened?"

"Nothing. That's the point. I went back to the bathroom and got dressed. Afterward, we met downstairs, and he acted as though nothing different had occurred between us. He made chocolate milk shakes," she added, and grimaced.

"Didn't you talk about it?"

"Not right then. I was confused and frightened. I felt so strange, like my existence had been denied. Can you understand that?"

"Yes," Sally said, even though she wasn't sure what Audra meant. "When did you talk about it?"

"A week or so later. He apologized. He said he had things on his mind, and it had nothing to do with me. He said all sorts of nice things about me, but things became different and not long afterward . . ."

"He hanged himself," Sally said, providing the conclusion.

"Yes."

"But that couldn't be why . . . I mean, you're not blaming yourself in any way."

"No. I'm not blaming myself."

"Wow," Sally said, and started to lie back.

"Then came Jonathan," Audra continued, and Sally shot back up as quickly as she would had she been stuck with a pin.

"Don't tell me the same thing has happened."

"Quite the contrary," Audra said, her face finally breaking into a smile. The realization of what she meant settled in on Sally immediately.

"Audra! So quickly?" Sally thought for a moment. "Then, why did you say yes and no when I asked you if you like him?"

"Because sometimes I get this weird feeling that he was there before, watching Solomon and me, and he knows just what has to be done. He knows what excites me, what I like, but most importantly, what I want . . . maybe even need." She looked at her friend. "Does this make any sense to you?"

Sally's face turned serious as she thought. Then she nodded.

"It's something you're imagining because of the resemblances and because you're seeing him in Solomon's house, even in Solomon's room. It's your imagination, that's all."

"That's what I thought. That's what I thought you would say," Audra replied. She looked disappointed by the confirmation.

"But you know differently," Sally said. Audra and she locked their gaze for a moment. For Audra it was as though she were exposing her innermost self to someone she truly trusted, and for Sally it was as though she had suddenly found the power to look behind words and uttered thoughts.

"Yes," Audra said. "I know differently."

One of the results of Sally and Audra's tête-à-tête was Sally's promise to be more observant and perceptive when it came to Jonathan. She didn't really have to promise to do it; she thought the agreed-upon assignment was one of the most exciting things to happen to her this school year and maybe even her entire high school senior's life. She couldn't have been more anxious to participate, even vicariously, in Audra's love life.

And, she had been somewhat less than revealing herself that night she slept at Audra's. She didn't tell her about the number of times Jonathan had sought her out to talk to her privately, because during a few of those occasions, she thought she might have told him things about Audra that Audra might not have appreciated being told.

For instance, he was very interested in what Audra had been doing since Solomon's death. Jonathan knew about Steve Salvio, too, and was very inquisitive about Audra's relationship with the New York guy. Since she hadn't told Audra about these discussions immediately after having them, she was sure Audra would be very upset and might even feel betrayed. Right now, Sally didn't want to do anything that would jeopardize her exciting new assignment, and, as far as she could see, the information she had given Jonathan was common knowledge anyway. If he didn't get it from her, he would have gotten it from someone else in the crowd.

And then there was something else, something she definitely didn't dare tell Audra—she had begun to believe that Jonathan might have some romantic interest in her. A few times during the week, she caught him staring at her in class, and when he spoke to her privately, he always managed to touch her in some way, whether it was by taking her hand, or placing his hand on her shoulder, or just brushing up against her. Also, he never spoke to her without complimenting her on something—her hair, her eyes, even her posture. Couldn't this mean something more?

Right from the beginning of the week, Audra managed to work things out so that she, Jonathan, and Sally would spend more time together. They sat together in the lunchroom; Sally was always nearby when Jonathan stopped to talk to Audra in the halls, and twice during the week, Audra had Sally over when she and Jonathan got together to study something.

If he sensed being under observation, he didn't show it. On the contrary, he looked amused and flattered by all the added attention. He even went so far as to invite Sally over to the Sterns' the night he had asked Audra over. She accepted, of course. This was something Solomon had never done, even though he had been almost as friendly. There were times when she felt he might, but it never came to anything. Jonathan had done it and had done it so quickly and so nonchalantly, she wasn't sure what to make of it.

But Audra had her suspicions, suspicions Sally was beginning to believe were definitely manufactured in Audra's imagination. They nearly had an argument about it right after Jonathan had invited her to join Audra and him at the Sterns' house. Both of them remained in school and went into one of the audiovisual labs in the library.

"He knows what we're doing," Audra concluded. "He's deliberately being very cooperative."

"That's ridiculous. I don't see that," Sally said.

"Why else do you think he invited you over, too?" Audra asked, not realizing how cruel the question sounded. Sally blanched.

"I think he just likes me," she said, her voice humble and small.

"Solomon·liked you, too," Audra said, "but he didn't play with you like this."

"He's not playing with me," Sally said indignantly. Audra was so wrapped up in her own perceptions, she didn't see Sally's reactions.

"He is very different, isn't he?" Audra asked. "You see that now, don't you?"

"Why shouldn't he be? He's a different person."

"But you heard some of the comments he made about the others. We talked about them. He says so many of the things Solomon said. Look at his evaluation of Gary Kaufman. He called him a latent homosexual."

"I told you, he's not the first to say that about Gary. Kirk Michaels said he wouldn't catch himself alone with Gary in the boys' locker room, didn't he?"

"Solomon told him that, and he never forgot it. All they know about each other, Solomon taught them," Audra said, "and now Jonathan is telling them the same things." She stopped talking and took a closer look at Sally. "I thought you would be able to see these things. That's why I asked you to be more observant."

"I see them," Sally said. She looked down at her notebook. On the other side of the big glass window, Mrs. Bobchick, the librarian, glared at them. She was very suspicious about why students remained after school whenever they did. The fifty-four-year-old librarian didn't trust any teenager, no matter how well he or she did in school and no matter what the other members of the faculty said. Even a valedictorian was not above doodling in a library book or using the library to slip someone drugs or be handed drugs.

Sally cleared her throat and began writing notes quickly. Audra looked up and smiled at the librarian, who did not smile back. She hesitated and then moved on to check on some students near the card catalog.

"Mrs. Bobchick, the academic paranoid," Sally said, and Audra seized her wrist.

"There," she said. "That's another example."

"What do you mean?"

"What Jonathan said at lunch today when I told him I was staying after school to do research on my economics paper . . ." Sally didn't say anything. "He said he heard the academic paranoid was having the school buy her one of those X-ray machines used in airports so she could check students on the way in and out of the library."

"I remember," Sally said, smiling.

"But don't you see . . . he called her 'the academic paranoid'; that was Solomon's name for her."

Sally thought for a moment.

"So what? He probably heard one of the others call her that and just picked up on it. I don't know, Audra; I think you're getting carried away with your own paranoia," she said. Audra thought for a moment and then relaxed in her chair.

"Do you?"

"So far, I must say, I do."

"Maybe you're right," she said. She stared out the window for a moment and then turned to her selection of filmstrips and cassettes. "I guess I'd better get the research done," she said.

"Okay," Sally said, gathering her things together. "I'll see you later at Jonathan's."

"Uh huh."

"Of course," Sally added, "I won't be able to make too many comparisons while I'm there because I was never there before with Solomon. He never invited me," she said.

Audra looked up at her, getting the first inkling that perhaps this conscription of Sally into the scene was not a good idea after all. Jonathan, just like Solomon, was too much for her. He was just as clever, just as shrewd, just as manipulative. Maybe it was even dangerous for her to be so involved. He might end up taking unfair advantage of her naive friend, she thought, and it would be all her fault.

"You haven't said anything to him that might have given him any ideas, have you, Sally?"

"What do you mean?"

"I don't know. I'm just very confused right now," she added quickly, and then looked up again and smiled. "Just be careful," she said.

"My God, Audra, you make him sound like Jack the Ripper or someone."

"I can't help it," Audra whispered, but Sally had already turned away and started for the door of the audio-visual lab. She didn't hear what Audra had said.

Audra looked into the monitor of the personal filmstrip and cassette machine and put on her earphones, but when she turned the knob and brought up the first slide, she didn't see the picture from the filmstrip, she saw Jonathan's face merging with Solomon's face.

The same thing had happened in the back of Gary Isaac's car. She had been pleasantly surprised by Jonathan's aggressiveness. Unlike Solomon, he didn't hesitate to put his arm around her and draw her closer to him as soon as she was beside him in the backseat.

Gary was with Paula Simon. They had been dating for four months or so, and Audra knew that they would be quite intimate with each other rather quickly because she knew Paula as a rather sensuous and forward girl who had been sleeping with boys since the ninth grade. Audra was one of the few people, probably the only other high school girl, who knew that Paula had had an abortion last year.

Audra thought that when someone went on a double date, especially someone who didn't know everyone that well and that long, it would be expected that he would be tentative and unsure of what the other couple would be like. But right from the start, Jonathan was not like that. He seemed to know immediately that Gary and Paula were not the types to be embarrassed by the passionate contact of their companions.

It was he who suggested they forget about the movie and go right to Paula's house. He picked up on something she had said during the day and knew her parents weren't going to be home. She had an older sister in college, so they would have the house to themselves. Audra couldn't remember Solomon once making such a suggestion. She was both surprised and excited by it, and Gary and Paula were more than amenable.

"I thought you might want to wait until after the movie," Gary said.

"It's not important to me," Jonathan said. He brushed his lips over Audra's left temple and kissed her softly on the forehead while his hand moved up her waist. She tightened up, and he didn't go further. They continued down the highway and reached the outskirts of the village, where they picked up the illumination of streetlights. As the car passed from the darkness to the light, Audra looked into Jonathan's face, and that was when his face began to merge with Solomon's.

Of course, she attributed it to her imagination, but as the marriage of physical characteristics continued, she found herself drawn closer and deeper to him. She was fascinated and mesmerized by the evaporation of time. Was she in the present? Was she in the past? Or was she caught in some magical moment when past and present vanish and one lives only in what one feels during those seconds, during those minutes, during those hours? Whatever it was, she felt inebriated. Her head was spinning, but she wasn't dizzy; she was light, carefree, like the time she and Solomon had gone running up the hill behind his house. Her body tingled with the memory of what could have been, and Jonathan seemed to sense it.

He was at her again, kissing her with more demand, his hands moving over her breasts as he turned her toward him. It turned out that they were the couple, not Paula and Gary, who couldn't wait to get into the empty house. Jonathan didn't opt for any preliminaries. Paula suggested they drink some of her parents' booze, but Jonathan wasn't interested in that. They split up immediately, she and Jonathan taking the den and Paula and Gary going to Paula's room.

Jonathan turned on the little reading light that was on the desk in the far corner. It cast just enough illumination to put a glow over his face and cut the shadows out of the darkness, delineating shapes on the walls and the ceiling, creating an audience of faceless spirits, voyeurs from another world, perhaps the world into which Solomon had entered that fateful day.

As Jonathan stepped toward her, he seemed to emerge from this darkness. She had the vague understanding that he came from out of the darkness of her own mind, where dwelt all her erotic fantasies and lived all her erotic dreams. He wore Solomon's shiny black jacket with the wool cuffs and the silver zipper. She always had thought he looked dangerous and handsome in that jacket.

Jonathan zipped it down slowly and peeled it away from his body. She was on the soft cushioned couch, and when he came to her, he knelt beside her to first lay his head on her thighs. She threaded her fingers through his hair, and when he looked up, his face was cloaked in darkness. He wore it like a mask. Who was behind it? she wondered. It was the last thought that had anything to do with hesitation, for when he rose and brought his lips to hers, she felt herself soften and lay back with an obedience that surprised even her.

They didn't make love like teenagers groping for new excitement, rushing into climaxes out of a fear that it might somehow be interrupted. They made love like a couple with years of sexual experience, touching each other knowingly, wisely, strengthened by an awareness of what was to come. Jonathan's kisses were filled with confidence; his touch was assured. She couldn't even remember the details of how her clothing was stripped away, but when they were naked together and her mind went back to that day in Solomon's room when they had embraced after taking showers, she found herself picking up the memory where it had been disappointing and attaching these moments to it, as though it could be true . . . she could meld the two boys into one very satisfactory boy and finally celebrate the ecstasy of her own sexuality the way she had wanted to celebrate it.

Later that evening they all went out for ice cream at the Old-Fashioned Shoppe in Monticello, and suddenly, as if he had been repossessed by his kindred spirit, Jonathan slipped back into an aloof demeanor more characteristic of Solomon. He sat farther away from her; he didn't take her hand or embrace her in the back of the car. There was only what she would best describe as a perfunctory good-night kiss at the evening's end. She felt terribly confused by it all, and that was when she had first gotten the idea that she had to share her experiences with someone and called Sally.

Now, once again, she wondered if she had done the right thing. She even considered the possibility that it was too late anyway. She had this intense sense of dread, as though things that had been started could not be stopped, but she had no concrete idea why she should feel this way. She just did, and it made her sad and depressed. Worst of all, it was playing havoc with her imagination.

Even now. Here in the library. Through the earphones connected to the audiovisual machine, she heard Sally Kantzler's voice over the telephone that terrible day.

"My father just told me he heard Solomon hanged himself. Is it true?"

Is it true?

Is it true?

Mrs. Bobchick tapped vigorously on the window of the audiovisual lab because Audra, without realizing it herself, had just screamed.

10.

The morning after what Joe considered to be Martha's animated nightmare, he waited anxiously at breakfast for some further reference to it. She said nothing about it, not even when Jonathan wasn't at the table with them. He decided to make no mention of it, hopeful that the gruesome image would not reappear in her memory.

When he was doing all that reading about suicide, he read a number of psychological studies and theories, and one researcher claimed that the mind had a way of protecting itself during the conscious hours by repressing the uglier and more depressing images and thoughts. They were always there, but during the waking hours, the mind threw up blockers and prevented them from penetrating.

It was a different situation after people fell asleep, for during sleep, those blockers were relaxed and those second-level thoughts could move freely out of what the researcher called "the dark corridors of the mind." Joe, who always related things to some mechanical or electrical device or another, thought of the mental blockers the way he thought of a surge protector on a computer. Once that surge protector was turned off, the electricity could flood the mother board and damage chips as well as blow out the monitor. In his mind, something similar to that had happened to Martha the night before, and therefore it was understandable that she wouldn't have any recollection of it now.

It wasn't until he left the house that morning that another, even more logical, reason for Martha's gruesome nightmare occurred to him. Thinking about the date and planning out his work calendar, he realized that they were only five days away from Solomon's birthday. It would be the second anniversary of his birthday since his death. The first time had been only months afterward, his death still stinging and still as ugly as an opened wound.

Of course, they went to the cemetery. For the longest time while they were there, Martha did not cry. She stared at the tombstone; she walked around the gravesite, but she did not cry. It was a gray, cold day, and Joe remembered that the wind seemed to burrow in under his skin as well as under his clothes, yet Martha looked undisturbed and untouched. She had the top two buttons of her jacket undone and wore nothing on her head. He spoke to her, but she didn't hear him. Finally he put his arm around her and drew her close to him, as much to keep himself warm as her.

"I don't feel he's here," she said. "I look at his name on the stone, but I don't feel he's buried under it. It's just a stone stuck in the ground. Solomon's somewhere else."

"I know," Joe said. "It's hard to accept the reality."

"I don't accept it," she said, but she put her fingers on the engraved words and the date, and soon afterward the tears came.

He took her home and put her to sleep with a sedative. It was a terribly dark day. None of Martha's family called, nor did any of their friends. He could understand their reluctance. When his mother called, she cried throughout most of the conversation. He was tempted a number of times to take a sedative himself, but he thought it would be better if one of them was alert, so he suffered through the silence, crying only when he recalled the early birthdays when Solomon sat on his lap and they both blew out the candles.

Now, he thought, even though she had Jonathan to look after, she was certainly conscious of Solomon's upcoming birthday, and that awareness was bringing on the nightmares. He expected there would be more, and he expected her to grow solemn and withdrawn as the birthday drew closer.

But she didn't. Instead, she kept very busy and was very energetic. She took Jonathan to the dentist and to the hairdresser, and that day she had her hair done herself. It was something she hadn't had done since Solomon's death. He was surprised when he came home from work on Wednesday and found her wearing her hair in a completely new style—cut short, the bangs straight, the color darkened. He didn't like it, but he tempered his dissatisfaction because he suspected she had done it to ward off the impending blues.

He was angrier when he discovered that apparently wasn't the chief reason.

"Jonathan likes it this way," she said. "He showed me the picture of a model in a lipstick advertisement in a magazine, and I brought it to Barbara Jean when I brought him to get his hair done. She made time for me. Didn't she do a good job?"

"I was always fond of your hair on the long side," he said. She grimaced.

"So was Solomon," she said. "Remember how he would never let me even think of cutting it. Long hair is a lot more work, you know. He never thought of that, though, did he? As long as everything was his way. Mindy Baker was right . . . I didn't think enough of myself. I was too . . . sacrificing."

Joe didn't respond. He stared at her, not sure he was hearing right. Martha, admitting she was too devoted to Solomon?

"On the other hand," she said, looking at her reflection

in the glass door on the bookcase, "Jonathan is more understanding and far less demanding. He keeps chastising me for working so hard to please him."

"Is that right?" Joe asked dryly.

"It is. Do you know what he said when I told him about my postponing my intentions to become a real estate agent?"

"What?"

"He told me to go to the community college and take that realtor's course after all. He said it would make him prouder of me if I accomplished something like that." She paused and smiled like someone about to divulge a major secret. "I bet you don't know I met Judy Isaacs for lunch twice and not only began to talk again about taking the realtor's course at the community college, but brought home some of the books Judy wanted to loan me."

"Really? I didn't notice any of those books."

"They're in Jonathan's room. He's been helping me study. We have a pact," she said. "If I take the course next semester and do well, he will be on the superintendent's honor roll every quarter. I don't doubt that he will anyway, but I let him make the offer."

"So you're definitely going to take the course?"

"It's a matter of balance," she said, like someone who had memorized it. "A woman today has got to balance the needs and demands of her family with her own needs and demands in order to remain healthy, both physically and mentally."

Joe laughed.

"I don't think that's funny. Jonathan found it in an article in a magazine at school and brought it home for me to read."

"Jonathan brought it home? Why would a young boy be reading articles about women and their self-images?" he asked.

"He's like Sol—he has varied reading interests," she said. "Anyway, I think it was a good article."

"I'm not saying it isn't. I was just surprised Jonathan would read such an article."

"I'm not," she said.

He didn't pursue it, nor did he say anything more that was critical of her new hairdo. Thinking more about the psychology of all this, he concluded that she didn't realize herself why she was doing these things. It was part of her mind's defense against the realization that Solomon's birthday was fast approaching. As it drew closer, he anticipated it with dread.

And then it came. He woke first that Saturday morning, but he didn't get out of the bed. Instead, he lay there waiting for her to open her eyes, realize what day it was, and begin to cry. He expected they would go back out to the cemetery where they would relive the day of Solomon's suicide and the funeral. Martha would close into a tight fist and spend the remainder of the day in bed.

He wondered how Jonathan would react to the air of depression that would fall over the household. He would just have to be understanding, Joe thought. It might even be wise for him to go to one of his newly made friends' homes for the day.

Martha stirred and then turned over onto her back. He watched her open her eyes and stare up at the ceiling. He could almost read the thoughts on her face. When Solomon was only three, he would be conscious of his birthday and come running into their bedroom as soon as he woke up, anticipating the gifts and the party. There was no more important day in their lives, at least in Martha's way of thinking. Usually, she did so much in preparation for it. Not his birthday, nor hers, nor their anniversary could compare.

"Joe," she said. "Do you know what today is?"

"Yes," he said softly.

"It's Saturday . . . Saturday, and tonight is Jonathan's first school party."

"What?"

She sat up abruptly.

"And I forgot to pick up his slacks and sports coat at the cleaners!"

He watched her get out of bed quickly and rush about like someone who had overslept and would be late for work. He didn't get out of bed while she showered, and he didn't get out while she dressed. All the while she was so intent on her purpose that she didn't appear to notice or care about his loitering. Just before she left the room to go down to make breakfast, she turned to him.

"Are you going to sleep all day?"

"No," he said, but he didn't make any move to get up. She shrugged and went out.

After a while he sat up and scrubbed his head with his fingers. He looked about the room like a man waking after a night of heavy drinking. He did feel the weight of a hangover of sorts. He wasn't sure what he should do next.

Should he go on and pretend, as she was obviously doing, that this was no special day? Was that the best way to get over the hump of sadness and depression? He could do that, and there would be no gray sky, no cold wind, no dark shadows. Of course, throughout the day he would wait, anticipating her realization. It would be like waiting for the falling of that inevitable second shoe. Could he stand the tension?

Or he could force her to face it by reminding her that today was Solomon's birthday. He didn't have to say it in so many words. What he could do was simply ask her if she wanted to go up to the cemetery at any special time. At least that way, he would get it over with once and for all.

He couldn't explain all the reasons for his choice. In the back of his mind was the idea that Solomon was, after all, his son, too. He wanted to consider Martha's feelings and Martha's needs, but he had feelings and needs. He didn't think he could face himself, knowing he deliberately ignored his son's birthday. Joe thought there was still the real possibility that Solomon did what he did because he had ignored him too much. Joe couldn't help wondering if he had given up sooner than he should have. How could he ignore him now?

Joe was also driven by the conflict in his feelings about Jonathan. In one sense, he was happy that Martha was so involved with the boy that she would be able to avoid depression and sadness; but in another sense, he was indignant about the way Jonathan had so completely seized Martha's attention and imagination that she would disregard the memory of her dead son.

In the final analysis, it might have been the way she and Jonathan were carrying on at the breakfast table when he arrived downstairs that made him decide. She had made a big breakfast: bacon and eggs, grits, and muffins. Neither of them looked up at him to greet him when he stepped through the kitchen doorway. Jonathan had just said something under his breath, and Martha was laughing hysterically, pieces of the muffin caught between her lips, her body shaking, her eyes closed.

Joe didn't move. He stood there until she realized his appearance.

"Hungry?" she asked. He couldn't help but recall breakfast on this day last year. He could barely get her to take a sip of coffee, and when she returned from the cemetery, she drank only the water that she took with the sedative.

"Not very, no," he said.

Jonathan turned around and looked at him. There was something immediately sly about his demeanor. His eyes were small and the left corner of his mouth was drawn up, giving him an expression closer to a sneer than anything else.

" 'Morning," he finally said. Joe nodded weakly.

"What's the matter with you?" Martha asked. "Are you sick? You usually get up earlier than this, and you're always hungry on Saturday and Sunday mornings."

"Not this Saturday," he said, expecting the hint to be

enough, but she either didn't know what he was getting at or she was deliberately ignoring him. She turned to Jonathan.

"Want more grits?"

"Yes, please. They're great."

"Solomon hated them," Joe said. It came out like an involuntary burp or a hiccup. He couldn't believe himself that he had said it. Martha and Jonathan paused and stared at him as though he were crazy.

"Not everyone has the same tastes, Joe," Martha finally said. "I, for one, always liked grits."

"I always liked it, but you never made it much."

"Well, I made it today. Do you want some?"

"I . . . no, I'll just have some coffee for now."

"Whatever you want," she said. She got up to get Jonathan more grits, and Joe sat down. He poured himself some coffee and stared ahead blankly for a few moments. Martha sat down, but no one said anything. She watched Jonathan eat.

Joe looked at him closer, drawn by the glitter around his neck. He hadn't noticed it until now, because until now, he had worn his collars closed and the chain was hidden. But today his collar was open, and he wore no undershirt. The sight of it was the final thing to push him over the edge. He turned to Martha.

"I was wondering what time you wanted to go up to the cemetery," he said. Jonathan stopped eating and looked at Joe, but Martha kept her attention fixed on Jonathan.

"I'm not going up to the cemetery," she said.

"But . . . you know what today is."

"Today," she began, and then smiled. "Today is Saturday," she said, and Jonathan smiled.

Joe looked from one to the other. The chill that climbed up his back felt more like an enormous hand carved out of ice, the thumb and pinkie clamping down on his ribs. He couldn't breathe. He felt the blood rush into his face.

"Saturday?" he said. It was all he could get out.

"I don't want anything to ruin the day; I don't want

anything to ruin our happiness," she said. She turned to him, her eyes metallic and cold; determination and anger were woven together into a rope of intensity and purpose. "We don't deserve any more unhappiness," she said.

He didn't move. His elbow was on the table; the coffee cup was clutched in his hand and frozen in the air before him. After a beat, Jonathan tapped his fork on the plate as he scooped up the remainder of the grits, and Martha smiled.

"He loves grits," she said. "With lots of butter. Are you sure you don't want any, Joe? I'm only going to throw it out."

"No," he said. "Thanks." He lowered his coffee cup to the table and got up slowly. "I'm going out for some air," he said. Neither she nor Jonathan replied, but when he was halfway to the front door, he heard them both laugh. He moved quickly until he was outside and the door was closed behind him.

For a long moment, he just stood there, grateful for the silence. Even the birds were respectfully quiet, and there was no traffic on their road.

Then he went around to the rear of the house and stared dumbly at the tree from which Solomon's body had dangled in death. It seemed to him that his son would punish him forever. He had even found a way to do it through the new boy. Perhaps he was reaching both of them through that damn computer, he thought. It would fit his sardonic sense of humor to do so. Joe resolved to go after the password to that file again, if for nothing else than to satisfy his curiosity.

Martha didn't need Joe to remind her about the significance of the day; Solomon had been reminding her in little ways, not the least of which was his humming of "Happy Birthday." She heard it Monday afternoon while she was taking the clothing out of the dryer. Images from the night before had been recurring all day, shooting across her eyes with lightning swiftness, turning a thread into a rope, a plant into a tree, a pair of pants into a pair of dangling legs and the creak of the stairway into the creak of a branch straining under the weight of Solomon's body.

Joe thought she had had a bad dream. Of course, he didn't see what she had seen, so he wouldn't understand, just as he wouldn't hear the sound of Solomon's humming. She looked up from the basket of dried clothing and listened. When she went to the doorway, he stopped. But as she carried the clothing upstairs, she turned and saw him at the foot of the stairway.

He was looking up at her and wearing one of those funny little party hats they used to buy when they had birthday parties for him. They had those parties up until his eleventh birthday, after which he insisted they stop making it into a national event. He settled for a private celebration without any of the accoutrements.

"You would have been sixteen," she told him. "Sixteen. A high point of your young life. Joe would have gone with you to motor vehicles to get your driving permit, and he would have spent time teaching you how to drive. You would have gotten your license this year, and maybe I would have talked your father into buying you your own car."

"Saturday," he simply said. "This Saturday."

"Salt upon a wound," she said. "That's what you're doing by reminding me."

"Happy birthday to me; happy birthday to me."

"Stop it." She turned away and left him below. But she heard him singing it again and again. She chose to ignore it, or at least pretend to ignore it.

"What good is reminding me of your birthday?" she demanded when he appeared in the living room on Thursday, still wearing that silly party hat. "Can I invite your friends over to celebrate? Can I buy you a wonderful present since it's your sixteenth? Can I be happy for you?

You went behind this house and murdered all your birthdays." She turned away from him.

"Happy birthday to me; happy birthday to me."

"No," she said, the tears stopping at the edge of her lids without going over to run down her cheeks. "It's not your birthday anymore."

"You can't stop birthdays," he said.

"Oh, no? Maybe I can't stop them, but I can replace them. In two months and four days, it will be Jonathan's birthday, and we'll sing happy birthday to him. Happy birthday dear Jonathan; happy birthday to you."

Did she laugh? She couldn't remember, but when she turned back to him, he was gone.

And now he was coming back at her through Joe, she thought. He couldn't get satisfaction by addressing her directly, so he was planting the ideas in Joe's head. Why else would Joe have been so upset about her refusal to be sad and depressed? She was conscious of all Joe's efforts to make her happy. Joe hated to be reminded of the tragedy. He would do anything to avoid any reference to it, and she thought she could count on her fingers the references to Solomon he would initiate. It had always been she who refused to let the wounds heal.

It had to be Solomon speaking through him. Joe would never have made that comment about Solomon's not liking grits, she thought. And now she had no other choice. As cruel as it would seem, she would have to be indifferent and hard all day. She might even have to ignore Joe, since he wasn't in complete control of his own thoughts and words. It was their best defense. In the end, he would understand, and he would be grateful.

She didn't want to tell Jonathan that Saturday was Solomon's birthday. Why burden him with the sadness, especially since it was going to be a special night for him? But he found out on his own, and, bless his soul, she thought, he was determined to do what he could to ease her pain and suffering.

"I know about Saturday," he told her on Thursday. Her first thought was that Solomon had appeared to him to tell him, and now he knew that his spirit haunted this house.

Joe was downstairs, watching television and reading. He had a knack for doing both at the same time, looking up from his book or magazine whenever something that would interest him appeared on the screen. He told her it was auditory discrimination.

"You tune into a certain frequency, just the way our garage door opener does, and ignore all others."

She wasn't sure she wanted to be compared to a garage door opener, but she knew what he meant.

Jonathan knocked on her open bedroom door. Dressed in only her bra and panties, she was sitting at her vanity table, studying herself and considering a comment Jonathan had made earlier that week about women who use cosmetics creatively.

"Everybody says Joan Collins would look plain and unattractive without her makeup on," he said, "but the truth is she is beautiful with it on."

"You think Joan Collins is beautiful?" she asked him. Now that she realized it, he didn't talk much about movie stars or television personalities, and he didn't go out and buy any new posters for his room. Just like Solomon, he was friendly with Audra Lowe and, Martha had to admit, Audra Lowe was an attractive young lady. Audra and she had a similar look: the natural look. Unlike other teenagers her age, Audra did not go in for heavy and dramatic makeup. So why then did Jonathan suddenly make this comment about Joan Collins? Were his tastes changing? Would Solomon's tastes have changed?

"In a way, she is very beautiful. Sure," he said.

She had watched "Dynasty" a number of times and seen Joan Collins in many magazines, so she was familiar enough with that look. That was why she was now studying herself in the vanity table mirror: she wondered what she would look like with eye shadow, longer lashes, brighter lipstick, face makeup, and blush.

"What?" She turned to face him in the doorway.

"I just wanted you to know I know about Saturday, and you don't have to do anything special for me that day. I can take care of my own things. I understand how difficult a day it will be for you."

She didn't say anything for a moment. He stepped into the room.

"If you want, I'll go with you and Joe to the cemetery," he added.

"Oh." She turned back to the mirror. "I don't know if I want to go to the cemetery this time," she said. Almost on cue, Solomon's face began to appear over hers in the mirror. She fought back the dissolve, determined not to let him come between her and Jonathan. Then she wondered how Jonathan had found out. Joe certainly hadn't told him, she thought. "How did you know about Saturday?" she asked.

"I found his birthday cards. He saved them all, even the ones people sent him when he was only one."

"Oh."

"I couldn't help looking at them. I'm sorry."

"That's all right. There's no harm in your seeing his cards. I'm just sorry you learned about Saturday. Now, forget about it," she said, "because that's what I intend to do."

"Really?"

"Yes. I don't want to wallow in sorrow any longer. I didn't tell him to go out there and do something so stupid," she said. Jonathan didn't reply. She realized she had raised her voice and probably appeared mad, so she smiled quickly. "Besides, Saturday is going to be a big day for you. I want it to go well."

"Thank you."

When she looked into the mirror again, she saw Solomon standing across the room, glaring at her in his unique way. She looked at Jonathan, but she could tell that he couldn't see him. All she had to do was ignore him.

"I bought some makeup yesterday," she said. "I've been thinking about experimenting with my looks."

"Good," Jonathan said. "Can't wait."

He left her, and she did put on everything she bought. Solomon stood behind her the whole time, staring in silence, smirking and sometimes smiling disdainfully. She continued to ignore him.

"You look ridiculous," he finally said.

"To you maybe, but not to Jonathan."

"He's ridiculous. How would he know any different?"

"We'll see," she said. She wasn't going to lose her temper; she wasn't going to get excited. That was just what he wanted. She might even cry, and everything would smear, and then she would look ridiculous.

"Wait until Joe sees it."

"He'll like it."

"Just like he liked your hairdo."

"It just takes getting used to. Anything new does."

"Ridiculous," Solomon repeated.

"Yes," she said, turning around, "almost as ridiculous as putting a rope around your neck and tying it to a tree. You want to talk about looks? About bulging eyes and swollen noses and lips?"

He said nothing, and when she turned back to the mirror, he was gone.

She didn't leave the bedroom wearing the makeup, however; she was still insecure about the new look. It was so different from what she had been to this point in her life that it was almost like looking at a stranger. Besides, she wasn't sure she had done everything correctly. It would take a few more experimental sessions before she would be confident enough to show Joe and other people.

On Saturday afternoon, when she probably would have gone to the cemetery if Jonathan hadn't come to live with them, she went up to the bedroom and experimented with her makeup for hours. She had even found a full-page close-up of Joan Collins and tried to imitate some of her cosmetic style. Afterward, she washed it all off, but she felt a good deal more secure about what she had accomplished.

The late part of the afternoon was spent helping Jonathan get ready for his party. He had trouble styling and blow-drying his hair to look as good as it did the day he came back from Barbara Jean's, so she sat him down at her vanity table and worked on it until they both agreed she had gotten it right.

Joe walked in and out twice, but he said nothing to either of them. He had been quiet and withdrawn all day. He left the house in the early afternoon and didn't return until nearly four-thirty anyway. She had gone to the dry cleaners and done some other shopping, so when he did return, she told him she hadn't prepared anything for their supper.

"I guess we'll go out," she told him. She was setting him up for a surprise. He was totally taken aback by the idea.

"Go out? To dinner?"

"Of course, Joe. It is Saturday night. People do go out to dinner on Saturday night, don't they?"

"Yeah, but . . . where do you want to go?"

"I called Mindy and Kevin."

"You did?"

"Uh huh. They didn't go to that new place in Goshen after all, and they thought it would be a great opportunity to do so, so Mindy made reservations for the four of us," she said quickly. He didn't reply. "They're coming by at seven-thirty to pick us up. Okay?" she said. He still looked stunned. "I said, is that all right?"

"Yeah, sure, I guess so."

"Fine. I'll get back to Jonathan," she said, and she went upstairs. It was her idea to give him one of Joe's pinkie rings to use just for the evening. She asked him if he could, and he said as long as the boy took care not to lose it. She gave him the blue onyx in the white gold setting. It went well with Solomon's watch and chain. That afternoon she had bought him some cologne, too. He picked out Solomon's favorite. She tried to talk him into another scent, but he seemed determined about it.

"Audra likes it, too," he said. She felt heat come into her face, but she didn't want to argue about something so seemingly insignificant. She couldn't very well stand there and explain to him that every time she smelled that scent, she thought about Solomon. A few times she had smelled it first, and then Solomon appeared to her. She concluded that if she did tell him such things, she would only be permitting Solomon to dictate what she should buy for him and what she shouldn't buy, and she was determined not to give him such control of their lives. He had had that control when he was alive; she'd be damned if he would have it now.

After Jonathan put on his clothes, he came back to her bedroom for her final inspection. When she saw him dressed in Solomon's finest slacks, sports jacket, shirt and tie, and black leather loafers, with his hair styled and the jewelry glittering, she was rendered speechless. She brought her hands to the base of her throat and stared in admiration. A tingle of electric warmth traveled up her waist and under her breasts.

"Well?" he said.

"You're a very handsome young man, Jonathan."

"Thank you," he said. "I'll go down and talk to Joe. They'll be picking me up in fifteen minutes."

"Have a good time," she said.

"You, too."

"And thank you for helping me get through the day."

"It wasn't hard. You're stronger than you think you are," he said. How she loved him for it. She wanted to kiss him, but she was afraid to draw him closer to her, afraid that if she embraced him, she wouldn't let him go.

"See you later," he said, and left. She stood there

staring at the empty doorway for a few moments. Then she realized the scent of Jonathan's cologne wasn't just lingering. Solomon was behind her, lying on the bed, his hands behind his head. She tried to ignore him. It was time to think about getting dressed herself. Joe had already put on his clothes and gone down to wait.

"He's a pretty boy," Solomon said. "A very pretty boy." She didn't look at him. She knew he was smiling sarcastically.

"Much more handsome than you were. Your clothing and your jewelry never looked as good on you."

"Think he's sexy, huh?"

"He's sexy."

"Does he understand sex? Does he understand it the way you understand it?"

"Shut up."

"Does he need explanations, comfort? Is he coming to you with his problems?"

"He might," she said, spinning around on her vanity table chair. She glared at him, and for a long moment, she heard nothing and said nothing. Then Solomon turned to lean on his propped-up elbow. He used to spend hours lying on her bed like that, watching her work, watching her dress.

"Will you help him like you helped me?"

"You're spiteful. I never realized how spiteful you were. What did I ever do to deserve it?"

"You're breaking my heart. Anyway, he doesn't need your help. He's been around. He comes from the gutter."

"He does not come from the gutter. He's had a hard time, but he's not a low-class person."

"He might even have been sexually abused."

"Ridiculous," she said. She turned away and began working on her makeup. "You can tell when someone's been sexually abused."

"What is sexual abuse, Mother?"

She didn't say anything. Her heartbeat had increased so

rapidly, she was having trouble breathing. There was almost no need to put the blush on her cheeks; they were red enough as it was.

"What is sexual abuse?" he repeated. She didn't look back at the bed.

"I'm glad you hanged yourself," she said in a loud whisper. Then she raised her voice. "I'M GLAD. I'M GLAD, I'M GLAD." She turned to him, but he was gone, and she was shouting at an empty bed. A few moments later she heard Joe calling from the bottom of the stairs.

"Martha?"

"Yes?"

"Are you calling me?"

"No."

"I thought I heard you yelling."

"I just . . . I just cursed my curling iron for taking so long to get warm. Sorry."

He didn't reply. She took a deep breath, bit gently on her lower lip, and went back to her makeup.

Joe was in the living room watching the national news when she came down the stairs. Jonathan had long gone. She stepped into the doorway and waited for Joe's reaction. He turned away from the set slowly and then took a double take.

"My God," he said, "what have you done?"

"I decided I needed a new look. Well?"

"You look like you're wearing a ton of makeup."

"All I have done is highlight things, Joe. What do you think?"

"Highlight? You smothered them, is more like it."

She didn't cry; she didn't even get angry. She nodded slowly, expectantly.

"You're a beautiful woman, Martha. You don't need all that paint on your face."

"It's all right, Joe. I understand."

"Understand what? I'm telling you what I honestly think."

"It's not you talking," she said.

"Huh?"

They heard the sound of a car horn.

"The Bakers are here," she said, and started to turn toward the front door.

"Wait a minute. What do you mean, it's not me talking?"

"You can't help it, but it doesn't matter. I'm strong enough to deal with it. Just as Jonathan said, I'm stronger than I think I am," she added, and smiled with such assurance that it gave Joe the chills. For a long moment, he was unable to raise himself out of the chair.

He looked back into the house before he closed the front door behind him because he thought he heard the voices of little children gathered around the table in the kitchen as they began to sing, "Happy birthday to you, happy birthday to you. Happy birthday, dear Solomon, happy birthday to you."

He closed the door to shut away the sound of little hands clapping.

11.

Audra felt herself cringe in the backseat of Gary's car as Jonathan came out of the Sterns' residence. Her involuntary movement didn't surprise her. It was as though she were two people now: one very much infatuated with Jonathan, and one very much afraid of him.

But why afraid? she wondered. Was it simply because of her mixed emotions and her confusion about him, or was there something else, something more frightening that she sensed, but couldn't express, even to herself just yet?

Her hope that Sally Kantzler would be of some help faded the night the two of them went to the Sterns' house to study with Jonathan. All week she had sensed that Sally was losing her objectivity. The reason for that was understandable. Jonathan was paying her more and more attention, and Jonathan was a good-looking boy with a strong personality.

During the short time he had been at their school, he had firmly entrenched himself with Solomon's old friends and won more than their respect. He had their adoration. They literally battled with one another to get closer to him, to have more private talks, to win his approval. Audra was beginning to find their behavior disgusting. Had they no self-pride? All Jonathan had to do was suggest one of them get him another milk or loan him a pen, and they all rushed to do it.

And even when they weren't with him, she saw that he still held their attention. Their conversation was filled with "Jonathan said this" and "Jonathan said that." Nothing seemed more precious to any of them than an original Jonathan statement. She felt sure that some of them were fabricating just to outdo the others. How would it end?

Solomon had been confident, maybe even somewhat arrogant, she thought; but he was nothing like this. He didn't have to dominate their every word and thought, and he didn't turn them into his personal slaves. Another thing that she concluded: Solomon wasn't as conniving. He hadn't been as clever about manipulating them and working them against one another to his own advantage. In fact, she recalled many times Solomon had been embarrassed by too much attention and ridiculed it.

But Jonathan's appetite for it was insatiable. He couldn't tolerate anyone around him being indifferent to him. She saw that. If he spotted such a person, he would turn his full energies on that individual until he was satisfied the individual was sufficiently within his shadow and reach.

Furthermore, she had been hearing some bad stories about him concerning the junior varsity basketball team. Although he was good enough to make the team, he was apparently not that good. Consequently, it was a given that he would not be one of the starting five players. In this area, at least, he wasn't up to Solomon's achievements.

But apparently instead of working harder and contributing as a team member, he was creating dissension among the other second and third string members. During lunch one day, she overheard a conversation between Steve Jacobs and Tommy Williams, two of the starting five. Steve said that he had listened in on a conversation Jonathan was having in the locker room with two other second-stringers, Billy Sennet and James Grady.

"He told them the coach was just using them to spell

Kratch and Cumbie," Steve said. "He said the coach wasn't giving them a fair chance because his mind was made up a long time ago. 'No sense in breaking your ass out there during practice,' he told them. I heard it all," Steve said.

"What did you do?" Tommy asked. Audra leaned toward them to hear the answer.

"Nothing. If those assholes want to listen to him, let 'em."

Afterward she asked Jonathan about the team just to see if he would say anything similar to what Steve Jacobs had overheard. His response was just the opposite.

"I love it," he told her. "Coach Martin's a sharp guy, and a fair guy, too. It's easy to play for him. He makes you want to give it your all," he said, and she wondered if Steve Jacobs had been talking about the same Jonathan.

If she was so confused about him, why should she be surprised or disappointed about Sally's reaction? she thought. But that night when she and Sally were at the Sterns' almost ended with her having nothing more to do with him.

When Sally and she first arrived, Jonathan was sweeter than ever to Sally. At first, she thought it was very nice of him to be so considerate of Sally. He could sense she was obviously very nervous about coming to the Sterns' house. Jonathan didn't cut her out of their conversation or ignore her in any way. In fact, before long it was she, not Sally, who began to feel slighted.

She saw how Sally was becoming more and more excited by his attention. Her face was flushed; she couldn't turn away from him long, and she welcomed every opportunity to touch him or brush up against him.

They all ended up lying on the bed, their notebooks opened, eating from a big bowl of hot buttered popcorn Martha Stern had made at Jonathan's request. After a while, they all got a little bored with the homework, and when Jonathan suggested they spice it up a little, both she and Sally were receptive. It was what he suggested that startled them.

"I know what we can do," he said, sitting up and slapping his hands together. "Let's play trivia striptease using the material for the English test."

"What?" Audra asked. "Did you say striptease?"

"Uh huh. Me against the two of you. That's fair."

"You can't be serious."

"Why not? What's the big deal? It'll certainly put some excitement into this junk," he said. "Right, Sal?"

He had been calling her Sal all night, and she loved it. It was something Solomon used to do. She looked at Audra and bit gently on her lower lip.

"I don't know."

"What's the problem? You two are the brains of the class, and it's the two of you against me."

Sally laughed nervously, but Audra noticed she wasn't looking for a way to retreat. Jonathan was a seducer, all right, she thought.

"You're crazy," Audra said, but she had to admit to herself that she was a little intrigued and titillated. What would Sally do?

"Sal?"

"If Audra does it."

"Okay, then. Audra?"

"I don't believe this."

"Here are the rules: I can ask only one question, and the two of you can answer after conferring. You two can confer on the question you ask me. The only thing is we all have to keep to the notes and the textbook material. No out-of-the-way information. Each missed answer costs one article of clothing. You two can alternate. Okay?"

Sally nodded and sat up on the bed. Audra thought she looked hypnotized, her gaze now locked on every move Jonathan made.

"Sally, you really want to do this?"

Sally turned to her and then looked quickly at Jonathan.

"I don't want to force anyone," he said, smiling.

"No, it's all right. Really. I want to," she said, turning back to Audra, a look of annoyance forming.

Jonathan got up and went to the bedroom door. He turned the lock and smiled.

"Martha's liable to get curious. Okay, you two can be first."

"What will we ask him?" Sally said immediately. Audra, still a bit stunned, shook her head. "Start with authors," she finally said.

"Okay. Jonathan, who wrote *Sinners in the Hands of an Angry God*?"

"That's easy. My namesake, Jonathan Edwards," he said, and the game began.

Audra was suspicious throughout the questioning. She felt Jonathan was always in control, and even when he missed answers, he did so because he wanted to. Ten minutes into the game, they had missed only two, but he had missed four and taken off his shoes and socks. He caught them on a question concerning a character in *The Crucible* and then he missed what Audra thought should have been a relatively easy question about Nathaniel Hawthorne. Of course, they expected him to take off his shirt, but instead, he took off his pants.

Sally's face reddened, and Jonathan's next set of questions were all good examples of legitimate trivia, the kinds of questions Mr. Stanley would ask on one of his unit tests. By the time they were finished with the round, however, they had been caught on enough questions to force Sally to take off her blouse. Audra knew what that would mean to her.

"That's it," she said. "We had fun. Let's stop."

"Unfair," Jonathan said, looking at Sally.

Sally hesitated.

"It's all right," she said, her voice so soft they could barely hear her. "Jonathan's right. It wouldn't be fair."

"Sally."

"No. What's fair is fair," she said, and unbuttoned her blouse. Jonathan sat back triumphantly as she stripped it off. Audra felt the blood rush into her own face in sympathy with Sally.

"All right," Audra said, her temper riled. "Who's considered the father of the American short story?"

Jonathan looked at her, a wry smile on his face.

"That's easy," he said. "Poe."

"Wrong. Washington Irving. Check your notes."

"Oh, I believe you." He shrugged and stood up. Then, looking directly at Sally, he began to lower his briefs. She screamed and buried her face in her hands.

"Jonathan!" Audra said. "Stop it."

"What's fair is fair. You got me."

There was no question in Audra's mind that he was about to take off his underpants and would have if Martha Stern hadn't yelled up to announce Sally's father had just pulled into the driveway.

"Saved by the horn," he said, and Sally rushed to get her blouse back on.

Jonathan put on his pants and began to put on his shoes and socks as Sally hurried to do the same. Before she left, she smiled at both of them.

"It was fun," she said, and left. Jonathan was hysterical.

"I don't think you were very funny," Audra told him. "You know how she is."

"I know what she needs," he said.

"No, you don't. You're not God, Jonathan. You don't know everything about everyone. You haven't known her that long, anyway," she said.

"No, but Solomon knew her well."

"What do you mean? How do you know what Solomon knew about her?"

"You want me to show you?"

"What? Show me what?"

"What he thought of her," he said. She stared at him a moment.

"You found something he wrote?"

"Uh huh."

"Where?"

"There," he said, pointing at the computer.

"I don't understand."

"You will. Come over here."

He sat her down in front of the monitor and turned on the computer. Then he taped out the passwords for the software and got to the menu, which was a list of various things Solomon apparently wrote and committed to the computer's memory bank. The name of one file was simply "Sal." He called it up, and Audra began reading. She stopped after the second page had been scrolled.

"I don't believe this," she said.

"I found it and read it," he said.

"Solomon never said any of these things."

"Maybe not to you, but he said it to the computer. Listen, this is like a personal diary."

"I don't want to read any more," she said, and got up from the desk.

"Okay." He shut the computer down. "I just wanted to show you that my thoughts about Sally weren't just mine."

"All right," she said. They heard the car horn and knew it was her father. "I've got to go."

"Listen, Audra. This was just some innocent fun," he said. "If I knew it would really bother you or Sally, I wouldn't have done it."

She looked at him. He seemed so sincere.

"I hope you're telling the truth."

"I am. Really. Let's forget about it. In fact, let's keep some distance between Sally and us for a while, okay? Just to keep her from getting the wrong ideas."

"Okay," she said.

It wasn't until she was in her father's car and on her way home that she wondered if Jonathan had done all that he had done just to make her one faithful friend and otherwise intelligent and perceptive witness ineffectual.

But then she thought, he couldn't be that much of a conniver, could he?

She was sure it was partly the indecision about that answer that made her cringe as he came out of the house to get into the car the night of the party. But then, when she saw him, all dressed up in Solomon's sports jacket and his hair styled close to the way Solomon's was, she couldn't help but soften. That part of her that was infatuated with him took control. The memories of their lovemaking were vivid again. And when he got into the car and sat beside her, he put his arms around her and greeted her with a passionate kiss. He was truly Solomon the way she wanted him to be. How could she turn away from that now?

You have nothing upon which to base such a rejection, anyway, her alter ego told her. Why can't you enjoy something without analyzing it to death? That's been your problem all along.

Embracing her firmly, Jonathan held her against him.

"You look fantastic," he said. "You're the most beautiful girl in this school," he whispered. He kissed her on the neck, and all the dark thoughts and worries she had had seemed to disappear like smoke thinning into air.

Audra was surprised to see Sally come to the dance. She rarely came to one before. Audra and Jonathan were there a good hour before Sally arrived. Just as he went across the gym to get her some punch, Sally entered.

Audra had never seen Sally dressed this way. She imagined Sally had just recently bought the jeans, tank top, and off-shoulder sweatshirt. She had put in her contacts, something she said she hated to do, and put on some makeup as well. She was wearing a glossy pink lipstick, some eye shadow, and even a little Indian Earth to darken her otherwise pale cheeks. At first, Audra did a double take, almost not recognizing her. The girls around Audra parted and stepped back as Sally approached her, everyone buzzing about her. The normally self-conscious seventeen-year-old appeared oblivious of the turned heads and smiling faces.

"Hi, Audra. The committee did a great decorating job, didn't they?"

"I can't believe it's you. You look . . . good," Audra said.

"Thanks. I'm so nervous."

"You don't look it. Why didn't you mention you were coming to the party when we talked about it?"

"I wasn't. Until this afternoon."

"What changed your mind?"

"Jonathan."

"Jonathan? When did you see him?" she asked her. She was somewhat skeptical. Jonathan had promised to avoid Sally during the remainder of the week in school. Whenever she and Audra were together, he deliberately spent time with other students, and his greetings and acknowledgments of her were perfunctory.

Yet Sally didn't seem to notice any difference. Audra kept expecting her to complain about him, but she said nothing derogatory, and when she did turn to Jonathan to return a nod or a wave and then turned back, Audra had the underlying feeling that Sally thought there was something special going on between herself and Jonathan. It was as though she knew why he was behaving this way.

"I saw him, but he didn't say anything in school. He has a wonderful sense of time and place, don't you think?"

"Oh? So when did he talk to you about the party? What was the proper time and place?" she added, growing annoyed with Sally's new air of superiority. What had he done to imbue her with such arrogance? Audra wondered.

"He called me to ask me about Palmer's homework, and we talked awhile. He mentioned the party, but I didn't want to come. You know how I feel about these . . . these parties, but he was so insistent. I think he feels bad about the game we played in his room," she added. "I told him I didn't do anything I didn't want to do." She paused and

looked across the gym at Jonathan. She neglected to tell
Audra that she had told Jonathan what Audra had wanted
her to do. She told him it was why she had been staring at
him all the time, even though that wasn't the real reason.
She didn't think he was mad about Audra's request for
her to spy on him because he just laughed. "He's so
sweet."

"Yes," Audra said. She looked across the gymnasium,
too, only her eyes were filled with fire. "Jonathan is so
sweet."

Jonathan was by the punch bowl, talking to some of
whom Audra still thought of as "Solomon's crowd." They
had gathered around him, and they stared at him with rapt
attention as though he were their guru.

Usually the Student Government Association provided
only soda, pretzels, and potato chips at these dances, but
this evening they had put out three bowls of punch. The
seniors and some of their friends had spiked one bowl with
vodka. Jonathan and she knew about the special bowl, and
he had gone over to get some of the "good stuff."

When he turned around, he saw Sally and waved. Then
he poured another cup of spiked punch and came across
the floor. Audra felt the heat building in her face.

"Hi, Sal. Thought you'd like a punch," he said, and
winked.

He handed Audra her cup of punch. She took it without
saying anything, but her eyes were ablaze. Jonathan smiled
and looked surprised at her reaction. Sally swallowed almost the whole cup in one gulp.

"Hey, take it easy," he warned. "That stuff's potent."
She laughed.

"He means they put vodka in it," Audra said. Sally was
surprised. "Don't you taste it?"

"No. I guess I'm just too excited about being here. But
it's good," she added, as though she were used to spiked
drinks. She started moving seemingly in rhythm to the
music, only there wasn't any being played at the moment.

Audra looked at her with a half-amused expression on her face. Was this her withdrawn, somewhat introverted friend Sally Kantzler? "Where's the music?" Sally asked. "Or are we supposed to make our own?" she asked Jonathan. His smile widened.

Audra's amazement at her friend continued to be fueled. Sally sounded and looked a great deal more sophisticated than Audra knew her to be. What could have brought about so quick a metamorphosis? Had it been going on all week without her realizing it?

"The DJ took five. He's outside smoking a joint," Jonathan said.

"Doesn't Sally look good tonight?" Audra asked, punching her words out emphatically. If Jonathan sensed her anger, he didn't show it.

"She sure does. Thought you'd look good in jeans, Sal."

"Thanks. Oh, there's Dede. Excuse me a moment, will you. I want to tell her something," Sally said, and went off to her right. Jonathan watched her and shook his head.

"One of these days, she's going to break loose."

"Why did you tell her to come to the party? She thinks you practically invited her."

"Tell her? What are you talking about, Audra?"

"She says you called and told her to come tonight."

"You're kidding. First of all, she called me, and all she talked about was the party. Coming here was entirely her idea. I just didn't discourage it. How could I?"

"That's not what she said."

"So? She's fantasizing. Solomon said she would."

"Solomon said? What do you mean, Solomon said? When do you talk to Solomon?"

"It's not that I talk to him, exactly. I showed you."

"You mean that stuff in the computer?"

"Yeah. But now that you ask . . . in a strange way I do feel like I'm talking to him when I turn it on and read his files."

"Files." She looked away, and then a thought occurred to her. "Is there a file on me, too, Jonathan?" He didn't reply. "Well? Is there?"

"Not exactly."

"What does that mean, not exactly?"

"I've seen references to you here and there, but no file like Sal's."

Audra continued to study him. Was he telling the truth? Suddenly she understood what she had felt in Solomon's old room as she sat before that computer monitor and began reading the words about Sally. She knew why she didn't want to continue to sit there and read. It wasn't only because of what was said; it was because of how it was said. It was like "The Twilight Zone"; it was eerie because as she read the sentences, she could hear Solomon saying them.

She imagined Jonathan was addicted to the computer, drawn to it by spiritual magnetism. Her imagination began to go wild. She knew so little about computers and had such little interest in them. They seemed too impersonal, too mechanical; but she was well aware of what Joe Stern did for a living, and in her mind, because computers were still relegated to some magical part of technology, she saw him as being more of a magician than a technician.

She recalled that Solomon rarely talked about his father's work, but when he did, he always cloaked his conversation in metaphors. "My father is just another piece of machinery," he once said. She thought that was a terrible thing to say about one's father.

"You don't understand," he went on. "The machines dictate to him. When they break down, he goes. He's at their every beck and call."

"You make it sound as if they are another form of intelligent life."

"You'd be surprised," he said. And then smiling, he added in a soft, subtle admonishing manner, "You'd really be surprised."

Jonathan finished his cup of punch and put it on the seat beside them. The DJ returned, and the music began again. Almost immediately the lights were dimmed, and the floor became crowded with dancers. Sally, who was usually quite shy about these things, was out there dancing with Larry Elias, but she kept looking their way.

"Were there files on other kids, Jonathan? Solomon's other friends?" Audra asked. She had to bring her face very close to his because the music was so loud. The scent of Solomon's old cologne was so strong. If she closed her eyes, she went reeling back through time. Jonathan didn't respond immediately. He continued to look out at the dance floor as though he hadn't heard her.

"Jonathan?"

"Not exactly."

"What is this not exactly? Don't you know one way or the other?" she asked, the irritation evident in her voice. He turned to her.

"I haven't read it all, Audra. There's quite a bit, and I'm just getting the hang of that computer. Joe's given me a lesson or two, that's all."

"You handled it pretty well the other night."

"I learn fast," he said. "Come on, let's dance."

"No, I don't feel like it just now."

"Really? Mind if I go out there? I feel like it."

"Go on," she said. She watched him make his way into the crowd until he was close to Sally. Before long, she had turned away from Larry, and she was dancing with Jonathan. Audra watched the way he moved his head, eyes, and shoulders. He's teasing her, she thought, or tempting her. Was that what the computer told him to do?

She gulped down the remainder of the cup of punch Jonathan had brought her, and then she made her way across the gym through the dancers and got herself another cup. In a moment, Paula was at her side.

"I don't believe Sally Kantzler. Is that the Sally Kantzler we all know and love dancing with Jonathan?"

"I'm not sure who she's dancing with."

"What?"

"Nothing," Audra said. She took a long sip of her punch. "Where's Gary?"

"Billy Marcus had some pot, so they went into the boys' locker room."

"Amazing. What would they do if they had only music and food and beautiful cars and great clothes and parents who kept giving them everything they wanted?"

"Jesus, you sound angry."

"Well, I am angry. I'm sick of this. We came to have some fun, not to go off in our own little worlds."

"Excuse me," Paula said. "But you and Jonathan had no trouble going off into your own little world at my house the other night."

"Thanks, Paula. I knew you could be discreet."

"Huh?"

"Forget it. If Jonathan ever comes off the dance floor, tell him I had a headache and went home."

"Are you serious?"

Audra didn't respond. She finished the cup of spiked punch, slapped the empty cup down on the table, and sauntered across the dance floor again. When she looked back at Jonathan and Sally, she saw that he was dancing very close to her and that someone had gotten them both another cup of punch, too.

From this angle, with the lights dimmed and the crowd of young people massed together in what looked to her to be an orgy of rhythmic and suggestive movement, Jonathan and Solomon began to dissolve into each other again. After all, Jonathan had Solomon's hairdo, wore Solomon's clothes, and just about had Solomon's height and build. She rushed away from the image.

She went to the pay phone in the lobby of the school and called her father, telling him she wasn't feeling well, but she didn't want to spoil things for the others. He said he would pick her up in a few minutes, and she told him she would be waiting in front of the school.

She went out the front door, which was not the entrance for the party. Students were supposed to come into the school through the gym entrance only. Consequently when she closed the front door behind her, it locked automatically, and she couldn't get back into the building. The custodians had put lights on only by the gym entrance. She found herself standing in the darkness on the steps of the school.

Perhaps it was because of the two cups of spiked punch, or perhaps it was a result of her anger and disappointment, or maybe it was the effect of the anxiety that had been created when she and Jonathan talked about Solomon's computer . . . it could have been a combination of everything, but whatever it was, it suddenly made her skin cold and her heart beat madly.

She would swear later that she sensed another presence, and since she had always been a sensible and intelligent girl, no one would simply tell her she had imagined everything. Her parents would just nod silently in understanding and continue to comfort and calm her.

The overcast skies permitted no moonlight. Except for an occasional passing vehicle on the highway in front of the school, there was no illumination whatsoever. The world she now saw around her was a world filled with enormous liquid shadows, rearranging their shapes in the flow of the cool, autumn night air, pouring their darkness into one form and them emptying it quickly into another.

The school lawn was a sea of blackness from which emerged faceless night creatures, some of which crawled quickly up the front of the building. They were gathering out there, drawn from their sleep by her intrusion into their world. They oozed over the long, circular driveway, driving away any barriers between her and them.

She even imagined she could smell them. Their scents were sickly sweet and suggested the stickiness of honey and molasses. If she took a step forward, she imagined she would be sucked down into their putrescence. She would drown in the sea of rotting organic matter. Her body would peel away like the skin off a grape, and she would be left screaming in the night, a pulsating body made of only exposed red flesh, her eyes two molds of jellylike matter threatening to burst and pour into everlasting blindness.

The images terrified her, but froze her into a statue on the top steps of the school. She willed her legs to move forward, but every appendage of her body was in mutiny, angry and defiant because of what she had permitted her imagination to do. She saw herself to be a prisoner of her own body, locked within and at the mercy of muscles and tendons. She pleaded with her bones, begging them to press against the recalcitrant sinews.

First she heard someone in the shadows on her left, and then she heard his voice. There was no doubt about who it was. He pronounced "Audra" in the same manner he had always pronounced it, elongating the "a" sound just a little more than needed, having told her at one time that Audra sounded deific, like some mythological goddess such as Phaedra or Diana. He used to tease her sometimes, but she loved it. "Audra of Sandburg, Goddess of the High School. Your wish is my command," he would say, and perform a sweeping, European bow.

Was that her laughter or his? The sound trailed off into the darkness and was quickly absorbed by the night creatures. They fed off the living in every way possible, fueling on the sounds of laughter, of conversation, and especially the sounds of fear and sorrow.

She heard it again, but she didn't turn toward it. Her neck was immovable. The chill over her body was driving her blood back toward her heart in a hysterical retreat. She felt her chest grow heavy. It was getting harder and harder to breathe.

He called again and again. And then there was that

distinct laugh. He sounded so close. All she would have to do was turn her head, and he would be there beside her.

But she had gone to the funeral, and she had seen the coffin lowered into the earth.

She closed her eyes hard, and when she opened them, she was able to burst forward and break free of the shackles of fear. She charged down the steps of the school and ran madly across the driveway, sensing him right behind her. The night creatures tried to hold her back, but she pressed onward with such intensity that their grips were easily broken. Only, she could feel their cold fingers sliding from her ankles and waist, and occasionally, even her neck.

She broke onto the highway and continued to run, disregarding the oncoming vehicles that swerved to the right to avoid her. Tears were streaming down her face now, but she wasn't even aware of the sounds of her own sobbing. Finally a car came right up behind her, and the driver leaned on the horn. She moved over to the side of the road and waited for it to pass, but it didn't. It pulled up beside her, and her father emerged quickly.

"Audra. What the hell are you doing? Audra?"

She was spinning around, waving her arms about like someone battling an attack of honeybees whose hive had been disturbed. Harry Lowe finally had to seize and embrace his daughter vigorously to get her to stop, and even then he had difficulty getting her to understand that it was he and not some horrible monster who had wrapped its arms around her.

Finally she collapsed in his arms, and he got her into the car. Something told him he had better take her right to the hospital emergency room. They had to take her in on a stretcher. While Audra was being examined, he called his wife, even though he wished he could hold off until he found out exactly what was wrong. However, he knew she would wonder what was taking him and Audra so long to get home.

By the time she arrived in her car, the emergency room doctor had a preliminary diagnosis.

"Someone slipped her something," he said. "Looks like acid."

"Christ," Harry Lowe said. "At a school party."

"That boy," Stephani Lowe muttered, but Harry didn't hear her. He called the police immediately, and they went right to the school and seized possession of the punch bowls.

By the next day, it was learned that one of the punch bowls was indeed spiked with vodka, but as far as the police and the school authorities could determine, no one else had been given any drug-related substance. Some students were drunk, and some had vomited afterward, but that was the worst of it. Nothing compared to what had happened to Audra Lowe.

12.

Kevin and Mindy Baker were quite shocked by Martha's new look. Both were politely complimentary, but Joe saw immediately that like him, neither of them approved. However, Joe sensed that not only didn't they like it, but they both saw it as characteristic of Martha's emotional instability. To them she appeared to be some madwoman, perhaps a schizophrenic who was now in her second identity. It made the entire evening fragile. The Bakers handled Martha, and even him, like thin china. He could almost hear the tinkle of delicate wineglasses.

At first the Bakers hid their faces behind frightened smiles, their eyes dancing with anxiety as they looked quickly from him to Martha and back to him. Mindy was overly solicitous; her voice was filled with high-pitched sounds, making it seem as if she were talking to a child. Kevin was restrained, obviously afraid to make his usual witty remarks. Joe felt sorry for them, but he didn't know what to do to ease things.

Martha, who was normally the quietest of the four whenever they did go out together, was loquacious, babbling like someone on uppers. And her entire conversation was about Jonathan. From the moment she got into the car, to the moment they arrived at the restaurant in Goshen, nearly an hour away, no one could introduce any other topic. Kevin tried twice, but each time she managed to turn what he said into a reference to Jonathan.

She began by giving them a remarkably detailed account of all the things Jonathan had done since his arrival. Her narrations were filled with minutiae that even surprised Joe. It was as if she had been at the boy's side from morning until night, studying his every move. Joe recalled that she had often talked at great length about Solomon when the Bakers and they were together, but nothing she had said before seemed comparable in detail or even in enthusiasm.

Mindy picked up the fact that something Jonathan had said had been the catalyst for Martha's new, cosmetic look.

"Solomon even hated me wearing lipstick," Martha said.

"Then Jonathan's quite different from Solomon," Mindy concluded. Joe saw that Kevin would rather Mindy had not fueled the discussion, but her own natural curiosity about all of it was overpowering.

"Oh, yes." Martha laughed. It was a short, dry laugh, the laugh of someone who had caught her fugitive or trapped her victim. "In the beginning, we thought he was remarkably like Solomon, but as we got to know him, we realized he is, as you say, quite different. Right, Joe?"

"Maybe the Bakers want to get a word in about their own kids," Joe said gently. This time Martha's laugh was more natural.

"Of course. How are the boys? What's happening in your house?" she asked, but almost immediately after Mindy said something, Martha had a comment about Jonathan. It seemed impossible to turn her away from the topic.

When they arrived at the restaurant, they were able to change the conversation to a discussion of the decor, the music, and the selections on the menu. Here, in a better-lit setting, Martha's exaggerated makeup was even more grotesque. She had mentioned Joan Collins, because Jonathan had mentioned her; but Joe thought Martha looked more like a caricature of Joan Collins and other television stars than an imitation of them. How could she look in the mirror and not see it? he wondered. What did she see?

Now that they were among other people, the Bakers were more demonstrative about the embarrassment and sympathy they felt for him. Twice Joe had to ask Martha to lower her voice when she broke out into anecdotes about something Jonathan had done or something Jonathan had said. Before long, he and the Bakers were devoting all their attention to handling Martha—showing her that they were interested in her stories, keeping her voice down by keeping their own voices down, easing her into other topics as best they could.

When Mindy suggested that she and Martha go to the ladies' room, both Joe and Kevin looked at her with an expression of relief and gratitude. At first, Martha wasn't going to go, but then Mindy mentioned the need to freshen up her own makeup, and that did the trick. Kevin and he watched them walk off, and then Joe sat forward, put his elbows on the table, and rested his head in his hands.

"This was a mistake, Joe," Kevin said. "Wrong day to take her out."

"It wasn't my idea. It was hers. I didn't want to go."

"Really?"

"You don't know what's going on. Do you know that I went to Solomon's grave by myself today? She wouldn't go."

"You don't say." He thought for a moment, and then added, "Well, maybe she couldn't take the pain of—"

"Pain? No pain. She wanted to ignore the meaning of today because it might spoil the happiness she's having taking care of Jonathan. She didn't go because of Jonathan," Joe added, unable to keep the bitterness out of his voice. Kevin nodded, but it was evident he didn't really understand Joe's point.

"She's still treading on thin ice. The loss was too great. I imagine the new boy is merely a distraction."

"Oh, no, Kev," Joe said. "He's become much more than that. You heard her. He's more of an obsession."

"Well, what kind of a kid is he?"

Kevin sat forward, both his forearms resting on the table. Kevin was a stocky man with wide shoulders and a thick neck that made him a natural on a wrestling team. Although he had developed something of a middle-age paunch he still worked out periodically. He kept his rust-colored hair cut short on the sides, but never gave up the pompadour in front for which he was famous in high school. In fact, in their yearbook, "pompadour" was next to Kevin's name for "Most noted for."

Because of reddish-brown hair and a light complexion, Kevin always looked flushed or excited. He had a ribbon of tiny freckles over both his eyes, but nowhere else on his face. He had very light blue eyes and a square jaw that emphasized his slightly thicker lower lip.

"He's bright. Doing well in school. Handy around the house. He's made friends quickly."

"So? That's all good."

"Yeah, but . . ."

"But what?"

"I don't know. His friends are all Solomon's old friends. He's even taking out Solomon's girlfriend, Audra Lowe."

"Nothing wrong with that. I know the Lowe girl," Kevin said, pulling the left corner of his mouth up into his cheek.

"There's more. It's . . . weird."

"Look," Kevin said, sitting up. "It probably wasn't the best idea to take in a boy so close to Solomon in age. All the rest feeds your imagination."

"I told her that would happen, but she was stubborn, and I thought . . ."

"It'll work out," Kevin said, tapping him on the arm. The women were returning. "Just give it time."

"Sure," Joe said.

Something happened to Martha after dinner was served. She quieted down considerably and contributed very little to the ensuing conversation. In fact, as the evening wore on, she looked more and more distracted and aloof. At times, Joe caught her staring blankly across the restaurant. When he looked at Mindy, she closed and opened her eyes gently as if to say "Leave it be."

Even Kevin's descriptions of some of his more dramatic new cases, one malpractice case, and one terrible divorce, didn't bring her back into things. Joe, who had been embarrassed because of the way Martha had dominated the conversation earlier, was now embarrassed by her total indifference. He was happy when dinner was finally over and they had paid the bill.

On the way out, he had an opportunity to step back and whisper to Mindy because Kevin had taken Martha's arm and escorted her out the door.

"What happened to her in the bathroom?"

"She started to talk about Jonathan again," Mindy said, keeping her eyes on Martha, "and then she stopped as if someone were standing right behind me. I actually turned around. Then she went into a stall. Maybe she took something. Is she on anything?"

"Not for quite a while. Not since we decided to take in the foster child. Although, we have plenty of tranquilizers in the house."

"Sorry, Joe. This wasn't much fun for you."

"It's all right. It's not your fault. This was the wrong day to go out. She thought she could do it."

"I understand," Mindy said. "I'll call tomorrow."

"Thanks."

The ride home was the antithesis of the ride to the restaurant. Whenever Kevin or Mindy spoke, it was obvious they were forcing conversation. Martha said she was tired and sat back with her head tilted against the seat, her eyes closed. Joe had to announce their arrival when Kevin pulled into their driveway.

"We'll keep in touch," Kevin said.

Joe helped Martha out of the car. The good-nights were said, and they entered the house.

He asked her if she was all right. She said she was, but she went right up to bed. When he looked in on her, she was sound asleep, and she hadn't even taken off her makeup. He checked the medicine cabinet and discovered one of the bottles of tranquilizers was indeed missing. He found it in her pocketbook.

He stood by the side of the bed looking down at her. Her face was in deep repose. The heavy eye shadow made her eyes look almost sewn closed. Her breathing was slight but regular, and he thought she looked so soft and vulnerable that his heart went out to her.

Poor Martha, he thought. She believed she could ignore the significance of this day, but it crept over her and took hold. He knelt down and kissed her on the cheek and then went downstairs to watch some television until he, too, was tired enough to sleep.

Actually, he fell asleep in his easy chair and didn't wake up until the station he was watching went off the air. It was a local network, and the sound became a low-pitched hum. He opened his eyes slowly and looked at the snowy picture. Realizing what happened, he sat up, rubbed his face, and then turned off the set. It was close to four in the morning.

He turned off the front light and locked the door. Then he went upstairs. When he reached the landing, he paused before Jonathan's room because he thought he heard the clicking sound of the computer keyboard, yet there was no light coming out from under Jonathan's bedroom doorway. He stepped closer and listened. No question about it, he thought. That's the computer. He knocked very gently. The clicking ceased.

"Jonathan?"

There was no response. He waited. Then, his curiosity still piqued, he turned the handle of the door very, very slowly, expecting to open the door gently and look within. But the door was locked. He waited a few more moments and then went on to his own bedroom.

Martha was still in a deep sleep when he crawled into bed beside her. She looked like she hadn't even turned once. He brought the blanket to his neck and closed his eyes, but then he heard it again, distinctly . . . tiny little clicking sounds. The keyboard was going. He looked at the clock. Four-thirty in the morning? Why would Jonathan be up using the computer? Surely it had something to do with Jonathan's attachment to Solomon. Those secret files . . . they loomed larger and larger as the key to all this. He felt sure of it.

He lay there listening until he grew so tired again, he couldn't keep his eyes open. He didn't open them again until late Sunday morning when the telephone rang. The moment he lifted the receiver from its cradle and put it to his ear, Harry Lowe began screaming something about drugs in his daughter's punch.

"I used to tell Solomon," Martha began, "that that girl was no good for him. I spotted it right away. There's something weird about her. She's very unstable."

"She's very unstable?" Joe said. Martha had been quiet during the entire ride to the police station, but just before he made the turn into Sandburg proper and headed for the government building, Martha came to life.

He had wakened her immediately after hanging up on Harry Lowe. Moments afterward, the chief of the town police, Paul Dawson, called and requested they bring Jonathan to the station. A number of high school students were being asked to come in for questioning.

"Of course. It wouldn't surprise me to learn that she put the drugs into the punch herself and then drank it."

"For Christ sakes, Martha."

"Well, it wouldn't," she said. She turned back and looked at Jonathan. Joe looked at him through the rearview mirror. He had been like a zombie from the moment they woke him, and he was half-asleep in the backseat now.

"What time did you actually come in, Jonathan?" Joe asked him. Jonathan didn't stir, but there was a slight flicker in his eyelids. Joe squeezed the steering wheel so tightly his knuckles whitened, but he waited patiently.

"A little after one," Jonathan finally said, without opening his eyes.

"What time was the party over?"

"About twelve."

"So where'd you go?" This time Jonathan didn't reply. Joe turned into a parking spot. From the number of cars in the parking lot, he surmised there were already some other parents at the station with their children. Joe turned around before turning off the engine. "If the party ended at twelve and you came home a little after one, where did you go?"

"Joe. He's here to be questioned by the police, not you," Martha said.

"Went parking," Jonathan said. "Couldn't you figure that out?"

"You're embarrassing him, Joe," Martha said. "How would you like it if your father had asked you all these questions after a night out?"

"My father didn't have to bring me to a police station," Joe said dryly. He turned off the engine but thought about what Jonathan had said. "Parking?"

"It's been done before," Jonathan said. Martha laughed, and Joe felt his face redden.

"But didn't you go to the party with Audra?"

"She left early. Told Paula she was sick."

"So who did you—"

"Joe?"

"They're only going to ask him inside."

"Sally Kantzler."

"Jonathan," Joe said, turning around in the seat to face him, "before we go in there, is there anything you know about this?"

"JOE!"

"It's better if he tells us now, Martha."

"I don't believe you could even ask him that."

"I'm just trying to—"

"It's all right," Jonathan said. "No, I don't know anything about it. Let's get it over with," he added. He opened the door and stepped out of the car.

Martha grabbed Joe's arm before he opened the door.

"How could you ask him that? Can't you see he's very upset?"

"All he looks to me is very tired," Joe said. He got out, and the three of them went to the station. Sally Kantzler was in the lobby, sitting on a bench with her mother and father. Some of the other high school students were standing in a small group in the right corner by the bulletin board. They were comparing one another to the faces of the wanted criminals. A few turned with interest when Jonathan appeared.

Bernie Kantzler looked up and shook his head. Sally had her head buried in her mother's shoulder. She stopped sobbing when Joe said hello. When she turned around and looked up at Jonathan, Joe caught something in her face that told him she was terrified. He looked at Jonathan, but Jonathan was inscrutable, his face a blank slate ready to have some expression of emotion stamped on it at any time.

"Helluva thing," Bernie Kantzler said. "Can't even send 'em to school parties and feel safe anymore."

"How is she?" Joe asked.

"She's in the hospital," Kantzler said, as if that were all that had to be said. Joe nodded.

"Sally go in yet?"

"Yeah, but they asked us to wait. They have a couple of other kids in there. No one seems to know anything. Little bastards."

"Come on, Jonathan," Martha said, taking his arm. "I don't intend to be kept waiting here all day."

"Martha." Joe watched her go right to the desk and demand attention. He shook his head. When he looked back at Sally, he saw she was sitting back, her face tight like the face of one expecting to hear her own death sentence. He joined Martha at the desk.

"We're going in with him, Joe," Martha said. "The chief and some state detective will see him next." She looked disdainfully at the patrolman behind the desk. "I told this man we're going in with him."

"You don't have to. I can go in myself. It's okay," Jonathan said.

"No, it's not okay. I know what they think here," Martha added, continuing to glare down at the patrolman. "Just because you're a foster child, you're the most likely suspect. Or should I say the easiest one to suspect? They think you don't have a family."

"Martha, come on," Joe said. He took her by the elbow to pull her away from the desk, but she broke free of his grasp.

"Things like this have happened to him before, Joe. But he didn't have decent protection then. He didn't have someone who cared about him. If you don't want to go in, don't go in. I'm not letting him become any kind of scapegoat."

"Jesus." Joe glanced at the young patrolman. He looked sympathetic and patient. Joe thought that despite his youthful appearance, the patrolman probably had years of experience and had dealt with women like Martha before. Not that there could ever be anyone like Martha, he concluded.

"How much longer will it be?" Martha demanded.

"I don't know, Mrs. Stern."

"So why did they ask us down now?"

"We need everyone's cooperation, Mrs. Stern. This is a serious incident," the policeman said firmly but patiently.

"We're cooperating. We're here, aren't we?"

"So let's be cool about it and wait our turn," Joe said. "Come on." He tried again to turn her toward an empty bench. She glared at him, and then she took Jonathan's hand and headed for the bench directly across from where the Kantzlers were sitting.

Joe noticed that Sally was staring at Jonathan intently, although Jonathan seemed indifferent to her. He sat back, folded his arms across his chest, and closed his eyes, a look of boredom and indifference still on his face.

"How late did you stay up last night, Jonathan?"

"He told you. He was home a little after one," Martha said.

"He didn't go to sleep then, or if he did, he woke up again."

"What are you talking about?"

"Jonathan?"

"I fell asleep almost immediately," Jonathan said, speaking with his eyes still closed. "Slept until you woke me."

"I heard the computer going at four in the morning."

"What?" Martha smiled widely. "Are you crazy? Four in the morning?"

"I heard it," Joe said softly. He saw that the Kantzlers were watching them and straining to hear their conversation. "And I think I know what a computer sounds like."

Martha stared at him a moment. Then she looked at Jonathan.

"Did you hear it, too, Jonathan?"

"What do you mean, did he hear it, too? He'd have to be the one using it, wouldn't he?"

"Jonathan?"

"I was dead to the world," he said. "The last thing I would have done was work on that computer."

"Now, wait a minute . . ." Joe started to turn to him when two boys from the high school senior class emerged from the chief's office. They looked unruffled. Both nodded at Jonathan, and he lifted his hand weakly in response.

"The chief will see him now," the patrolman at the desk announced.

"Let's go," Martha said. She got up quickly, eager for combat.

"Martha, hold up," Joe said softly, hoping to slow her down. She didn't hear him. She walked right beside Jonathan to the office. Joe followed meekly and looked over at the Kantzlers one more time. Sally was biting down gently on her lower lip and watching intently. Bernie and his wife looked dazed.

Paul Dawson stood up behind his desk as they entered his office. Joe didn't recognize the tall, olive-skinned man in the dark blue suit who stood just to the right of the desk, but he had known Paul Dawson all his life. Paul was a local boy who had served in Vietnam in the military police. He had been on the Sandburg police force before he was drafted, and when he came out of the service, he returned to the force and quickly moved up the ranks until he became chief of the township police.

Joe always thought Paul Dawson to be the military type. Even in high school, he walked with a soldier's gait—his shoulders back, his chest out, making him appear more then five-feet-ten-inches tall. He kept his hair shorter than everyone else's and always looked as though he had just come home on leave from boot camp. He replied to his male teachers with "sir" and his female teachers with "ma'am." He wasn't an exceptional student, but he was a good student, responsible, efficient, dependable. He was the kind of teenager liked more by adults than by other teenagers, but that never seemed to matter to him. He had his mind set on his goals and refused to permit any distractions.

After high school, he studied police science for a year and a few months, but he had to give it up when his father died unexpectedly. An only child, he returned home to work and care for his mother. He had no trouble getting a job on the local police force, and people appreciated the professional manner with which he handled himself, even as a small-town patrolman; so it came as no surprise to anyone, least of all Joe, that Paul moved up quickly and became chief of police when the opportunity arose. Now married with three young children of his own, he was as stable a part of the community as the most respected town fathers.

Paul extended his hand when Joe stepped out from behind Martha and Jonathan.

"Joe, Martha. Thanks for coming down. Everyone, please take a seat. This is Lt. Diana from the state police division handling substance abuse." Lt. Diana nodded, but Martha did not smile at him or Paul.

"So," Paul began, sitting down after everyone else had, "this is Jonathan. I've been hearing a great deal about you, Jonathan," he added, smiling tentatively. Dawson still wore his hair very short. Dressed in a tapered, short-sleeve white shirt, blue tie, and dark blue pants, he looked as trim and muscular as he did the day he returned from his stint in Vietnam.

"The others are blaming him, is that it?" Martha asked quickly.

Dawson glanced at Lt. Diana and then at Joe before responding. Joe sensed that there were some real suspicions.

"No, Martha. No one has placed any blame on any-one." Dawson leaned forward and turned to Jonathan. "But there's no question someone's to blame, right, Jonathan?"

"I suppose so," Jonathan said. He sat up straighter in his chair and looked more wide-awake.

"You knew about the vodka being in the punch, didn't you, son?" Lt. Diana asked. The abrupt way in which he entered himself into the conversation turned all heads.

Joe thought the state investigator looked more like a corporate executive. He wore a rich-looking gold watch on his left wrist and two rings on his fingers: a gold wedding ring and a tigereye pinkie ring in a gold setting. He had a trim, full head of thick black hair, and although he was cleanly shaven, his dark beard was visible and threatening just at skin level. There was no question he had to shave twice a day.

"I heard about it, yeah," Jonathan said. "But I didn't put it in there. It was already spiked by the time we got to the school."

"How did you know it was spiked?" Dawson asked.

"Someone told me."

"Who?"

"I don't know. Everyone knew. I think it was Abe Hodes who told me first."

"And you told Audra?" Lt. Diana asked.

"Uh huh."

"And she wanted some?"

"She didn't say no."

"So you got it for her?"

"I got her a couple of cups, yeah. Then I started dancing, and she got her own."

"Why didn't you dance with her?" Dawson asked. "She was your date, wasn't she?"

"She said she didn't want to dance. I did."

"Why would he want to put anything in his date's drink?" Martha blurted. She sat forward and directed herself to Lt. Diana. "Obviously, it had to be someone else. It's only logical."

"Kids do illogical things," Lt. Diana said. "Can't rule something out because it seems illogical to us."

"Are you accusing him?"

"Martha," Joe said.

"As the chief said," Lt. Diana replied, looking unruffled by Martha's aggressive manner, "we're not accusing anyone yet, ma'am; but we are looking for information. All right, Jonathan, did you see who was with Audra while you were dancing?"

"I don't know. There were a lot of kids around her. Larry Elias was there. Philip Kotin. I saw Brad Rosen."

"They were all drinking from this punch bowl?" Dawson asked.

"Yes, sir." Jonathan's use of "sir" raised Dawson's eyebrows. He looked at Lt. Diana.

"Did you see Audra leave with anyone?" Lt. Diana asked.

"I didn't see her leave. Paula Simon told me she left. She said she was sick."

"Didn't you try to find out?"

"Find out what? Why should she lie about that?"

Everyone was quiet for a moment. Paul Dawson looked down at his desk and then up at Jonathan.

"You didn't see anyone do anything unusual around Audra, then?"

"No, sir. As I said, I was dancing."

"Uh huh." Dawson studied him a moment and then sat back, pressing the tips of his fingers against one another. "Jonathan, how was your behavior at the last school you attended?"

"What does that have to do with anything?" Martha asked quickly. Joe thought she sounded more and more like a defense attorney. "He was living in a different kind of a home then. He's with people who care about him now."

"I understand, Martha, but the principal at our school mentioned—"

"That's terrible. What did I tell you, Joe?" she asked, turning to him. "A scapegoat." She spun around to face Dawson again. "The real culprits here are the school authorities who can't protect the children. How did that vodka get into the punch to begin with, huh? Why don't you ask the principal that while you're at it?" Her face was bright red, and she looked as if she would fly off the chair. Dawson did not respond. He looked at Joe.

"Martha. You've got to calm down."

"Calm down? While they work to frame Jonathan?"

"Nobody's framing anyone, Martha," Paul said. "Look . . ."

"Did someone accuse him? Was there a witness who claimed he did it?"

"No, Martha."

"Then what else do you want to know? He told you everything he saw and heard."

"All right," Paul said, sitting back. Joe saw that Martha's aggressiveness had pushed him faster along his plan of questioning. "Jonathan, you brought Audra at least two cups of punch, is that correct?"

"Yes, sir."

"I'll ask you this only once. If it comes up again, it will be because I have uncovered evidence and things will be different when I ask you again. Do you understand?" Paul Dawson's gaze was intense. He had the hard look of a professional policeman talking to a hardened criminal now.

"Yes, sir." Jonathan pulled his shoulders back as though readying himself for a blow.

"Did you put anything in those cups before you gave them to Audra Lowe?"

"No, sir, I did not." Jonathan matched his inquisitor's determined look. The boy's in no way intimidated, Joe thought, but he wasn't sure whether that proved him innocent or confirmed his guilt.

There was a moment of silence. Dawson sat forward.

"Is that it?" Martha asked.

"For now," Paul Dawson said. Martha shot up out of her seat. Jonathan got up slowly, but Joe hesitated. He felt overwhelmed.

"You know," Martha said. "More and more young people are taking drugs themselves these days. They don't need someone to slip it in their drinks. They slip it in their own drinks. Have you considered that?"

"We're on it, Martha," Paul said politely but dryly.

"Good," Martha said. She put her arm around Jonathan and looked at Joe. He stood up.

"So long, Joe," Paul Dawson said. "Thanks."

"Right," Joe said. He followed Martha and Jonathan out of the office.

Sally Kantzler and her mother were not on the bench when Joe, Martha, and Jonathan stepped into the lobby.

Bernie Kantzler looked up expectantly. Martha walked right up to him.

"I'd advise you to watch the way they handle your daughter," Martha said. "Obviously Harry Lowe's money is speaking. They're looking to pin this on someone other than Audra."

"Huh?"

"See you, Bernie," Joe said. He wanted only to make a quick exit. He said nothing until they were all in the car and he had backed out of the parking lot. "I don't think you did the boy any good in there, Martha."

"What? Why not?"

"You didn't give them a chance. You made it seem—"

"Seem like what?"

"Like you were afraid of what they would ask."

"Did you ever hear anything like this?" Martha asked Jonathan. He was sitting back, his eyes closed again. He opened his eyes and then closed them. She turned back to Joe. "Don't you realize what they were trying to do?"

"They were trying to do their job, that's all," Joe said. He was tired himself and decided that would be all he would say about it. Martha decided silence was the best route to take, too. No one said anything until they reached the house.

Jonathan went directly upstairs to his room, mumbling something about being tired. Joe went into the living room, and Martha went up to take a shower, complaining that she had to rush for nothing this morning and never got a chance to get washed and dressed properly.

"All because of some spoiled brat," she added.

Joe didn't respond. He lowered himself into his easy chair as though he would never be able to pull himself up and out of it. He didn't turn on the television or pick up a magazine. Instead he simply sat there staring at the silent set. He felt a strange weakness in the pit of his stomach that reminded him of the times in his life when he was frightened by something or felt a great foreboding. He sat there desperately trying to understand it and forced himself to find an analogy with something in the mechanical world.

All he could imagine to give him a similar feeling was driving along in his car and suddenly having the steering go out. What it would mean was everything was beyond his control; he would be carried along by whimsical fate or some dark force that took pleasure in his plight.

Joe was now convinced some dark force had indeed entered his house in the guise of this new boy. He had to find a way to rid them of the evil before it was too late. Perhaps it was too late already. He had let his own ambivalence render him helpless for so long that now he wondered if he had what it would take to do battle.

As if in response, he heard Martha and Jonathan laugh. It was the laughter of strangers, the kind of laughter that left him feeling alone.

He had lost Martha once and then thought he had regained her, but now it seemed he was in danger of losing her forever. He didn't know exactly what he could do, but in his heart, he understood that something had to be done and done soon.

13.

Even though the mirror was covered with mist from the hot shower, Martha saw Solomon's reflection in the glass. She stepped out of the stall, reached for her towel, and caught his image clearly outlined beneath the film of water. It was like seeing him through a heavy fog. She smiled to herself, took the face towel from the rack, and wiped the mirror to bring him out clearly, but when she looked behind her, he wasn't there. He was only in the mirror.

The noose was around his neck again, with the remainder of the rope dangling. It looked more like an umbilical cord. Blood seeped out along the woven twine, the cord taking on a fleshy texture. Except for his face and the underside of his chin, his body was as pale as a corpse. It was as if death were creeping up, reclaiming him an inch at a time. She thought his eyes looked more glassy and his lips paler and more swollen than they had during any of the previous times he had made a ghostly appearance.

It wasn't unusual for her to see him in her bathroom before, after, or even during one of her showers. Until he was thirteen, they occasionally took showers together. Often he was impulsive about it. He would come in while she was getting ready for a shower, and after she undressed and stepped into the stall, he would undress and step in, too. She never discouraged it, and they had a thing about washing each other's back.

She recalled how upset Joe would get whenever he heard about them doing it or saw it being done, especially during the last year or so before Solomon stopped doing it himself. It infuriated her to hear him say it was indecent. At first she concluded that Joe was merely very puritanical. After all, it was his so-called straight-arrow character that had attracted her to him in the beginning and had made him so popular with her parents, too.

But then she concluded Joe was simply jealous of her relationship with Solomon. It wasn't her fault that the boy wasn't as close to him as he was to her. She knew he resented it, and she admitted to herself that his resentment was understandable. Hadn't she tried so many times to get them to be closer to each other? However, a great deal of the problem was Joe's fault, too, only he wouldn't admit it.

In any case, she disregarded his complaints. She wasn't going to turn her boy away from her and put up all these artificial barriers just because Joe thought she should and just because Joe had trouble being affectionate. The mother-son showers finally stopped, but they stopped when Solomon wanted them to stop.

Even so, he didn't avoid talking to her while she showered or while she dried herself. She never locked her bathroom door; she never asked him to wait outside. Therefore, it didn't surprise her when Solomon made an appearance now in the bathroom while she was taking a shower. He couldn't wait to take pleasure in the present difficulties, she thought. The truth was she had expected him. She had anticipated and even welcomed his coming, even though his image was apparently trapped in the bathroom mirror.

"Still think he's an innocuous waif?" he asked. When he smiled, she noticed that his teeth looked so gray. Usually Solomon's teeth had been so white. He took such good care of them that even the dentist had to remark about it. He had had only one cavity all his life and that was, in the dentist's words, "only a pinprick." There had never been a problem about getting him to go for his regular checkups. In fact, he usually reminded her about it.

Martha realized something different was happening here. He looked more ghoulish than at any other sighting. Only this realization didn't sadden or frighten her. It cheered her. He's losing it, she thought. Soon, he'll be completely gone again, and he won't be coming between me and Jonathan.

She smiled back at him.

"Solomon, poor Solomon. Deluding yourself again. Did you really think I would fall for all this? Did you really think I wouldn't understand what you did?"

"What I did?"

"It was a pathetic . . . no, it was a juvenile attempt to besmirch Jonathan. Perhaps, under different circumstances . . . if he were still with the Porters, for instance, your plan might have succeeded. They would have thrown him to the wolves to protect themselves. In fact, they did. But here things are and will be different for him. No matter how you use Joe," she added.

"Use Joe?"

"Come on now. I can see through that. I saw through it when you were with us. Why shouldn't I see through it now? Joe's so . . . what should I say . . . easily manipulated?"

Solomon shook his head. Tiny lines of blood trickled out from under the rope and crisscrossed down his neck before disappearing under his shirt collar. The smile left his face, and the underside of his chin, which had been crimson and alive a few moments ago, turned as pale as the flesh beneath.

"That's not true," he said. "You've got to start being more observant, Mother, and see things for what they are."

"That's what I'm doing, dear Solomon. That's exactly

what I'm doing," she added, smiling. His image grew a size or two smaller.

Martha started to dry her body more vigorously. She ran the towel down between her breasts and over the small of her stomach. Solomon's eyes followed her activity.

"Want to dry my back?" she asked. "Oh, I forgot. You can't. I'll have to ask Jonathan."

"You're making a mistake, a terrible mistake. You're being blind again."

"Again?"

"Yes, again. I didn't do anything to Audra Lowe. He did it."

"Doesn't surprise me that you chose to use her. You used her before to hurt me, didn't you?"

"You're wrong."

"Am I?" She wrapped the towel around her waist and tucked it in so it would serve as a skirt. Then she brushed back her hair, looking past him in the mirror. He was well off to the left now, growing smaller and smaller. "Jonathan was right about my use of makeup. Everyone liked it."

"They didn't; they were only being polite. You looked foolish." Solomon's voice was thinner, weaker, more like an echo in a deep tunnel.

"That's what Joe thought, but it was you speaking through him, wasn't it? Don't worry, I'll always know when it's you. There's no point in your doing that anymore." She took another towel and draped it over her shoulders so that the ends of it would just fall over her breasts. "I've got to get my back dried," she said.

"Mother, don't do it. Believe me," Solomon said. She paused for a moment before leaving the mirror. He was much smaller, and his voice wasn't filled with his usual confidence. That gave her some hesitation, but she pushed it aside. "Mother," he cried one final time as she turned away. She hurried from the bathroom to frustrate his further attempts to dissuade her and went to Jonathan's room.

He was lying on his back, his hands under his head, staring up at the ceiling. When she entered, he turned her way.

"Do me a favor and dry my back, will you?" she said. He sat up quickly, and she sat on the bed, her back to him. He took the towel from her shoulders and wiped her back in firm, small circles. She closed her eyes and moaned with pleasure. "That's good. Better than . . ."

"Than Solomon used to do it?"

"Yes," she said. When he finished, she put the towel back over her shoulders and pulled it down over her breasts. She turned to him. "I told you about that Audra Lowe," she said. "I told you how she used to chase after Solomon and how I had this feeling she was not a nice person."

"Yeah, I know."

"I was right, wasn't I?"

"Uh huh."

"She probably did put the drugs into her own cup. I'm not saying she was doing it to get you into trouble, but she didn't think what might happen. She just didn't care. Right?"

Jonathan shrugged. "I don't know. It's not important anymore."

"Exactly. It's not important anymore. I promise you, they're not going to blame you for it. I won't let them."

"You were great in there," he said. "Those cops never knew what hit them."

Martha smiled.

"I suppose I can stand up for what I believe when I have to," she said.

"Joe was kinda . . . upset," he said.

"Frightened is more like it." She smirked.

"I know. I was a little disappointed. When I first came here, I thought you were the weak one and he was the strong one. But things are starting to look different."

"Joe is too nice sometimes. Polite at the wrong times."

"He means well," Jonathan said. "But I can see why Solomon was disappointed with him sometimes."

"Oh, yes."

"It's a shame. But," Jonathan said, smiling, "you're not disappointing. You make up for it."

"Well, just don't go hanging around with people who can get you into trouble anymore," she said. She ran her fingers through his hair. "Choose your friends more carefully."

"Right. Thanks for everything."

"You don't have to thank me." She leaned over and kissed him on the forehead. "Let's forget about it now," she said. "Put it behind us and think only of good things."

"Okay." He smiled. "But it's going to be hard to forget how you put it to those cops," he added, and laughed. She laughed, too. "And the way Joe sat there with this look of shock." Both of them laughed again, their laughter much louder.

She stopped when she thought she heard something fall in her room.

"What was that?"

"What was what?" Jonathan asked.

"I don't know." She listened for a moment. "I'd better get dressed. There's plenty left to do today," she added, and went back to her bedroom. For a moment, she stood there looking around. Then she realized the bathroom door was open. Hadn't she closed that?

She went to it and looked within. Was it her imagination, or did that look like a drop of blood in the sink beneath the mirror? She stared down at it a moment and thought of Lady Macbeth. "Out out, damn spot."

She started to laugh at the literary allusion and then stopped. The drop of blood looked too real. She wanted to touch it, even smell and taste it, but she couldn't get herself to reach into the sink. Instead, she turned on the faucet and watched the water wash it down the drain.

•   •   •

For Joe the Audra Lowe incident and the subsequent interrogation at the police station marked a major turn of events. Suspicions that had been running like a polluted stream below the surface of his consciousness began to emerge. The boy wasn't only a conniver, he was a parasite, because he lived off the heartaches and pains of others.

Right from the start, he knew how to worm his way into Martha's heart. He knew the things she wanted to hear and the things she wanted to see. He sensed where she was vulnerable, and he struck at that vulnerability. She wanted Solomon alive, so he gave Solomon to her. But with what accuracy . . . what eerie accuracy.

And he even got to me, Joe thought. He knew I was ambivalent about my son's death, and he took advantage of that ambivalence. He played up to my own doubts about myself. When he had to stroke me, he stroked me . . . like when he made a big deal about wanting to accompany me on a service call. Or when he pretended interest in sports. He was always conniving, plotting, working at getting in with us until it was difficult to see him for what he is.

A cold feeling came over Joe. He could see him for what he was, but how would he ever get Martha to do so? He had worked it so every time Joe criticized him, it looked like his only motive was jealousy. He would need solid, irrefutable evidence. But where would he look for that? All that the boy did, he did subtly.

Martha refused to permit any further discussion of the drug-related incident. When Jonathan and Martha had come downstairs for lunch, Joe commented about the fact that apparently only one student had ingested a hallucinogenic drug.

"We're putting that behind us, Joe," she said in a tone of reprimand. "Placing doubts in our minds about Jonathan is just what he wants us to do."

"He?"

"The police," she said quickly. "Let's not talk about it anymore. In fact, I forbid discussion about it," she added.

"You forbid?"

"We won't answer any questions or acknowledge any comments relating to the incident," Martha said, sounding like a defense attorney again. Joe looked at Jonathan. He looked inscrutable, but Joe thought his eyes betrayed an inner satisfaction. To emphasize her point, Martha turned away from him and began to discuss some new designer shirts she had seen at the Orange Plaza Mall. "Colors by Julian," she said. "There was this one design that would highlight your eyes, Jonathan . . ."

Joe felt his face flush. He realized that when they had come down for lunch, she hadn't even called him to come eat. She had made herself and Jonathan some sandwiches and actually had sat down at the table before he entered the kitchen. He made himself a sandwich and joined them. Now they were carrying on a conversation as though he weren't even present.

"I know what we should do," Martha concluded, her face animated with excitement. "All the stores are open in the mall today. Why don't we take a ride and you'll try on one of the shirts."

"Sure," Jonathan said. "Just give me a half hour to knock off some math homework." He glanced at Joe, but Joe said nothing. Martha began to clean off the table. She looked at Joe as though she just realized he was there.

"Are you coming along with us?" she asked. He could see she didn't really care whether he did or not.

"I thought I'd finish the trim work Jonathan and I started last weekend."

"Good," she said. "You should finish that before the weather gets so miserable, you can't do anything."

His decision apparently cheered her. She turned on the radio and began to sing to the music. Jonathan excused himself, and Joe went out to the garage to remix the paint and get out the ladder and paint rollers. He was well into the work when he heard the garage door open and saw Martha back out the car. He paused for a moment to watch them drive away.

Jonathan was staring out the car window, and Martha was gabbing away, apparently being just as loquacious as she had been the other night with the Bakers. Just before Martha shifted into drive and headed down the road, Jonathan caught sight of Joe watching them.

They stared at each other for only a split second really, but in that short moment, Joe definitely experienced a foreboding premonition. Jonathan had such a cold look of self-satisfaction and arrogance. Joe thought the boy already knew he had taken a significant grasp on their lives. Holding his head back, his face unsmiling, his eyes as still as fake-glass orbs, he brought the left corner of his mouth up into his cheek and turned to Martha as they drove off together.

Joe watched the car disappear and then went back to his work. He moved more slowly, his mind occupied with other thoughts. He kept coming back to the accuracy with which the boy had taken on Solomon's ways, an accuracy that enabled him to win Martha over so completely. It was almost as if Solomon had come back from the grave to whisper in his ear, but Joe knew that couldn't be so. The dead don't come back. They just don't . . .

Unless . . . he looked up at the house . . . unless they've left their words to be heard. That's it, he thought. That's it. Excited by his realization, he walked into the house quickly and rushed up the stairs to Jonathan's room.

He entered, but stopped in the doorway. The computer monitor stared at him as though it anticipated what he was about to do, what he had to do. He rushed to the keyboard and searched all around it. Nothing. He looked behind the machine and even looked under the computer table to see if something had been stuck there. Nothing. He stood up and stared down. Where could it be?

Gingerly he lifted the keyboard. There was the slip of

paper. He picked it up slowly and read the symbols, feeling a certain electricity when he realized what they meant. This was the password into Solomon's secret files.

Without delay, he turned on the computer and called up the menu listing the files. It seemed to him that there were a number of new ones, but he brought the cursor to the ones that had been inaccessible to him, and when he typed in the symbols from the paper, he found that he had indeed entered into his dead son's secret files.

He sat down at the computer and began to scroll the pages. As he read the lines rolling before him, he understood why Jonathan would think he had brought Solomon back from the dead. Suddenly the computer had become The Lazarus Machine. He could hear Solomon speaking as clearly as if he were standing beside him.

"My father's life seems so vacant and empty, filled with endless hours of watching basketball games, fixing the house, occasionally reading a computer magazine. He's devoted to the family, but when I think about him, I wonder if he doesn't at times feel the emptiness, the uselessness, of his activities."

He scrolled down further, and read on. "Watching him makes me think about my future. Despite my good school grades, what makes me think I'll be any different? There seem traps in the adult world, a pattern of ceaseless, pointless activity that never really satisfies . . .

"Sex is a brutal antidote they use to forget their vain, empty lives . . . and here I am, an experimenter of sex, but not an enjoyer. Not the enjoyer my own mother is."

Pressing the button again, he got more text, a chill rising up his spine. "I've been thinking a lot about life and . . . death lately. I don't want to believe that this is all there is. Death seems too final and yet . . . I went to the library to do some research on the subject and read *The*

Undead by Dr. R. R. White and *Black Numerology*. I like the idea that life after death is eternal and contains only the most beautiful aspects of life . . . things that are pleasing linger with us forever. At times—maybe I'm going crazy—it seems peaceful, the peace I seek.

"There's an interesting idea in the numerology book: If you die on the day of your birth, you'll obtain blissful afterlife. Didn't Thomas Jefferson, or was it John Adams, die on his birthday? How did he know? How can you guarantee that you'll die on your birthday? Maybe I'm getting jaded, but these questions have lingered with me since childhood . . . the puzzle of it all.''

Pain traveled up Joe's spine. He felt stunned and struck by the maturity of his son's secret voice. Was this inside the boy all that time? Shaking his head, he scrolled back through the file, feeling the dreaded chills again as he read his son's thoughts, and saw the path to his final solution.

He scrolled more deeply into the file, stopping here, stopping there. His son had maintained a virtual computer diary, recording his every thought and feeling. The diary was divided into days, and recorded in a way that he could call up any section at will.

One entry made him pause long. It read: "Audra was talking to Donald Pedersen again today. I could feel my anger growing, recalling all the stories I'd heard about the way he treats women. He uses then discards them, and I didn't like the way he was peering into Audra's eyes. I've also observed him bullying and taunting some of the more helpless students, like the science whiz Henry Wilson . . . when old man Corde's barn burned down to the ground two months ago, destroying several horses and goats caught inside, everyone knew Pedersen was behind it. Fortunately Audra had put on her 'pleasant,' polite facade, and when I arrived, he backed off. But I will say this, if I were to go, I would enjoy taking him with me . . .''

•   •   •

Joe sat back, his apprehension growing. "Take him with me" echoed again and again in his mind, along with other memories.

He recalled the night of the Pedersen accident. Was it an accident, after all? He recalled he thought he had smelled gasoline after Jonathan returned that night.

He looked at the computer screen again, locked into the passage he had just scanned. Now the glow of the machine was more than mesmerizing; now the glow was evil.

Chilled to the bone, Joe realized that the pieces fit all together. In a horrible, twisted way, Solomon was possessing Jonathan. Through the computer. Solomon had indeed reached back from the grave and fed his thoughts into a mind most eager to receive them.

Who was really to blame for Donald Pedersen's death? Jonathan or Solomon? Actually, now it no longer mattered. Joe had to do something. The boy was dangerous. What if there were other references to violence in here? he wondered.

He sent the computer's memory to the final chapter and scanned Solomon's thoughts on suicide again. It was bone-chilling to read the entry. His fingers could barely work the keys to move the pages forward.

When he had read enough for now, he paused. He had to read all of it, but he didn't want to do it in here. He took a disc from the rack and copied the file. He would read the rest of it at his office.

He wasn't aware of how much time he had spent at the computer until he looked outside and saw how far the sun had descended. He went outside to clean up his painting material. By the time he returned, the house had grown depressingly dark, too. He went about turning on lights. The mall to which Martha had gone was only a half hour away. He knew how long she could be when she went off with one of her girlfriends to shop in the bigger malls in New Jersey, but he couldn't imagine her spending so much time with a teenage boy in the local mall, a mall that had a quarter of the stores.

He was also getting very hungry. From what he could see, Martha hadn't prepared anything for dinner yet. He opened the refrigerator and picked on some leftover chicken, but he grew increasingly annoyed by her absence as the minutes ticked on. When the phone rang, he expected it to be her, but it was Kevin Baker.

"We heard about the disaster at the school party last night," he said. "The boys were just talking to their friends about it. Lucky it didn't happen to Jonathan, too."

"Yeah. I hope it was only luck."

"What do you mean? You think he might be involved with drugs?" Kevin asked, taking on the tone of an investigator for the prosecution. "Have you found anything on him or in the house?"

"No."

"Well, does he seem stoned at any time?"

"Not really, no."

"Is he hanging around with kids who might be into that sort of thing?"

"No. Like I told you, all his friends so far are Solomon's old friends, and from what I could see and from what I still see, they're pretty straight kids."

"So what are you talking about?" Kevin asked. Joe debated about telling Kevin about the computer files, but he didn't think he'd understand. Who would unless he had lived here and seen the subtle things Jonathan had done?

"I don't know. I get these bad vibes."

"Not very scientific, and for you to be unscientific . . ."

"I know, Counselor. I know."

"How's Martha today? Mindy was going to call, but she went shopping in Jersey with her sister, and she's not back yet."

"Martha's not back yet, either. She went shopping with Jonathan. I'm afraid she's getting too involved with this boy," Joe said.

There was a long pause.

"I asked my boys about him. They say he's cool."

"He's cool all right."

"Look, Joe. If you're feeling uncomfortable with him, then maybe you should have a good conversation with Martha."

"Don't know if I can. Don't know if she'll listen, and the last thing I want to do to her now is get her emotionally upset a day after Solomon's birthday."

"I understand. Well, if there's anything we can do . . ."

"There's something," Joe said, the idea coming to him quickly. "When we were at the police station, along with other parents and students this morning, Paul Dawson mentioned something about Jonathan's previous records. Do you think you could find out if he had any run-ins with the law?"

"He's a juvenile, Joe. There aren't going to be any records like there would be on an adult offender. If he had problems in previous schools, the principal here might tell you about them."

"I'm looking for more serious things."

"Sometimes it's better not to look," Kevin said. "Anyway, from what the boys tell me, he's doing very well here."

"He is."

"Maybe you're just getting uptight for no reason, Joe. With Martha under tension, with you under tension . . . Harry Lowe called me a little while ago. He wants to sue the school, so maybe I'll be talking to Jonathan myself."

"Good," Joe said. He wanted someone with Kevin's insight and intelligence to talk to the boy. "Maybe I can arrange for it this week."

"I'll see. This might be one of those cases that I settle with a phone call."

"What did he say about Audra? How is she?"

"Apparently she's still having reactions. Hallucinating, talking about creatures on the school lawn, and . . ."

"What? I can take it," Joe said in anticipation.

"Solomon. He's in the hallucinations." There was another long pause, and then Kevin added, "This is the main reason I called you, Joe. You're liable to hear it one way or another. Stephani Lowe blames it on her going out with Jonathan, going back to your house, being with a boy about his age. She was babbling about all kinds of resemblances that Audra sees between Jonathan and Solomon, but from what Martha said last night . . ."

"There are some similarities," Joe said, and almost laughed after what he considered to be an understatement.

"Stephani was wild on the phone. Harry couldn't keep her off. I never heard anything so stupid. She was threatening to call you. You might want to say something to Martha and prepare her just in case she does make such a call. She'll certainly tell her thoughts to other people. Stephani Lowe's beside herself. Understandably, I suppose."

"Yes, it is understandable. Thanks for the warning, Kev."

"Unfortunate situation, all around. I'll try to resolve the legal end of it as quickly as I can and get things back to normal. I'll be in touch," he said, and hung up.

Joe went back to the living room and stared out the front window. Darkness was falling quickly now. The shadows were coming out of the forest to reclaim the road and the lawn. He could see the first stars appearing. When he looked at his watch, he saw that it was six-thirty. He was annoyed with Martha for not calling, but then he thought maybe they had gone to another shopping center and picked up a pizza. They would be home any moment, and the delay would be explained.

He tried watching some news to keep his mind off the two of them, but when they didn't appear by a quarter after seven, he gave up on the pizza theory. Although he was aggravated, he was also hungry, so he went into the kitchen and made himself some eggs. He had just sat down to eat when Martha and Jonathan drove up the driveway.

He heard the garage door open and close, and a moment later, he heard their excited voices and laughter.

They were still laughing when they came in from the garage. Both of them were carrying bags, and both stopped immediately when they saw him. He sat back and lifted his hands in exasperation, palms upward.

"What?" Martha said.

"What? Where the hell have you been? That's what."

"You knew where we went."

"Yeah, I knew you went to the mall, but you didn't say anything about not coming home for supper."

"Jonathan and I decided to eat in that German restaurant."

"I waited and waited and finally made myself some eggs."

"I knew you could take care of yourself."

Jonathan started to laugh, but stopped and kept it at a wide smile. Joe blanched.

"That's not the point, Martha," he said calmly. "You wouldn't want me to do such a thing to you." He looked pointedly at Jonathan and added, "And it's not the kind of thing you've done in the past."

"Oh, my God. To carry on over something as insignificant . . ." She put her hand on Jonathan's shoulder. "Go on up with the clothing and forget about showing it to him."

"Fine. I'm the one who's wrong here," Joe retorted. He looked down at his eggs, his appetite quickly dissipating. Jonathan moved quickly through the kitchen and to the stairs. Martha waited and then came to the table.

"I had succeeded in getting him to forget the depressing time he had last night and this morning, and now you ruined it."

"I ruined it? And what do you mean, depressing time he had last night?" Martha stared at him for a moment.

"He finally told me about Audra Lowe. There's no question she gave herself the drugs."

"What?"

"That's right. She had offered them to him a few times before, only he says he's seen what drugs can do to people. He's had some terrible experiences, Joe. You can just imagine what nightmares were revived for him because of this episode."

"What about Audra's nightmares?"

"They're her own making."

"I don't believe that, and neither do the police."

"They will, once their investigation is completed."

"Harry and Stephani Lowe won't buy it. Kevin called earlier. They're suing the school."

"Figures. They want to shift the blame from themselves to someone else. Typical pattern for parents who are into themselves. They can't see what's going on right under their noses."

"The Lowes aren't like that."

"Well, how do you know they're not?"

"How do you know they are?"

"I told you what Jonathan said," Martha replied.

"How can you believe him?" He wondered if he should tell her about Solomon's files, but then he thought she'd want to read them, and the pain involved in that would be overwhelming. First he'd have to find another way to get her to see what Jonathan was.

"I can believe him," she said slowly, "because I have won his trust. It didn't happen overnight, and it didn't come easy, but now that I have his confidence, do you think I should give him the feeling I don't believe him?"

"Martha . . . Jesus, it *is* overnight. How long has he been here? You can't think you know all you have to know about him. It's more complicated than that."

She smiled, but in such a way as to make his blood cold. Then she nodded slowly.

"I understand," she said softly, "from where your doubts come. It's all right. Everything's going to be all right."

"What the hell are you talking about? Didn't you hear

what I said before? The Lowes are very upset. Stephani Lowe wants to blame us,'' he added, speaking under his breath.

"Us? Whatever for?"

"For . . ." He paused. How would he say it? Should he come right out and say "for finding someone who made himself so similar to Solomon in so many ways that it drove Audra Lowe mad? She thinks taking in a boy about Solomon's age is bizarre."

"Well, who the hell does she think she is?" Martha said. "Who the hell . . . I have a good mind to call her and tell her about her precious goody-goody daughter."

"They're going through enough, Martha. Let's be a little sympathetic."

"And do what? Give up Jonathan? Send him back to some home where the people couldn't give a damn about him?" Her voice began to climb toward a hysterical pitch. He sensed its coming and closed his eyes. "Well?"

He shook his head. "I don't know," he said. "Everything worries me."

"Well, it doesn't worry me."

He couldn't look up at her. She looked furious, and that ferocity made her ugly.

"All right," he said. "All right. It's been a bad day all around." He looked down at his cold eggs. When he looked up, she seemed placated. The redness had gone out of her face, and her eyes weren't as big.

"I bought this shirt for you," she said, "but it wasn't my idea to buy it. It was Jonathan's." She pulled the shirt out of the bag. "It's nice, isn't it?"

"Yes," Joe said.

"It'll go well with your dark blue slacks and gray sports jacket. Jonathan has a good sense of color coordination. He really is a remarkable young man, Joe."

"That he is," he commented but she didn't hear his meaning.

"Please, Joe," Martha said, approaching him. She took his hand into hers. "Try to fight it."

"Fight it?"

"The urge to blame him for things, the urge to hate him. Don't let anything influence you. Make your own decisions."

"That's what I do," he said, but she took on that cold smile again.

"I'll go up and change, and we'll have coffee. I bought something in the bakery. Okay?"

"Okay," he said. Then he looked down at the shirt. The conniving little bastard, he thought. He had to find a way to get rid of him. Their lives literally could depend on it.

14.

Sally Kantzler walked slowly across the hospital lobby and approached the front desk. She had called the Lowes first to ask them if she could visit Audra, and they had asked their doctor. Although Audra hadn't experienced any drug-related hallucinations for nearly twelve hours, she was still suffering from what the hospital psychiatrist had diagnosed as delusions of paranoia, which he termed a residual effect of her substance abuse. The doctor thought one of her close peers might help to relieve some of the tension and give her some reassurance. So the Lowes told Sally it would be all right for her to make a short visit.

Actually Sally had been hoping they would say she couldn't come. She felt guilty for telling Jonathan that Audra had wanted her to spy on him, and now she felt even more guilty because she had been with Jonathan the night before.

Sally's fantasies about Jonathan had begun almost as soon as he entered her school. She had once secretly hoped for a romance between her and Solomon, but she had always been afraid. She wanted a romance to occur between her and Jonathan, but she had envisioned something more uplifting. She certainly didn't want it to be something done behind Audra's back.

All week long she had been sensing that Audra was growing disenchanted with Jonathan. She felt certain that this whole idea about her observing him closely to look for evidence of something strange was Audra's way of validating her impending decision to have little or nothing to do with him. Because of some of the things Jonathan had asked her about Audra, and because of the attention he had paid to her during the week, Sally was convinced Jonathan was growing just as disenchanted with Audra. It confirmed her belief that he was really more interested in her. So when Jonathan invited her to the party and when he began to dance with her and ignore Audra, she thought it was all logical and good.

He wasn't even concerned about Audra's absence. After he and Sally stopped dancing, they met Paula at the punch bowl, but Jonathan didn't ask her where Audra was, even though it was clear that she was no longer in the gym. Paula gave him Audra's message, but all he did was shrug and go off to talk to some of his friends. For a while, she had thought he left the party, too; but then he suddenly reappeared and asked her to dance again.

She didn't know how many of those cups of punch she actually had drunk because some she finished and some she sipped and left on the tables. Just before the party ended, Jonathan invited her to go with him, Billy McDermott, and Christy Dobbs up to the Neversink Reservoir. They could park just off right of the dam and look out over the water.

Her initial response was "It's a cloudy night; it won't be so nice." The looks on Billy's and Christy's faces told her, even in her somewhat inebriated state, that that was of no importance and it was the height of stupidity to bring it up. Not wishing to appear totally unsophisticated in front of Jonathan, she laughed quickly and agreed to go. It wasn't until she was in the backseat of Billy's station wagon that she realized she hadn't called her parents. Her father was expecting her to call him to have him pick her up at the school.

But when Jonathan embraced her and kissed her, those thoughts evaporated. The events that followed happened so quickly she wasn't sure of the sequence. Jonathan's hands had been all over her body during the trip to the reservoir, but she had put up only token resistance. Her head was spinning from the spiked punch, and she was confused by her conflicting emotions. After all, a dream was coming true—she was with Jonathan.

Some time after they'd arrived at the reservoir, Billy and Christy took a blanket and left them alone in the wagon. Jonathan found a lever on the side of the seat and lowered the back so they could sprawl out. All the while she kept telling herself that she had to say or do something to end this before it became too late.

She had never gone this far with a boy, much less do the things that Jonathan urged her to do. The speed and intensity with which he came at her frightened her, and at one point she did begin to retreat. However, he didn't force himself on her; he became softer, more compassionate, and more gentle. After a while, she convinced herself that she wasn't resisting only him, she was resisting all her fantasies, and that was something she didn't want to do.

So she stopped pushing his hands away, and she no longer held back when she kissed him. She did not stop him from undoing her pants. She let it happen first inches at a time. After a point she thought it would be too late to retreat, but to her surprise that realization did not fill her with fear, but with an even greater excitement. In a moment, Jonathan was naked beside her. Intellectually she knew what to expect. She waited, thinking that what was about to happen was inevitable.

But nothing did. When he pressed against her, he was soft. His kisses grew shorter until he sat back. She wondered what she could be doing wrong. She couldn't see the expression on his face in the darkness, but he sounded angry when he spoke.

"You should have invited me into your house that night I walked you home, Sal," he said.

"What?"

He didn't say anything else. She heard him start to get dressed, so she did the same. Not long afterward Billy and Christy returned to the car, and they took her home. She apologized profusely to her parents for not calling them and for not telling them where she was going, and then she rushed to her bedroom, longing to be alone.

She crawled into bed and got under the covers quickly. Almost immediately Jonathan's words returned to her.

She sat up as if she had just heard them. When he had said them, she was so involved in her own feelings and what was happening to her that she hadn't really heard them. But now, reviewing it all, the words resounded and echoed in the darkness so vividly it was as though he were there with her. She even imagined she felt his breath against her ear.

"You should have invited me into your house that night I walked you home?" He never walked me home, she thought. Solomon. Solomon once walked me home.

What did Jonathan mean?

She could share the words and the experience only with Audra. Audra would understand her confusion, but Sally wondered if she would be angry because she had gone with Jonathan after Audra left sick. She might think I took an unfair advantage, even though she had grown disenchanted with him. She would have to take that chance.

Sally went to sleep intending to call Audra first thing in the morning and tell her everything, but her phone rang at eight o'clock in the morning. When Barbara Rosen told her what had happened to Audra the night before, she felt her face whiten. A little while afterward her father knocked on her door to tell her they had been called to bring her down to the police station.

"What's going on?" he asked. She felt sorry for the look of agitation on his face. His perfect daughter had betrayed him.

"I don't know, Daddy," she said. But almost immediately she started to cry. Her mother came in, and the two of them comforted her.

Later on, when she saw Jonathan at the police station and he didn't so much as acknowledge her, she had the most frightening feeling of all. It was as if she hadn't been with him the night before, as if it wasn't he with whom she had tried to make love. He had such a look of aloofness. He looked like a stranger.

It was as though she had really been with Solomon in the back of that car. Oh, Audra, she thought. Maybe you were right. There is something strange going on. I shouldn't have told him what you wanted me to do. She stared at him across the lobby. Who was he? She began to shudder, and the tears came again.

She couldn't explain it to the police, and she couldn't explain it to her parents. She was useless during the interrogation. They asked her all sorts of questions about Jonathan, but she found it nearly impossible to talk about him. It was even hard to pronounce his name, even though she suspected he had put the drug in Audra's drink. Everyone thought she was upset only because of Audra. She was glad to get out of there and go home.

Now she was taking the elevator up to Audra's room, feeling just as paranoid as her friend and wondering what it was they could say to each other to make things any easier.

Audra's mother and father were in her room, but after she entered, they said they were going down for coffee. Audra wouldn't let go of her mother's hand. Stephani had to coax her into it.

"Your friend's here. You can talk. She's been worried about you."

Stephani Lowe nodded at Sally, and Sally moved up closer.

"Hi, Audra."

To Sally, Audra looked small in the hospital bed. The drug seemed to have somehow diminished her. All but her eyes, that is. Her eyes were widened in what resembled a state of perpetual terror. She didn't smile when Sally said hello. She said hello, but she watched Sally move about her bed as if expecting her to do something threatening at any moment. It made Sally even more nervous.

"Here, take a seat beside her," Stephani Lowe said. She took a chair and brought it right up to the side of the bed. "We'll be right back. You two have a nice visit," she added. She winked at Sally, and then she and her husband left the room.

Sally put her hands on the metal sides that had been raised to keep Audra from getting off the bed, and for a long moment, the two friends just stared at each other.

"How are you feeling?"

"Why?"

"I just wanted to know if you're feeling any better?"

"I wasn't sick."

"I know."

"You know what they think happened to me?"

"Uh huh. The police have been questioning everyone about it," Sally said. "They called me in this morning."

"Did it happen to anyone else?"

"Not that I know of, no."

Audra nodded, confirming a thought.

"How did it happen to you, Audra? Do you remember?"

She turned away and looked up at the ceiling.

"The only one who gave me anything to drink was Jonathan," she said. Sally felt her spine turn into an icicle. The chill reached around her shoulders and ran down her arms, making her hands numb. Her fingers, still clutching the metal bars, began to ache as if dipped in a nearly frozen cup of water.

"I thought so," Sally said. "It's all my fault," she added in a whisper. Audra turned to her, even though she didn't hear the last statement.

"I keep expecting him to come here. Is he?"

"I don't think so. I don't know."

"Have you seen him?"

"Not since last night," she said.

"Good," Audra said. She looked away, her face softening. For a moment, Sally simply stared at her. Audra didn't fall asleep, but she looked like she was going into a daze.

"I've got to tell you something, Audra," Sally finally said. Audra did not turn back. "Are you listening?" Audra nodded. "I left the party with Jonathan." She waited a moment. At first she thought Audra hadn't heard her. Then Audra turned to her slowly. Her eyes weren't full of anger, but the look in them still frightened Sally.

"I knew you would."

"You knew I would?"

"I mean, I knew he would ask you to go with him. What happened?"

"We went to the reservoir," Sally said. She looked down quickly. When she looked up, she saw that Audra understood.

"Did you enjoy yourself?" she asked bitterly.

"Audra, nothing really happened. It was . . . the same as that time you were with Solomon."

"I don't believe you," Audra said.

"It's true. I wanted it to happen, but he . . . couldn't do it. Just like Solomon couldn't do it."

"You're lying. You did it with Jonathan."

"No. Honest, I didn't. Audra, I want to know something," Sally said, pressing herself closer. "Did you ever tell Jonathan that Solomon once walked me home?"

"Walked you home?"

"Yes, he . . . he wanted to come into my house, but I didn't invite him. I . . . I just didn't, and he never stopped teasing me about it."

"You never told me that," Audra said, pronouncing it more like an accusation.

"I was a little embarrassed. I don't know why I didn't tell you. I knew Solomon would tell you."

"He didn't. You're lying again. He never walked you home. You're making it up. You're making all this up," she added, her voice rising and taking on a shriller note.

"I'm not lying," Sally said, but Audra had started to sit up. "I've got to tell you something else," she said, looking down, but Audra was no longer listening.

"Who sent you here?"

"What do you mean?"

"Is he here?" she asked, and looked to the door.

"Who?"

"He's out there, isn't he? Waiting for the right moment."

"Who's waiting? Audra?"

"No," Audra said. She looked about the room wildly. "I don't want to see him."

"Audra?"

"NO," she shouted. She tried to push herself farther back in the bed. "NO!"

"What is it?" a nurse said, coming to the doorway.

"I don't know," Sally cried. She stood up and stepped away from the bed.

"HE'S HERE!" Audra shouted, looking at the nurse. Because the light in the room was dimmer than the light in the hall, the nurse's face was backlit and in some shadows. Audra started to swing her arms wildly before her. The nurse rushed to the bed.

"You'd better leave," she ordered, as she reached over the sides and started to restrain Audra. "She's having flashbacks," she muttered.

Sally rushed from the room. Another nurse came and then another. From what she could hear, she understood they were having a hard time restraining Audra. The shouting was terrifying because it didn't sound like Audra. Her voice was so shrill, and it was so incongruous for Audra, the most sensible and mature girl she knew, to be acting like this. Unable to take it any longer, she ran down the corridor. She didn't wait for the elevator. Instead she found the stairway and ran down the stairs until she was in the lobby.

Once there, she caught her breath. Her father was waiting in his car in the parking lot, but she didn't want him to see how disturbed she was. He hadn't been happy about her decision to visit Audra. She had had to practically beg him to take her. After she gathered herself together, she started out.

She was nearly halfway to her father's car when she saw him. At least, she thought it was he standing just in the shadows to the right of one of the pole lights at the end of the parking lot. He was standing there, staring up at the window of what would be Audra's hospital room.

She ran as fast as she could to the car and got in.

"What is it?" her father asked.

"Just go," she said.

"What?"

"Drive, Daddy. Please. Just go."

"What happened? Jesus," he said. He started the car and backed out of the parking spot. When they turned the corner and headed down the hospital driveway, she looked back at where she thought she had seen him.

It looked just like Jonathan.

Or Solomon.

Now there was no one there.

Maybe it was only my imagination, she thought. Maybe.

It was more like a hope.

"Jonathan's not going to school today," Martha said. "He doesn't feel well."

"Oh?" Joe said. He poured some cornflakes into a bowl and watched her prepare a cup of tea and some toast, which she was obviously going to bring up to Jonathan. "What's the problem?"

"He's getting a cold. It's best he stay home and rest."

"He seemed all right last night when you came back

from the mall. Maybe he shouldn't have left again to go bowling with Billy McDermott.''

"He felt all right then, and he wasn't out late," Martha said. "But I'll watch him." She put the tea and the toast on a tray and started out of the kitchen. After she left, he ate slowly, thoughtfully. The nervousness that he felt soon aborted his appetite, and he pushed his food away. He didn't even want to finish his coffee.

He waited awhile, but Martha didn't come back downstairs. Before he left for work, he shouted up to her. There was no reply, so he shouted again. She came to the top of the stairway and glared down at him with her hands on her hips.

"What are you yelling about?"

"I'm leaving."

"So?"

"I thought . . . you used to want to say good-bye."

"Oh, Joe. I'm taking Jonathan's temperature."

"Oh. I'll call you later," he said. She didn't reply. She turned away and went back to Jonathan's room. Joe stood there for a few moments and then left the house.

On his way to work, he permitted his imagination to have free rein. Usually he pulled away from these images and memories, but today he didn't want to resist them. He was too angry to deny them. All that was left was to accept the cause of that anger, which was something he was never prepared to do. He thought it might drive him mad.

Suppose Jonathan had some fever, he thought. She would have him strip, and she would take cool water and sponge him down. "There's nothing wrong with that," he muttered under his breath. He was entering into an argument with himself. It had happened many times before, but he had never permitted himself to lose. "Mothers do these things," he continued. "She had done it for Solomon when he was little and he was sick.''

But then he was fifteen and he was sick, and she was still doing it.

"Shut up," he told himself.

And you had gone by the room.

"No."

You didn't intend to look in . . . the door was slightly open.

"I didn't see anything unusual."

He was on his back, and she was bringing the sponge up the inside of his legs and . . .

"NO!" He brought the car to an abrupt halt and lowered his head to the steering wheel. "It wasn't anything; it was understandable; it could happen."

But it happened before. You know. You knew.

He sat back, his eyes closed, and shook his head.

It's happening now. Back at the house. Right now.

He shook his head more vigorously and brought his hands to his face. Then he lowered them slowly, finding the conclusion that he could accept.

"It's not her; it's him. He's taking advantage of her. She's still vulnerable. She's fragile; he knows. He's evil. He's dangerous. I can't permit him to stay. I've got to end it."

Right now it's happening again.

His heart was beating rapidly. He was falling into a terrible state of anxiety. He couldn't decide whether he should continue to the office or turn around. What would he do or say if he returned home? Where should he go now? How could he end it?

Drivers in cars coming up behind him began beeping their horns. He had stopped right in the middle of the highway. One passed him, the driver shouting angrily. An approaching car forced the second car to stop behind him, the driver leaning heavily on his horn.

Joe sat forward and accelerated again. He drove on, but continued staring ahead like one in a daze. When he arrived at the office, he barely spoke to anyone. He picked up the day's assignments, hoping that if he lost himself in his work, he would find some respite and escape from the images threatening to destroy his sanity.

But it was no good. His first job involved a Selectric III that wasn't printing properly. It required only a simple adjustment on the typewriter to bring it up to standard, but he sat there staring down at the keys as though he hadn't the faintest idea what to do. He nearly made things worse before he finally fixed it, and it took him twice the required time to do it.

Afterward, on his way to the next job, he tried to be logical about the problem. The objective, he told himself, is to get rid of Jonathan. The complication is Martha's attitude. She thinks he's a perfect child, full of potential that she is now helping to bring forth. The boy was too clever to do anything overt; consequently, it was difficult, if not impossible, for Joe to build a case against him. Anything he said to Martha now she interpreted solely as jealousy and cruelty. He had to find something concrete, something besides the computer files.

When he realized where he was heading for his next job, a possible solution occurred to him. Why did the Porters, Jonathan's previous foster parents who lived in Middletown, lock their bedroom door at night and eventually want to get rid of Jonathan? Maybe they would tell him something he could use to convince Martha that Jonathan wasn't all good. Of course, he could call Mrs. Posner at the agency and question her more about Jonathan's past, but that might get back to Martha, and he suspected that the head of the agency was so intent on finding homes for these children that she would leave out negative information. She was a bureaucrat only interested in making her job easier.

No, he thought, the best way to do this was to go visit the Porters himself; but when he stopped at a gas station and looked up the name Porter in the phone book, he found there were at least a dozen who lived in Middletown. His heart sank. Then he remembered that during one conversation about bike riding, Jonathan had mentioned a street, because, according to him, Mrs. Porter believed it was too busy a street to permit bike riding. He copied down all the addresses alongside the names, and when he reached Middletown, he went directly to the police station and found which address was closest to the street.

Congratulating himself on his logic and clear thinking, he set out for the residence of the correct Porters, Mr. and Mrs. Aaron Porter. He was encouraged by his ability to solve the problem. Surely this meant that he was up to the task, even though he was quite disturbed over the events taking place at his home. Minutes later, he arrived at the small Cape Cod–style house owned by the Porters. It was in what he considered a rather quiet, almost suburban neighborhood away from the city proper. Certainly there would be no difficulty about children riding their bikes here, he thought. This was no main thoroughfare. Jonathan had lied about it, but Joe wasn't surprised. If he had to, he would bring Martha to the street and prove the lie to her.

He would prove everything. This discovery, as simple and insignificant as it seemed, filled him with encouragement. The depression and anxiety that had taken hold of him this morning was in retreat. His old confidence was returning. He got out of his car quickly and crossed the sidewalk to the Porter house and pressed the door buzzer.

Moments later, the door opened, and he looked in through the screen door at a tall, middle-aged woman with apple-blossom white hair cut neatly at the base of her neck. She had a drawn, tired face with sad dark black eyes and a long, thin neck. Her collarbone was emphatically visible within the unbuttoned heavy cotton, light gray housecoat. She wore a pair of men's brown slippers with no socks. Her lips quivered before she spoke, as though it took great effort for her to pronounce her words.

"Yes?"

"Mrs. Porter?"

"Yes?"

"My name is Joe Stern. You don't know me, but—"

"What is it, Blossom?" a man asked from behind her. Joe saw no one in the little entranceway. Then Blossom Porter stepped to the side to turn around, and Joe saw Aaron Porter seated in a wheelchair.

Joe's heart sank. It was obvious why these people would give up a teenage foster child. Any teenager would be too much for them. They'd probably thought they could do it and then realized they couldn't. This was going to be a wasted trip. He felt like he should say he had made a mistake and just turn away and leave.

"I don't know, Aaron. I'm just finding out," Blossom said caustically. She turned back to him. "What can we do for you, Mr. Stern?"

He shook his head, and for a moment, he didn't speak. Aaron Porter wheeled himself closer to the door. His wife's face lightened as her eyes developed interest.

"You're the Porters who had a foster child, right?"

"Oh," Blossom Porter said. She brought her left hand to the collar of her housecoat and closed it.

"Who are you?" Aaron Porter demanded.

Joe looked down at what seemed to have once been a tall, powerful man. He had a stout upper body with very heavy shoulders and a wide neck. His chest strained the buttons on his flannel shirt. He had his sleeves rolled up to his elbows, revealing dark, hairy, muscular forearms. But even in the loosely fitted denim pants, his legs looked pathetic in comparison. Joe thought he could clearly make out the man's bony knees, and his ankles looked thin, almost underdeveloped.

However, the paraplegic had a rough, weathered face, the face of a man who worked in the outdoors. The lines in his face were deep like the facial lines of a fisherman's face, carved by the sharpness of constant sun and wind. He had a strong jawline and bright hazel-green eyes. His dark brown hair was only speckled here and there with gray hairs, and he wore it long and brushed back rather neatly. From the waist up, Aaron Porter looked strong and handsome, a candidate for television commercials set with the ocean or the mountains in the background.

In fact, Joe thought that Mrs. Porter looked older than her husband, despite his malady. Joe wondered if that couldn't be the result of having to care for an invalid.

"My name's Joe Stern," Joe repeated. "My wife, Martha, and I have taken in a foster child, too. I believe it's the same boy you had."

Neither of the Porters spoke for a moment. They stared at him with expectation, however. Joe struggled for the right words, now that he felt foolish for coming to this door. Aaron Porter wheeled himself back a few inches.

"Jonathan? Jonathan's living with you now?" he asked. Mrs. Porter released her grip on her housecoat collar and pressed the palms of her hands together as though she were about to offer a prayer.

"Yes," Joe said.

"God help you," Aaron Porter said, and Joe's face lit up. He had come to the right place after all.

15.

Joe entered the Porters' modest home and followed behind Aaron Porter as he wheeled himself into the living room. At Aaron's request, Blossom went to fetch some apple cider.

"My brother makes it himself," Aaron explained with some pride. "It's just starting to have a little kick to it."

"Thank you," Joe said. He didn't think it would be politic to refuse.

"Have a seat," Aaron said and Joe went to the blue-and-white-patterned Herculon couch. Aaron turned his wheelchair so he was facing him directly, then folded his hands on his lap and sat back.

Joe took a quick inventory of the room. Although the house was small, it didn't look to be the home of people on a restricted income. All the furniture was well maintained, the woodwork polished, the glass glistening. The knickknacks on the shelves and on the mantel above the small fireplace looked like valuable antiques and heirlooms. There was a rich-looking Persian oval rug on the floor and a rather good replication of a Remington on the wall across from him. Aaron Porter caught the look in his eye.

"That's an authentic Remington," he said. "Been in the family a long time."

"Really? Beautiful."

"I like paintings that depict real people in action. Don't go for these staged, postured shots," Aaron said. "What do you do, Joe?"

"I'm an IBM service technician."

"Don't say? Computers?"

"Oh, yes."

"Never even turned one on, but I guess they're like anything else—once you learn what they're about, it's no big deal."

"Exactly."

"How long has Jonathan been with you?" Aaron asked, his face tightening quickly.

"Not long. Less than a month, actually."

"It doesn't take long," Aaron said cryptically. Blossom entered the room with a pitcher of cider and some glasses on a tray. She set it down on the dark pine oval table and poured three glasses.

"Thank you," Joe said, taking a glass of cider. He sipped it quickly. "Wow, this is good."

"Thought you'd like it," Aaron said. "You're ever up around Hancock, stop at Michael Porter's Country Store."

"I'll remember that."

Blossom sat in the rocker to the right and stared at him. The intensity of her gaze made him uneasy.

"So?" Aaron said. "You want to know about our experience with Jonathan, is that it?"

"Yes."

"Did the agency send you over here?" Blossom asked.

"No. They don't know I've come. I tracked you down myself."

"Thought as much," Blossom said and smirked.

"Why is that, Mrs. Porter?"

"You can call me Blossom. Jonathan always did," she said. "Right from the start. Shoulda known something then. There wasn't any shyness in him."

"Shyness?" Aaron laughed without making a sound, his upper body shaking.

"They shoulda told us more about him, too," she said. "They just want to get rid of those kids as fast as they can."

"What's he doin' to you?" Aaron said. "Or should I ask, what's he done?"

"It's hard to say exactly."

"Uh huh," Blossom said. She started to rock in the chair.

"He's . . . like . . ."

"Like crazy, is what he is," Aaron said. "They shouldn't be shipping him around to innocent folks. They should be puttin' him in an institution."

"Why do you say that?"

Aaron looked at Blossom. She stopped rocking and sat forward.

"As you can see, Mr. Stern, my husband's an invalid. He wasn't always so."

"Jonathan didn't . . ."

"No. I have MS," Aaron said. "Multiple Sclerosis. It started slowly about four years ago, and it's finally reached this stage. Although, I don't doubt that kid could put someone in a wheelchair."

"My husband used to be the foreman at one of the bigger lumber companies here."

"And I did a lot of construction myself on the side," he said.

"I'm sorry."

"It's all right. We're living with it."

"Thing was," Blossom recounted, sitting back and rocking again, "we got to thinking we were doting too much on our problems. Our children are all grown and away. After Aaron got sicker, this house became very depressing for both of us."

"So, we thought we'd get involved with someone else's problems," Aaron said. "Friends of ours had taken in foster children and enjoyed the experience. Blossom was willing, even anxious, to do the same thing."

"And they sent us Jonathan," Blossom said. She stopped rocking and sat forward. Her eyes were cold, gray. Joe sensed the intensity of her anger and the battle to maintain self-restraint. "They thought we should have an older child, one who could be somewhat independent so it would be easier for us."

"In the beginning, I thought it was a wonderful idea. I got so I liked the kid, and I thought he liked me," Aaron said. "We both thought we had done the right thing then, didn't we, Blossom?"

"Yes, we did."

"What happened to change your minds?" Joe said, impatient for the resolution.

"What happened was kind of weird and sort of hard to explain, just like your situation, I imagine," Aaron said.

"The boy took on Aaron's problems," Blossom said quickly. She bit down on her lower lip and nodded as though her pronouncement had explained it all. Joe looked at Aaron, who was also nodding gently.

"I don't understand," Joe said. "What do you mean by Aaron's problems?"

"One day," Blossom related, leaning farther forward, "he got up in the morning and screamed. I ran into his room and found him on the floor."

"What was it?"

"He claimed his legs gave out from under him. For a few moments, I thought he was just joking. I was about to bawl him out for performing a sick joke, as a matter of fact, but he didn't laugh, and he didn't smile. He just struggled to get to his feet. When he did, he sat back on the bed, and I swear he was white as a sheet."

"What did you do?"

"I called Aaron in, and we decided he might have had a dizzy spell for some reason or another. He didn't want to go to a doctor. He just wanted to lay there for a while."

"She brought his breakfast to him," Aaron said. "He seemed to get better, so we forgot about it. But not long afterward it began."

"It began?"

"He means it started happening more often," Blossom said. "I called the agency and took him to a doctor. The doctor couldn't find anything wrong with him, so I brought him home, and he was fine for a few days. Then, one day, he claimed he couldn't get up again. I brought him his breakfast, and when he did get up that day, he hobbled about like Aaron used to do when he could still move about on his own."

"To tell you the truth," Aaron said, "I began to think the kid was just making fun of me. I have another wheelchair, you see, and one day . . ." He shook his head and smiled. "One day the kid was in it, wheeling himself about the house. I blasted him for mocking me, but he acted like I insulted him."

"Couldn't get him to stop imitating Aaron," Blossom said. "And when I tried, he became belligerent."

"He wanted her to treat him the way she treats me," Aaron said. "He was always making comparisons."

"He wouldn't go to the doctor again or to any other doctor. If I threatened to call the agency, he would be all right, and then some days he would be a worse invalid than Aaron. I'd be bringing him breakfast, lunch, and supper. I didn't know what to do. I thought maybe he does have a problem, and if so, I was being cruel threatening him like that, so I guess I put up with it longer than I should have."

"Incredible," Joe said.

"He was wearing her out," Aaron said. "We both felt he was getting very strange."

"I became frightened of him," Blossom said. "If I didn't believe him when he told me he was unable to get about, he would take on this look of vicious anger . . ." She looked at Aaron. "And with Aaron in a wheelchair, I just felt in danger. After he started doing other kinds of things, we made up our minds we were going to have to get rid of him."

"What other kinds of things did he do?"

"Of course, he denied it, but I know he did them. He stole Aaron's medicine. I couldn't find it when he needed it, and I had to go out and get replacements. He loosened the wheel on his chair. He denied it, but one day Aaron was wheeling himself along, and the wheel came right off. He took a spill. Could have been serious. It got so I didn't like leaving Aaron here alone with him. During the last week or so that he was with us, I'd lock our bedroom door at night."

"I understand," Joe said.

"Do you? We don't," Aaron said. "But we were happy when they came to take him away. I really thought he'd be going to some hospital for mentally ill kids."

"But you know what he did when they came?" Blossom asked.

"Yes, I think I do," Joe said.

"Oh, yeah, what?" Aaron said. He leaned forward in the wheelchair.

"He walked out of here like nothing was wrong with him and you people were the crazy ones."

"That's it," Blossom said. She sat back. "But I didn't care. At least we had gotten rid of him before something else happened. With someone as weird as that . . . you never know. I couldn't sleep, and when he got into that wheelchair, he'd come up behind me so quietly . . ."

"Good riddance is what I said," Aaron said.

"I'd like to say the same thing," Joe replied.

"What's stopping you?"

"My wife. She thinks he's wonderful. She doesn't see what a conniver he is, and how dangerous he could be. Do you think it might be possible for me to bring her around one day? I'll call first, and you can tell her your experiences. Maybe then—"

"Sure," Aaron said. "Be glad to."

"They should have told you more about it," Blossom said.

"Maybe they believed him," Joe said. The Porters were silent. "Maybe he told them you didn't know how to get out of the obligation once you had started, and he was too much for you. He's very bright and can be very charming."

"I know," Aaron said. "As I said, in the beginning I really liked the kid. He was very helpful around the house. Fixed a few things and learned fast."

"Aaron would spend time explaining this or that, and Jonathan would master it."

"Like a garage door opener?" Joe said.

"He told you, huh?"

"He fixed mine."

"How someone could be so wonderful at one time and then so weird at another . . ." Blossom mused, and shook her head. "Do you know I think he got to the point where he was even taking some of Aaron's medicine when he stole it."

"I believe it," Joe said. He looked at the glass of cider and then finished it quickly. "Well, I thank you for being honest and willing to talk to me."

"No problem," Aaron said. "And bring your missus around if you want."

"I will. I definitely will." Joe stood up. "I gotta get back to work. Thanks again." He started for the door. Blossom walked behind him, and Aaron wheeled himself to the living room entrance.

"One thing I came to believe after a while," Blossom offered as Joe opened the door.

"What's that?"

"He would do anything . . . anything to convince you he was who and what he thought he was. That was the weirdest part: He believed it himself!"

"I understand," Joe said. He looked back at Aaron. "Thank you."

"Get rid of him and fast," Aaron called out as Joe left the house.

He got into his car quickly. Despite the fact that he had

located what he now considered valuable allies in his battle to turn Martha against Jonathan, he couldn't help feeling nervous. His hands were actually shaking, so he clutched the steering wheel tightly to steady them.

What had he and Martha done?

They were like flies inviting a spider into their nest.

Martha wanted a boy who resembled and reminded her of Solomon. And here they had unknowingly found a schizophrenic who fed off other identities, who, with the hunger of a vampire, sought another personality, sucked out all of its characteristics, and absorbed them smoothly into himself until for some people he became nearly indistinguishable. Adding insult to injury, Martha encouraged it; but she didn't understand the dangers.

He cheered himself with the belief that he could now convince Martha of the dangers and the problems. She would understand, and they would send Jonathan away before it was too late. The Porters would help, and it would all come to an end. It would be like waking up before the nightmare really began.

Perhaps it was a premonition and not just a sense of déjà vu, but on the way home from work at the end of the day, Joe felt the same way he had felt that first day Jonathan had arrived and he was returning home. He was just as nervous, just as reluctant to make the turns and increase speed. He was not eager to get home quickly. He knew what awaited him and what he had to do. Conflicts with people had never been something he enjoyed.

If only this were a matter of fixing a part in a machine, he thought. But it wasn't, and no delay, no matter what its length, would make it any easier. As soon as he drove into his driveway, he pressed the button on his garage door opener, watched it go up, and drove in. When he entered the house, he was surprised at how quiet it was. There were some delicious aromas coming from the kitchen. Martha had a roast in the oven. She was baking sweet potatoes, and she had made a chocolate cake. His stomach rumbled in anticipation.

"Hi, Joe," she said when he stepped into the kitchen doorway.

"Where's Jonathan?" he asked. He might as well get right to it, he thought.

"He's over at Arthur Griff's going over homework. He's much, much better. He should be home any moment. Why don't you go up and clean up for dinner? You look so funny. Your hair is a mess."

He thought for a moment. This wasn't the time to tell her about the Porters, and besides, he had an opportunity to do something else.

"You're right," he said. "Be right down."

He went upstairs quickly and entered Jonathan's room. The computer looked more threatening than ever. He couldn't believe how something he dealt with nearly every day had suddenly become a terrifying thing. For a moment, he had the impression it would do something to prevent him from shutting the door to the dead. Perhaps it would electrify him the moment he touched it.

He approached it slowly and turned it on, watching anxiously as the monitor lit up. The screen glowed like a giant pupilless eye. He hesitated and then called for the menu. The commands at the bottom of the screen provided the courses of action. He entered the password and then, without hesitation, he ordered the computer to delete the files. As it was programmed to do, it asked him if deletion was indeed what he wanted. He tapped the Y key, and the files disappeared.

It was as if his son had been sucked back into his grave. Joe's heart was beating so hard, he thought it would thump through his chest. He took a deep breath. The computer returned to what it always was. Perhaps it was a marvel of science, but every part of it was easily understood. For him, there was no more. Solomon could no longer reach Jonathan, and Jonathan no longer had a script to follow. Perhaps without it, he would fall back on his real personality.

In any case, Joe was happy he had taken the first step. The rest would follow easily, he thought. Martha would soon be made to understand, the boy would go, and the nightmares would come to an end.

He heard the front door open and recognized Jonathan's voice. Quickly he shut down the computer and left the room. He went to the bathroom and washed up and brushed his hair. He heard Jonathan go into his room and then go back downstairs. Not long afterward Martha sent Jonathan to call up to him.

"HEY," Jonathan called from the bottom of the stair-way. "HOW MUCH LONGER UNTIL YOU'RE COM-ING DOWN? I CAN'T TAKE THE TEMPTING ODORS."

Joe heard Martha laugh.

"COMING."

He walked down the stairs, pausing at Jonathan's open doorway to contemplate the computer once again. It looked so innocuous to him now that he chastised himself for ever having those weird thoughts. How could the dead come to the living or the living go to the dead through such a mechanical thing? What was he thinking of—a high-tech séance? The idea made him smile.

Sure, he told himself as he walked on, you smile now but you should have seen yourself before you deleted those files. And what about those late nights when you awoke and heard the computer keyboard going? Maybe every night the resurrected spirit of Solomon sat there and tapped out new information, new commands, new madness, for Jonathan to follow. And Jonathan, schizophrenic and ea-ger, followed it all . . . right down to the murder of that Pedersen boy.

Who would believe these things? he asked himself. Certainly not Martha and certainly not anyone on the outside. It was better to talk only about the concrete facts—what the Porters told him. Stick to that. It was his only hope for winning Martha over and getting her to see the truth.

Jonathan was already seated at the dinner table and eating his salad. He was wearing Solomon's dark blue wool robe. For a moment, Joe was unable to speak. He looked so much like his dead son.

"Martha says you feel a lot better," he said, taking his seat.

"Yeah. The pills help." He looked up at Martha after he replied, and she smiled.

"Oh."

"How was your day?"

"It was a typical day," he said.

"Don't be afraid to talk about your work, Joe," Martha said.

"There's nothing special to talk about. It was a typical day," he repeated. He caught the look between her and Jonathan. It was almost as if they knew where he had gone. He decided he would concentrate on eating.

Martha and Jonathan excluded him from their conversation anyway. Neither directed any questions or comments at him. They talked about the food; they talked about Jonathan's homework. They even talked about an afternoon soap opera Joe gathered they had watched together.

As soon as the dinner ended, Jonathan excused himself to go up and finish his homework.

"No sense falling behind just because I was sick one day," he said. "Most kids use sickness as a crutch or a way to avoid responsibilities," he added, and left. Martha smiled and shook her head after him.

"Solomon, almost word for word. Remember? He had the same viewpoint."

"I remember, only I don't think it's such a coincidence," Joe said.

"What do you mean?" Martha asked. Joe saw the way the skin tightened at the sides of her eyes. Her shoulders came back as she straightened her posture defensively.

"Martha, I did more than just work today. I visited some people."

"What people?"

"The Porters."

"The Porters?" She blinked rapidly. "What Porters? We don't know any Porters."

"You know what Porters. The people who were Jonathan's former foster parents."

"Those people?" She grimaced. "You visited them? Whatever for?"

"I wanted to hear their side of it . . . why, for instance, Mrs. Porter felt she had to lock her bedroom door at night."

"A neurotic. Jonathan's told me all about them."

"No, she's not a neurotic. She had good reason to lock that door, Martha."

"What are you saying? They made up things about Jonathan, and you believed them?" Her voice started to take on a shrill note. Joe bit his lower lip and looked down. He wanted to keep things calm and logical. It was the only way.

"I thought we should know all we can about the boy," he said softly. "There's nothing wrong with that, is there, Martha?"

"We learned all we had to from Mrs. Posner at the agency."

"They didn't tell us everything. Perhaps they don't know everything."

"Oh, but the Porters do. I see."

"Listen, listen," he said. He reached across the table to take her hand, but she pulled away quickly. "All I'm asking is you have an open mind and listen. Will you do that?"

"Listen to what?"

"To what I have to tell you."

"If it's what they told you, I don't want to hear it," she said, and got up abruptly. She started to take the dishes to the sink.

"Martha, you've got to listen," Joe said. She turned her

back on him. "Martha. If you don't listen, then I'll have to go to the agency myself."

She spun around.

"You wouldn't dare. Why would you do that?"

"It has to be done. Things have to be clarified, and questions have to be answered."

"What questions? What are you talking about? From where did you get these ideas?"

"Martha, I think Jonathan's . . . unstable."

"What?" She smiled widely. Then she threw her head back and laughed. "That boy is unstable? An A average ever since he entered the school. Making friends so fast it can spin your head. All kinds of girls after him . . . a help around the house, polite, eager, clean . . . he's unstable?"

"Martha, you don't understand. You're blind to some things. You've got to—"

"I don't want to hear anymore, Joe. And God help you if you go to the agency and lead them to believe we are unhappy with Jonathan."

"I won't if you come with me to the Porters tomorrow and hear what they've got to say," he said.

"I don't need to talk to other people to know what kind of a boy Jonathan is, and I'm disappointed in you, Joe, that you went there. It's a betrayal. You've betrayed both of us."

"How have I betrayed us?"

"Not you and me," she said. "Jonathan and me."

He didn't speak. He stared at her, his face reddening quickly.

"You're not seeing clearly anymore," he whispered.

"I see very clearly. Actually, I'm disappointed at what you've done, but I'm not surprised. I should have expected it," she added, and looked around the kitchen. She nodded as she did so. "I should have expected it," she repeated, and returned to her dishes. He watched her work for a few minutes and then got up and walked out with his head lowered, his shoulders drawn up.

He went into the living room, but he didn't turn on the television set, nor did he start to read any of his trade magazines. He simply sat in his chair thinking. Not long afterward Martha came by. She stopped in the doorway and looked in at him.

"You gave me a headache, you know that," she said. "I was feeling so good, and you gave me a headache."

"Martha, you've got to listen to me. You've got to come with me to the Porters."

"I can't believe you're still saying that."

"If you'd heard what they told me, you'd understand why."

"Don't talk to me," she said. "Don't talk to me until you apologize for what you've done." She turned away.

"Martha."

She didn't answer. She went upstairs and left him alone. He didn't feel like watching television, and he didn't want to go up and argue with her in the bedroom. Instead he went out to the garage to straighten up some things and try to think of a solution.

He decided that maybe he would go to see Mrs. Posner at the agency and tell her everything. He would demand she have the boy examined psychiatrically, and that would bring it to an end. He had to do this now, even though it could create a great deal of animosity between him and Martha.

Buoyed by his decision to take a serious action regardless of the consequences, he went back into the house. He watched television until he got tired and then decided he would go up to bed and do some reading. He expected Martha would either pretend to be asleep or simply sulk.

Before heading upstairs, however, he realized that he hadn't closed the garage door and went back out to do it. Just as he hit the button that lowered the door, the garage light came on automatically as it always did, only this time something caught his eye.

Below Solomon's bike that hung on the wall, there was

a small chest for the bike accessories and tools. What he saw was just peeking out from under the chest lid. He went to it and opened the lid all the way to look in and confirm that it was what he thought it was.

The thick rope, similar to the rope Solomon had used that fatal Thursday, was coiled like a long, sleeping snake. The noose had already been tied on one end.

"Good God," Joe muttered. He seized it and rolled it up quickly. He put it in a plastic garbage bag and went outside to put it right in the can, but then thought again. He might need this as evidence after he went to see Mrs. Posner at the agency. He decided to take the bag back and hide it in the garage.

He had almost been too late in deleting those files and in going to the Porters. Perhaps he should show the rope to Martha, he thought. No, he thought. It would be too brutal. And besides, the way she was behaving and defending Jonathan now, she might accuse him of putting the rope there.

He started up the stairs again, but when he reached the landing, he heard voices coming from his bedroom and realized that Jonathan was in there with Martha. He walked softly to the partially opened doorway and peered in. Jonathan was lying beside her in their bed, just the way Solomon used to lie there, and they were talking softly.

He felt himself grow infuriated. He opened the door completely and stepped into the bedroom. They stopped talking, and Martha looked up at him.

"You'd better go back to your room now, Jonathan," she said.

"Sure. Good night." He slipped off the bed. Joe stepped aside as he approached. " 'Night, Joe," he said. As he passed, Joe thought he caught an arrogant look in his eyes.

When he turned back to Martha, he saw that she had already closed her eyes and pressed her face to the pillow. He said nothing. He went to the bathroom and then went to bed. He didn't bother to read. He wanted the darkness.

For a long time, he lay there staring into the darkness. Tonight he would not awaken and hear any computer keys being tapped, he thought. He had put his son back to sleep. He wished he could wake Martha and tell her about this and get her to understand what had been happening and what had to be done.

In a real sense, Solomon had returned to her through the computer and through Jonathan. He couldn't blame her for not wanting to end it. Thinking back to Jonathan's arrival, he recalled that he himself had had a longing for it all to succeed. It wasn't only Martha who'd created the environment for this to happen; he had to bear his share of the blame.

The difference was he was able to recognize it and end it. She was too fragile. When he looked over at her now and saw her sleeping so softly, he felt a great pain in his heart for the pain he knew she would soon experience.

You're going to lose your son a second time, Martha dearest, but he must go back to the dead. He wanted to reach over and kiss her and begin to comfort her now, but he knew that had to wait.

One of the most frightening horror scenes he could ever recall was in a vampire movie he had seen as a teenager. A father was confronted by his now-vampire son, who he'd thought was dead. He didn't see what he had become. He wanted to welcome him back, and his vampire son took advantage of that love and that pain.

Neither Solomon nor Jonathan will do that to Martha or me now, he thought. When I stripped the computer of those files, I drove a stake through their hearts.

16.

Joe must be purged of Solomon's spirit, Martha thought. The idea seemed so right to her now. She didn't like being cruel to him, but it was something she believed had to be done for his own good as well as for hers and also for Jonathan's own good, too.

She loved Joe. There was never a time when she didn't. It was just that he was so independent, so self-reliant. Right from the start, he could easily lose himself in his own interests and even forget she was in the same room. Before Solomon had been born, she enjoyed looking after Joe, but he didn't seem to appreciate her loving attention as much as Solomon did, and as much as Jonathan now did. She supposed it was only natural for children to be attached to and dependent upon mothers more than husbands were attached to and dependent upon their wives.

She tried to interest herself in Joe's work, but whenever he talked to her about the things he was doing, his conversation was filled with so much technical language, she quickly grew bored. He filled the house with these dull trade magazines and papers. One looked just like the other. She had to confess it simply amazed her how someone could get so excited about machines anyway, espe-

273

cially computers. There was nothing attractive about them and nothing dramatic.

But he was a gentle person, and she knew he would do anything to make her happy. He worked hard to give her a nice home and the things she wanted. There was never an argument about the money she spent, whether it was money spent on herself or on Solomon.

After Solomon was born, there were times when she thought she was neglecting Joe, but during Solomon's early years, he didn't seem to mind. If anything, she loved him more for his understanding and his willingness to sacrifice.

She'd always thought Joe was a handsome man. True, he wasn't as outgoing and as dynamic as, say, Kevin Baker, but he was attractive in his quiet way, even though being attractive was not a major concern for him. He didn't worry about fashions. Why, he would wear the same shoes out to dinner that he had worn to work if she didn't put up a stink about it.

Joe was a kindhearted man, and that made him vulnerable to Solomon when Solomon was alive and even more so now, she thought. What has to be done has to be done. It's going to be like a surgeon cutting into healthy flesh to get at the sickness. I'm going to have to be cruel to be kind, she concluded.

She began the next morning by not making him his breakfast. She laid out Jonathan's things but ignored his. He didn't say anything, but she knew he was hurt. He got his own bowl, found his cereals, made his own coffee, and ate silently. She didn't say a word to him. He left before Jonathan did, but she didn't respond when he said good-bye.

Jonathan sensed the change in her relationship with Joe immediately, but wise young man that he was, he said nothing while Joe was still home. After Joe left, he asked her about it.

"Does it have anything to do with me?"

"No," she said. "It's husband-wife problems."

"Oh. Is there anything I can do to help?"

"Dear Jonathan," she said. She kissed him on the forehead. "No, this is something Joe and I have to work out. Don't you worry yourself about it. You go off to school and do well."

He nodded, but she saw how disturbed he was and she only wished that Joe could see his concern. Then he would realize that the stories the Porters had created were all false. Then he would realize how necessary it was for him to work harder at resisting the urge to be critical of the boy.

All day she expected Solomon's spiritual appearance. Eager to avoid it, she showered, dressed quickly, and went out to do her grocery shopping. She met Sally Cirillo and Sandy Miller at the market. She hadn't seen or heard from either of her two friends for a while, so she was eager to talk with them. But both women seemed aloof and uninterested. She even had the feeling they were afraid of being seen with her. On the way home, she thought it might have something to do with the incident at the school party and the subsequent police investigation. Both women had children in high school. She realized they hadn't asked one question about Jonathan.

Fools, she thought. Simpleminded, vapid fools. So much for friendship. It occurred to her that she hadn't even heard from Judy Isaacs or Mindy Baker. Common decency should have dictated their concern for her. How did they think she felt about being dragged down to the police station just because that girl took drugs? She made up her mind that when it was over and the truth was out, she would give them all a piece of her mind.

She put her food away quickly and went upstairs to straighten out the master bedroom. Afterward she made herself a light lunch consisting of cottage cheese and fruit and then went into the living room to watch a soap opera.

Every once in a while she looked up at the doorway, expecting to see Solomon, but he didn't appear.

In fact, a strange thing happened. When she tried to envision him, she kept envisioning Jonathan, and when she recalled him speaking, she heard him speaking in Jonathan's voice. Even when she got up and looked closely at Solomon's picture on the mantel, she saw Jonathan's face and not his in the photograph.

Oddly, it didn't bother her. It seemed so natural that she accepted it. Maybe what she had suspected would happen had happened. Solomon had given up and gone back to his grave. Jonathan was too strong for him. The struggle was over. Perhaps Joe would return to himself, and he would no longer say terrible things about Jonathan. Maybe her anger and her silent treatment had already succeeded, and Joe, more concerned with her love and affection, had already purged himself of Solomon's influence.

Her thoughts were interrupted by the ringing of the phone. She half expected it would be Joe calling to apologize, but it was the school nurse calling to tell her that Jonathan had come to her office complaining of headaches.

"I should have kept him home one more day," Martha said. "But he was so worried about falling behind in his work. I'll be right there to pick him up."

During the drive to the school, she experienced déjà vu and recalled that shortly before his suicide, Solomon had complained about headaches. Twice during the two weeks or so before his death, the nurse had called for her to fetch him. Sinus tablets had seemed to help, so they hadn't taken him to the doctor.

Jonathan did look like he was suffering from similar symptoms. On the way home, she stopped at the drugstore and bought him some of those tablets. She gave him two, and he went up to bed. After he got in under the blanket, she massaged his temples, just the way she had massaged Solomon's. He said he felt better but wanted to sleep.

All of it helped just the way it had helped Solomon, because two hours later, he was up and around, the headache gone. Joe called to tell her he was going to be delayed on a job in Ellenville. She was polite, but not warm. She told herself she couldn't be warm until Joe offered some apology or indicated some remorse.

She and Jonathan had a quiet meal together. It reminded her of the many times she and Solomon ate dinner without Joe because Joe was held up on a job. Just like some of those other times, she found herself doing most of the talking. She did take note that Jonathan was quieter than usual. She attributed his melancholy mood to his sinus condition, which returned a little while after dinner. She gave him two more tablets, and he went up to his room.

It was close to seven before Joe got home. She had warmed up his food and expected to serve it to him, saying only the things she had to say. But when she looked at his face, she knew she would be unable to keep quiet. She sensed that something terrible was about to happen.

"What is it?"

"Where's Jonathan?"

"He's upstairs. I told you on the phone, he got sick again today. The food's getting cold."

"Forget the food. Just sit down." She didn't move. "Sit down, Martha," he commanded. She put the pot back on the stove and took a seat at the table.

"What is it?"

"I didn't have extra work to do," he began. He came farther into the kitchen. "I went to see Mrs. Posner."

She gasped and brought her hand to her mouth.

"I told her about the Porters, and she and I went to see them. She agrees now that the boy needs psychiatric help."

"No." Martha shook her head. Her eyes filled with tears.

"The agency has authority here. They have a responsibility to the child and to people serving as foster parents.

You've got to be strong, Martha. You've got to be strong for him as well as for us. You don't want him to hurt himself, do you?"

She shook her head. He went to her and put his hand on her shoulder. He saw the pain in her eyes, and his heart went out to her.

"I'm tired," she said. "Very tired."

"Go upstairs and take a little rest. I'll eat and clean up."

She nodded and stood up. He embraced her.

"You must believe that what I've done, I've done to help everyone. It's not out of any kind of jealousy, believe me. Please, believe me," he said.

She nodded. She looked defeated, exhausted.

"I'm tired," she repeated, and then she started out of the kitchen. "I'll just check on Jonathan and then go lay down."

"Don't say anything to him about tomorrow. Mrs. Posner is going to come early in the morning. She'll handle it. It's better that way," he added. She bit down gently on her lower lip and nodded. He watched her leave the kitchen, and then he served himself the food.

Afterward he tried to relax alone in the living room but found that the tension and strain had taken their toll on him as well. He decided he would go up and read in bed until he felt sleepy enough to fall asleep.

Jonathan's room light was on, and the door was closed. He stood by it, listening, for a few moments. There were no sounds. The boy was probably reading, he thought. At least, he wasn't reading Solomon's computer files.

Joe had half expected Jonathan would come out and seek his help to resurrect those files. Surely he didn't suspect that Joe had erased them. He didn't know Joe had found the password to make entry in the first place. Of course, Jonathan wouldn't want Joe to know he had broken into Solomon's files, but he thought the boy might ask him some general questions to see if he could figure out what was wrong with the computer.

When he entered his bedroom, Joe found Martha fast asleep. He saw from the open pill bottle beside her that she had taken a sedative. She didn't even hear him enter the room. He washed up and dressed for bed. Then he put on his small lamp light and read for nearly two hours.

Every once in a while he would stop reading and think about what had happened and what he had done. He went over and over the recent events, confirming in his own mind that he had done the right things. He felt confident, at least, that he had forestalled what could be a most tragic ending—Jonathan's committing suicide. He told himself he had prevented the horror of that possibility when he'd wiped out the computer files.

Maybe it didn't matter that he had removed the files: he hadn't removed them from Jonathan's memory, too, had he? Maybe the boy was lying there in the next room, remembering.

Joe thought his own constant rehashing of all this would drive him mad. He kept returning to his reading in hope that it would give him relief. Make yourself tired, he thought. Get so you can't think anymore. Stop this worrying. Shut off the echo chamber. You dumped the files. The computer lost its hold on the boy. You've done the right things. Everything's going to be all right.

The chanting in his own mind had become like an evening prayer: you've done the right things. Relax. You've shut down that computer. Solomon's words are gone.

He forced himself to concentrate on his reading, and when he didn't absorb a line, he went back and reread until he did. This was the only way to prevent himself from thinking. Martha barely stirred, and he heard no sounds coming from Jonathan's room.

Finally tired enough, he put out his light and went to sleep himself. Sometime during the middle of the night, he thought he heard the sound of the computer keyboard, but when he opened his eyes and listened, he heard nothing.

Just a dream, he thought. Soon even those dreams will end. I ended them when I cleared the computer of Solomon's words. That realization comforted him, and he fell asleep again rather quickly.

He awoke abruptly at sunrise. The rays threaded through the venetian blinds and merged on the foot of his bed. Martha was still in a deep sleep. When he saw how early it was, he thought he would just try to sleep some more, but for some reason he couldn't keep his eyes closed.

All the events of the day before seemed like a dream now. He seized on them like someone who didn't want to lose the dream, however. After all, he had taken the right steps. He had ended the hold that computer had on the boy. It was all right to wake up and face the day. It wasn't going to be as bad as it could have been. Thank God he had been decisive about what had to be done. Thank God that computer didn't mesmerize him the way it had mesmerized Jonathan.

He got out of bed and took a shower, expecting the noise would wake Martha. He was surprised that she was sleeping this long anyway. She was usually an early riser, especially when she had something on her mind. Surely she would want to be up early to prepare what in her mind would be Jonathan's last breakfast, he thought.

He went to the bed to check her. She was breathing regularly, but she was in an extraordinarily deep sleep. He looked at the bottle of pills. A hot flash came over him. How many of these pills had she taken last night? She could easily have been on the verge of an overdose. Why hadn't he checked it out last night?

He decided to wake her. He shook her shoulders.

"Martha. Martha, wake up. Martha."

She groaned, but she didn't open her eyes.

"Martha." He shook her harder. Her eyelids fluttered, but she didn't open them. "Damn. Martha." He got up quickly and went to the bathroom to get a cold, wet washcloth, which he then placed on her forehead. He shook her again. This time her eyes fluttered and opened slightly.

"Martha, you've got to get up. I think you've taken too many of those sedatives. Martha."

She groaned and turned over in bed. He was going to have to physically lift her out of it and carry her to the shower, he thought. He went into the bathroom and started the shower, adjusting the water first so it would be easy to just bring her to it. Then he started back to the bed.

Something made him hesitate before he crossed to it. Why hadn't he realized what was going on with her last night? How could he be so oblivious of it? If he overlooked that . . . no, he thought, I've done all the right things. Everything's going to be all right; we're all going to be all right. I stopped it; I ended it. This is just a little thing, her taking too many pills. It doesn't mean anything.

He bit down on his lower lip and clenched his hands into tight fists, beating back all contrary thoughts. But he couldn't hold them back for long. He felt like crying. His chest heaved, and his stomach ached from the tension.

Like one being forced to turn his head against his will, he looked at the nearly closed venetian blinds and then he looked back at Martha. His heart skipped a beat.

"No," he said aloud. "Can't be. I did all the right things. It's going to be all right; it's going to be all right."

He shook his head as though Martha had spoken. She didn't move. The shower was pounding against the tile in the stall. The sun was rising faster. Darkness was being washed out of the room. Reality was insisting on being recognized. All dreams and hopes were being returned to the deeper recesses of the mind. He had to go to the window.

He opened the venetian blinds completely and looked down. For a moment, he was unable to move. It seemed as if all the blood in his body had sunk to his feet, turning them into cast iron. He thought that when he looked down at himself, he would see himself standing in a red pool.

Jonathan dangled from the same tree. The early morning wind made the strands of his hair dance over his forehead. Incredibly, his head was up, and he was looking straight at their bedroom window. His eyes were open; he wore a look of accusation.

Joe shook his head. He put his hands over his eyes and pressed his fingers against them. Surely this was just a memory. He was reliving Solomon's death. When he opened his eyes again, the mirage would be gone.

But it wasn't. Jonathan had killed himself.

Or, Solomon had killed him.

"NO," Joe screamed. He turned from the window. Martha groaned, and when he realized what she would do once she saw this, he panicked.

He ran out of the bedroom and down the stairs as quickly as he could. It took him moments to go out and around the house. When he reached the boy, he stopped and looked up furiously. The boy's face was white. His hands were frozen in rigor mortis. He hadn't just done this. Sometime during the night, he had sneaked out of the house.

Joe recognized the rope. A chill rippled up his spine. Somehow the boy had found where Joe had hidden it, or . . . Solomon found it for him.

"WHY?" he screamed at the corpse. "I WAS GET-TING YOU OUT OF HERE, GETTING YOU HELP. WHY?"

And suddenly he realized that was why. Solomon knew Jonathan was about to escape. Joe had cut out the files. But then, how had Solomon reached him again?

Joe spun around as though Solomon were there.

"WHERE ARE YOU?" he screamed. "WHERE ARE YOU?"

There was only the sound of the morning wind weaving its way through the surrounding trees and bushes. Jonathan's body turned a little to the right and then swung back a little to the left. It was as though Solomon were doing it.

Joe backed away, shaking his head. Then he turned and ran back into the house, fleeing from both the sight of Jonathan's corpse and the fear of Solomon's spirit. He rushed up the stairs like a lunatic. He needed Martha; he needed someone.

But he stopped at the opened door to Jonathan's room. The computer was on. The lit monitor glared out at him defiantly. Why was it on? What could Jonathan have done with it after he had deleted those files? Had he heard the keys going last night after all? It hadn't been a dream?

He stepped into the room and slowly approached the computer. The monitor was displaying the menu. His eyes followed the lines down the list of files and stopped when he saw them.

"NO!" he screamed, and stepped back. "IT CAN'T BE."

The files were back!

Either Jonathan had entered them again from memory or . . . Solomon had returned to the computer.

In any case, the words and the thoughts were there again, and Jonathan had followed them to the end, just as Solomon had done.

Joe raised his fists and brought them down as hard as he could on the top of the monitor. The force shook the instrument. He struck it again and again and again until the light went out. Then he lifted it from the table and threw it to the floor. The glass smashed as the monitor bounced into the wall.

Exhausted, tears streaming down his face, Joe fled the room. When he returned to his bedroom, he found that Martha had dragged herself out of bed. She had made her way to the window and looked out. Then she had collapsed on the floor in front of it. He went to her and took her into his arms, holding her body and rocking back and forth. He brushed back her hair from her face and kissed her cheeks.

It's over; it's all over, he thought. It was his only thought until Mrs. Posner arrived and found them both still on the floor of the bedroom.

17.

Spring came early. Joe was happy to see the snow and ice go. The winter had been unusually depressing. He had gotten so angry about the weather that he took to keeping track of the sunny days. At the end of January and at the end of February, he reviewed his records as if to prove a point to someone.

Maybe he did it because whenever he visited Martha, their discussions began with the weather. He would go on and on about it in great detail, and then they would sit quietly, listening to the silence for a while.

Everyone said she was doing so well. Just after spring had officially begun, she did seem to blossom. Her face took on more color; her eyes were brighter. He knew how fond she was of spring, how she liked to get out and start planting her flowers. It was important to her that she start things growing again.

Their conversations began to liven up. He became very optimistic. The doctor told him she was talking more and more about home and about the things she wanted to do. Then one day when he arrived, she appeared to have regressed. She wouldn't come out of her room. She sat by the window staring out at the grounds around the hospital, and she wouldn't answer his questions.

He found out that a teenage boy had come to visit a patient and mistakenly come to her room. When Joe spoke to the doctor, the doctor told him to be patient.

"Let her deal with it. She has to come to terms with the past in her own way now. We've done all we can."

"She won't," Joe said.

"Maybe not, but we've got to give her some more time."

Joe couldn't help being impatient. The house was filled with too many echoes. He tried to get rid of them in his own way. One afternoon, he went into the backyard and cut down the tree. He spent days hacking away at the stump until he was able to cover the spot with fresh dirt. He knew it was foolish to take out his frustration on the tree. The tree's only fault was being there. What if Solomon would have hanged himself from the garage roof, he thought, would he have ripped down the garage?

He realized it was a matter of trying to escape from the past. He got everything associated with Jonathan out of the house. He gave the bike to the police department and told them to offer it to a deserving poor family.

But none of this ended the loneliness or drove away the images. All it did was provide less opportunity for the stimulation of a particular memory. As usual, he buried himself in his work; but that didn't solve the problem.

The problem was he missed Martha. He missed the sound of her laughter, the scent of her hair, the look in her eyes, and the warmth of her body beside his.

One day after she had gone into this regression, he came to her and told her just that.

"I know," he began, "that it's been a long time since I told you how much I love you, but I need you to know that."

She continued to look out, her back to him.

"I can't take it anymore, Martha. It's hard for me, too. I know you're going through terrible pain, and I know how guilty you feel, but you've got to come back. I need you. I always needed you . . . even more than they did.''

He brought his hands to his face and pressed his palms hard into his cheeks.

"There aren't any· more words, Martha. The doctors have said all the words. Words don't matter anymore. Feelings matter. Actions matter. I want to walk with you in the woods now that the leaves are back and you can smell the earth coming alive. I want to hold your hand and listen to you laugh. I want us to start over somewhere, somehow. I want it to be different. I want us to care more about each other than we care about anything else. I promise to hold you and to love you more than you could ever know.''

She lowered her head, but she didn't turn to him.

"Martha, the truth is I'm scared . . . not of ghosts . . . not even of memories . . . I'm just scared of being alone forever." He waited and then stood up.

"Joe," she said.

"Yes?"

"He's dead."

"He's dead, Martha. He's not coming back anymore, not as another boy, not as a ghost, nothing.''

"I don't hear his voice anymore.''

"That's good, Martha.''

She turned to him.

"But now I'm scared, too, scared of the silence.''

"It won't be silent when you come home.''

"I want to come home, Joe.''

"Thank God,'' he sighed, and he went to her. He embraced her, and he kissed her.

She did come home, and she looked out at where the tree had been. She didn't say anything about its disappearance, but he could see she was grateful for it.

It was hard at first. Some nights they fell asleep wrapped in each other's arms. Sounds stirred them. Shadows had to

be wiped away with brighter lights. The bright sun of
summer was a welcomed sight.

They spent almost every available moment together.
They took their walks; they took rides and visited relatives. They went on a vacation to Cape Cod and fell in
love over again. They spent more money on themselves,
buying themselves new clothing and a new car.

And then one August day, they went to the cemetery.
They held tightly to each other and prayed at Solomon's
grave. Martha prayed for forgiveness; Joe prayed for
understanding.

It was odd, but she never talked about Jonathan. It was
as if he had never come to their house. His time with them
had lost its separate identity for Martha. Joe thought that in
a strange and wonderful way, Solomon had absorbed him.
He thought that was as it should be.

And then at the age of thirty-nine, Martha became pregnant again. After the doctor had confirmed it, neither she
nor Joe knew what to say. The doctor had no ready
explanation as to why she had failed to become pregnant
during the earlier years and suddenly did now. They went
home to ponder it.

The first thought was she should have an abortion.
Perhaps it was too late to have children.

Both of them knew what the real fears were, but neither
said anything about them.

The days passed, and Martha announced her intention to
have the child. Joe didn't oppose it, even though he was
quietly terrified. He had nightmares about Solomon's second return. Martha had become pregnant in a supernatural
way. In his dreams, the baby was Solomon's exact weight
at birth: seven pounds, fourteen ounces, and his hair was
the same light brown.

The night she gave birth he was convinced they had
made a terrible mistake. He was even considering their

giving the child up for adoption. Other people in the waiting room assumed he was the usual nervous father, but his anxiety was the result of so much more.

When the nurse came out to tell him all was well, he did not smile.

"Mr. Stern," she announced, a half smile on her face. "Your wife and your daughter are fine."

"Daughter?"

"Yes, sir. A plump one, too. She's eight pounds, twelve ounces."

"A daughter?"

Everyone was looking at him now, but he couldn't help it. He started to laugh and laugh and laugh. The nurse had to help him to a seat.

When he calmed down, he went in to see Martha. She was tired, but she was beaming. The baby was in her arms, looking so new and so different from Solomon. Joe was ecstatic. His nightmares burst like soap bubbles.

"I want to name her after my grandmother," Martha said.

"Name her anything you want."

"There are so many changes to be made . . . colors, furniture . . ."

"Yes," he said. "So many changes."

When he left the hospital, he was still laughing. He didn't care about the people who looked at him as though he had gone mad. Never did the sky look as blue. "So many changes," he repeated, and got into his car to go home so he could begin.

Epilogue

Gussie put her shoulder to the attic door and pressed as hard as she could. She had been up here only a few times before, and each time the door resisted being opened as though it were trying to prevent her from seeing what was stored within. She had first come up here when she was eleven, simply out of curiosity. Her curiosity grew out of her father's command not to go up to the attic.

"I'm not sure about the floorboards," he told her. "You could step on a rotten one and fall through the roof."

For a long time, that was enough to keep her away. Then one day she heard him wandering about up there and realized if he could walk on those boards, she certainly could. He was so much bigger and heavier.

When she asked about it casually at dinner one night, her mother told her it was dirty and dusty up there.

"Who knows, you might catch some disease," she said, but then again she wondered why her father didn't have such fears. Why did he move about up there if such danger existed?

She realized eventually what the real reason was: They didn't want her seeing any of Solomon's things. According to her parents, they no longer had anything relating to Jonathan.

"He had so little that was his, anyway," her mother told her. "He used Solomon's things, and whatever we did buy him, we got rid of."

"Why?" she wanted to know, but her mother wasn't willing to talk about it, and when she asked her father, he asked her . . . no, he pleaded with her, not to talk about Jonathan.

"Some memories are painful," he said, "and you don't want to cause your mother any pain, do you?"

Of course she didn't. But still, why couldn't she know more about Jonathan and Solomon? It wasn't fair. Her girlfriends knew all about their brothers and sisters. She felt funny when they asked her questions about her dead brother and she didn't know the answers. Even dumb Wilma Pedersen knew about her own dead brother. How he was killed in that car accident. Who his girlfriends had been. And he had died before Wilma was born, just as Solomon had died before she was born.

For a long time she was able to keep her curiosity bridled. Lately, however, that was getting to be a harder and harder thing to do. She had just reached her fifteenth birthday, and there often were nights now when she would lie awake in her bed and look up at the ceiling thinking, the mystery of my dead brother is buried up there, hidden in old chests and closed away in cartons.

Sometimes, as eerie as it sounded, she felt as if he were calling to her, calling to the sister he had never known. She sensed another presence, even heard a voice . . . a whisper. Oh, it could easily be only the wind winding its way through the crevices and openings of the house, or it could be purely a product of her own overworked imagination. She knew that, but she couldn't help thinking about it.

The other times she had sneaked into the attic, she had been afraid to touch anything. All she had really done was stand there, just inside the doorway, and look around. She was afraid to walk across the room, afraid her father might be right about the floorboards. He could do it just because he knew the safe from the unsafe ones.

She held her breath, too, thinking there was a great deal of dust and dirt here. Just as her mother suggested, the attic could be a haven for all sorts of germs. It was hot and musty most of the time, a perfect environment for evil bacteria.

But these fears dissipated as she grew older. Now they seemed like silly, obviously fabricated reasons to keep a young child from endangering herself. But she was no longer a young child. She was becoming a young woman, and she had a right to be trusted. She had a right to know about her own dead brother, to know her past.

Just as before, the door squeaked, its hinges straining under her efforts. There was a single, uncovered light bulb at the center of the ceiling. She flicked the switch and sent the pale yellow light down and around the attic. Shadows seemed to retreat reluctantly and hover in the corners, angry with the intrusion of light. She waved the air in front of her. Something did smell awful up here. Maybe, as her mother once suggested, bats lived here.

She went farther into the attic and studied its contents more closely. She saw the familiar shapes of old pieces of furniture and boxes draped in gray sheets. This time, though, she went to her right and began to examine what was under those sheets. She discovered old clothing; she found old books. Taking some of the clothing out of the cartons and holding shirts and pants out before her, she was able to envision her brother's height and form. The clothing had belonged to him when he was at least fourteen or fifteen, she thought, judging the length of the pants and the sizes of the shirts.

She looked with interest at the books, impressed with the depth and scope of his interests. She found a box of model airplanes and cars and studied the intricate work that had been required to make a successful replica of a famous automobile or plane. What patience he must have had, she thought, and envisioned him alone in his room for hours, working meticulously on these tiny plastic parts.

She moved on to discover lamps and toys and then finally stood before a large carton draped in a heavier, dark gray sheet. The bottom of the sheet had been tucked in under the carton to wrap it even tighter. This was something special, she thought, and quickly pulled the sheet out from under the carton and off it. She undid the flaps and peered in to discover a monitor, cables, and computer. At first, in the dim light, she thought it was a broken discard, the glass of the moniter shattered, the plastic case cracked. But when she knelt down to look more closely, she saw that she was mistaken.

She had been introduced to computers just this year in school. Of course, knowing the work her father did, computers were not as frightening to her as they seemed to be to many of her girlfriends. She had become most proficient on the word processor in the typing room.

Why did her parents leave such a valuable piece of equipment up in this dingy attic? she wondered. Especially now, when she could make good use of it for her own schoolwork? Perhaps they had forgotten about it. It was certainly foolish to leave it up here.

She thought about it awhile and then made an impulsive decision. Actually, she felt influenced. She knew it was only her overworked imagination again, but she could clearly hear all the arguments her dead brother might put forward to get her to use this computer. "It will help you with your schoolwork. It's a waste of money to leave it here. You have the room in your room. Why not?"

Indeed, why not? She knelt down and embraced the carton, surprised at the light weight of the contents as she stood up with it in her arms. Looking around a moment, she nodded with confidence. She had beaten back all the childhood fears and, in a sense, reached through time, in order to have some contact with her dead brother. At least she knew some things about him now.

She carried the computer down to her room carefully. No one heard her. Her mother was in the kitchen, and her father wasn't home from work yet. Slowly, handling the monitor and cables like sacred objects, she unpacked the carton and set the computer up on her desk. When she finished, she stepped back and looked at the blank screen. She had to dust it off some, but basically the computer looked brand-new.

She sat down before it, pulled herself up to the desk, and turned on the computer and monitor. The amber screen came to life with a single beep. She looked down at the keys a moment and then, recalling the instructions she had gotten in school, began to explore.

As if it had a mind of itself, the computer took her to its files, buried in its electronic memory. When the words appeared, she sat and read them slowly. Then, fascinated with what they suggested they would reveal, she pressed the keys to draw up the text. Paragraphs flashed onto the screen. It was as if she could hear his voice.

And suddenly, it all began again.

Bestselling SF/Horror

☐	Forge of God	Greg Bear	£3.99
☐	Eon	Greg Bear	£3.50
☐	The Hungry Moon	Ramsey Campbell	£3.50
☐	The Influence	Ramsey Campbell	£3.50
☐	Seventh Son	Orson Scott Card	£3.50
☐	Bones of the Moon	Jonathan Carroll	£2.50
☐	Nighthunter: The Hexing & The Labyrinth	Robert Faulcon	£3.50
☐	Pin	Andrew Neiderman	£1.50
☐	The Island	Guy N. Smith	£2.50
☐	Malleus Maleficarum	Montague Summers	£4.50

Prices and other details are liable to change

ARROW BOOKS, BOOKSERVICE BY POST, PO BOX 29, DOUGLAS, ISLE OF MAN, BRITISH ISLES

NAME...

ADDRESS ....

....

....

Please enclose a cheque or postal order made out to Arrow Books Ltd. for the amount due and allow the following for postage and packing.

U.K. CUSTOMERS: Please allow 22p per book to a maximum of £3.00.

B.F.P.O. & EIRE: Please allow 22p per book to a maximum of £3.00.

OVERSEAS CUSTOMERS: Please allow 22p per book.

Whilst every effort is made to keep prices low it is sometimes necessary to increase cover prices at short notice. Arrow Books reserve the right to show new retail prices on covers which may differ from those previously advertised in the text or elsewhere.

A Selection of Legend Titles

☐ Eon	Greg Bear	£3.50
☐ Forge of God	Greg Bear	£3.99
☐ Falcons of Narabedla	Marion Zimmer Bradley	£2.50
☐ The Influence	Ramsey Campbell	£3.50
☐ Wyrms	Orson Scott Card	£3.50
☐ Speaker for the Dead	Orson Scott Card	£2.95
☐ Seventh Son	Orson Scott Card	£3.50
☐ Wolf in Shadow	David Gemmell	£3.50
☐ Last Sword of Power	David Gemmell	£3.50
☐ This is the Way the World Ends	James Morrow	£4.99
☐ Unquenchable Fire	Rachel Pollack	£3.99
☐ Golden Sunlands	Christopher Rowley	£3.50
☐ The Misplaced Legion	Harry Turtledove	£2.99
☐ An Emperor for the Legion	Harry Turtledove	£2.99

Prices and other details are liable to change

ARROW BOOKS, BOOKSERVICE BY POST, PO BOX 29, DOUGLAS, ISLE
OF MAN, BRITISH ISLES

NAME...

ADDRESS..

....

....

Please enclose a cheque or postal order made out to Arrow Books Ltd. for the amount
due and allow the following for postage and packing.

U.K. CUSTOMERS: Please allow 22p per book to a maximum of £3.00.

B.F.P.O. & EIRE: Please allow 22p per book to a maximum of £3.00.

OVERSEAS CUSTOMERS: Please allow 22p per book.

Whilst every effort is made to keep prices low it is sometimes necessary to increase cover
prices at short notice. Arrow Books reserve the right to show new retail prices on covers
which may differ from those previously advertised in the text or elsewhere.

Bestselling Thriller/Suspense

☐	Skydancer	Geoffrey Archer	£3.50
☐	Hooligan	Colin Dunne	£2.99
☐	See Charlie Run	Brian Freemantle	£2.99
☐	Hell is Always Today	Jack Higgins	£2.50
☐	The Proteus Operation	James P Hogan	£3.50
☐	Winter Palace	Dennis Jones	£3.50
☐	Dragonfire	Andrew Kaplan	£2.99
☐	The Hour of the Lily	John Kruse	£3.50
☐	Fletch, Too	Geoffrey McDonald	£2.50
☐	Brought in Dead	Harry Patterson	£2.50
☐	The Albatross Run	Douglas Scott	£2.99

Prices and other details are liable to change

ARROW BOOKS, BOOKSERVICE BY POST, PO BOX 29, DOUGLAS, ISLE
OF MAN, BRITISH ISLES

NAME...

ADDRESS...

....

....

Please enclose a cheque or postal order made out to Arrow Books Ltd. for the amount
due and allow the following for postage and packing.

U.K. CUSTOMERS: Please allow 22p per book to a maximum of £3.00.

B.F.P.O. & EIRE: Please allow 22p per book to a maximum of £3.00.

OVERSEAS CUSTOMERS: Please allow 22p per book.

Whilst every effort is made to keep prices low it is sometimes necessary to increase cover
prices at short notice. Arrow Books reserve the right to show new retail prices on covers
which may differ from those previously advertised in the text or elsewhere.